VISIONS OF LADY MARY

RACHEL ANN SMITH

PENFORD
PUBLISHING

First Edition March 2020

Developmental Edit by Gray Plume Editing

Edited by Victory Editing

Proofread by Jennie Ladd

Cover design by Impluvium Studios

Copyright © 2020 by Rachel Ann Smith

ISBN 978-1-951112-06-6

ALSO BY RACHEL ANN SMITH

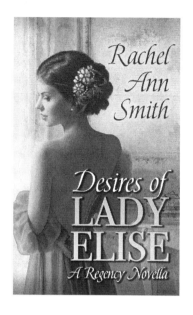

Desires of Lady Elise

He has the reputation of a rogue.

She is too busy with investigations to bother hunting for a husband.

But when the man who shattered her heart re-enters her world, will she be able to resist him?

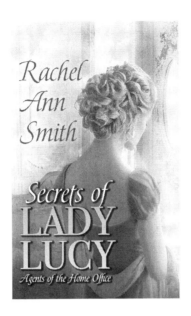

Book 1: Secrets of Lady Lucy

She is determined to foil an attempted kidnapping.

He is set on discovering her secrets.

When the ransom demand comes due—will it be for Lady Lucy's heart?

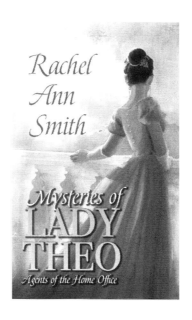

Book 2: Mysteries of Lady Theo

She must fulfill her family's duty to the Crown.

He prioritized his duty to the Crown before all else.

Will the same duty that forced them together be what ultimately drives them apart?

CHAPTER ONE

*D*ismounting from her horse, Lady Mary Eloise Masterson handed the reins to the stable master. "Thank you, Mac."

Nothing cleared her mind and invigorated her spirit like a good long early-morning ride. With a bounce in her step, Mary began to walk back to the castle.

Mac called out, "Yer aunt be lookin' fer ye."

She halted midstride and pivoted. "Aunt Agnes is awake?"

It was a bad omen if her aunt rose with the sun.

Mac's only response was to nod in the direction of the holding as he led her mare back to the stables. Mary's tummy rumbled. Better to deal with her empty stomach than hunt down her aunt. Headed for the kitchens, she paused as voices wafted around the corner. Altering her destination, Mary strode toward the castle's entrance. Her steps faltered at the sight of Aunt Agnes, who stood calmly in the middle of the crushed pebbled path. Footmen bustled about, loading what looked to be her traveling trunks onto a coach.

What the blazes was going on?

With each step toward her aunt, Mary's heart thumped harder. She faced the woman who had been her sole companion for the past six months. "Why is Greene outside on the steps, directing those footmen?"

Aunt Agnes glanced at Mary's maid and smiled. "She's ensuring you have everything necessary for your voyage. I'm shipping you off to France."

Wide-eyed, Mary stared at her aunt. "Beg pardon—did you say I'm to travel to the *Continent*?"

A chill ran down her spine. To be surrounded by all those poor lost souls—young men taken during the awful war. Aunt Agnes had lost her mind! It was bad enough she'd been banished to reside with her in this remote Scottish castle, dealing daily with century-old lairds who wandered around, protecting the grounds. Mary's stomach cramped at the thought of being on foreign soil, surrounded by strangers and tortured souls.

She shook her head. "Papa said I was to stay here. With you."

"Well, my dear. I will not stand by any longer and let him banish you to rot alongside me."

"But, Aunt, the Continent! With all those—"

Her aunt reached out and patted her arm. "It very well may be a challenge given the recent bloodshed, but I believe you will manage."

"I'll be surrounded by *strangers*. They will think I'm odd or even maybe—"

Aunt Agnes linked their arms, and they began to walk toward the fully laden coach. "Despite what our dear family may whisper, our ability to see and talk to the dead is *not* a sign of madness. It is a gift that has flowed through our bloodlines for generations."

A curse, more like it.

She wanted to give in to the temptation to stomp her foot and drag her feet, but she was six and twenty—no longer a child. Peering into the coach, she spied her sleepy-eyed maid, Greene.

The footman gave her a weak smile and held out his hand. As he assisted her into the coach, her brain screamed, *Turn! Run and hide in the woods!*

But Mary was no coward. Squaring her shoulders, she entered the coach. There was naught to do but to embrace her fate as she was raised to.

She leaned out the coach window. "How long have you been planning this?"

"Months, my girl. Months." Aunt Agnes cupped her cheek. "Be brave. Embrace what you know in your heart is to be." With a gentle pat, the dear old lady withdrew her hand. Before Mary could respond, a white parchment was waved before her nose.

She snatched it from her aunt's fingers. "Please tell me this is not one of your sp—"

"It's not a poem. This, my girl, is your future."

Mary warily unfolded the note. She gasped, recognizing the man in the drawing. He stood behind a woman whose head was bent, his lips upon the lady's neck, slightly below her ear. Mary inhaled sharply. It was as if she were peering into a looking glass.

"This cannot be!"

Her aunt grinned and stepped back. "I'm counting on you to make it so."

Mary glanced at the picture once more. The final frame showed her gazing at Gilbert Talbot, the Earl of Waterford.

There had to be a mistake.

The woman in the picture appeared infatuated with Gilbert, and Mary was long past any feelings at all for the

3

man she had once believed herself utterly in love with. No. She was no longer the naive thirteen-year-old, influenced by her brother's tall tales of a gallant young man by the name of Lord Waterford.

The coach lurched forward. Kind eyes twinkled at her as the heavy weight of a gray-haired visitor's transparent hand fell upon her shoulders. Thankful he had prevented her from falling to her knees; Mary smiled and settled back onto the coach seat.

Greene secured the covers of the coach window to the side. "My lady, the light will allow you to read better."

Mary's attention fell back to the parchment still held tightly in her hand. "No need." She folded the note and placed it between the pages of the book that Greene had stealthily placed upon her lap. "Tell me, Greene, how long have you known of our travel plans?"

Her maid squirmed in her seat. "Awhile, my lady."

"I see." Mary winked at her maid. "Well, it is good to know you are capable of keeping secrets."

Greene grinned and raised her own book to hide behind.

The impropriety of it all! Aunt Agnes had lost her wits—packing Mary's trunks, sending her off on a journey unchaperoned, *and* thrusting her in the direction of the man she'd happily avoided all these years.

Fustian! If France was her destination, then she would make it known she was not one who could be managed so easily *unless* it was in line with her own wishes. Her aunt's predictions might be correct, and Gilbert Talbot could well be in her future—but Mary was determined to set the terms.

She stared out of the window, oblivious to the rocky countryside that whizzed by.

How she wished she could change the past. But she of

all people knew that was not a feat that could be accomplished. No one could stop their fate from occurring, even if they tried. The images her aunt had sketched floated before her as she closed her eyes to rest. Waterford tenderly kissing her was, definitely, a figment of her aunt's overactive imagination. Mary might have been a naive thirteen-year-old, but there was no mistaking Gilbert's declaration that he would never consider her for marriage.

Mary vividly remembered the afternoon in the glen. She had been picking flowers when the vibrations of the ground alerted her that she was no longer alone. She'd raised her head to see who was casting a shadow over her.

A young man with near-black hair, a tad longer than convention would deem appropriate, and warm brown eyes stared down at her. She shook her head to clear both her vision and hearing.

She would never forget Gilbert's first words. "What the devil is the matter with your sister, Masterson?"

Phillip, her brother closest to her in every way, including age, jumped down from his horse. "Waterford! There is nothing the matter with Mary."

Thomas, Lord Roxbury, her eldest brother and heir to the Seaburn dukedom, glared at Gilbert while Phillip knelt next to her. As soon as she met Phillip's gaze, he smiled and assisted her to her feet. "I'm sorry if we startled you." Phillip's fingers dug into her. "Let me introduce to you my best friend from school— Gilbert Talbot, the Earl of Waterford."

From the corner of her eye, she had seen the perplexed, confused look on the man she had hoped to be her knight in shining armor. Focusing on her brother's features, Mary whispered, "When did you arrive home?"

"Not long ago. Tell me, how is my favorite sister?"

"Dorie is well."

"Not Dorie. You know very well whom I was inquiring about."

It had been no secret that Mary was Phillip's favorite sibling. She wasn't sure why. Maybe he pitied her for her condition, what their aunt called the family gift. Or maybe —as she very much suspected—Phillip too was burdened by what Mary would always call the family curse.

Gilbert's gravelly voice interrupted their tête-à-tête. "She's obviously not well. The lass is white as a ghost and clearly not in her right mind."

"Waterford, are you blind?" Phillip turned and guided her to stand before Gilbert.

Mary raised her chin in defiance.

"My sight is perfect. Look at her!" Chocolate-brown eyes scanned over her. "Her hair is in disarray— her frock, rumpled and stained. Explain why she had that odd blankness in her eyes." His jaw dropped, then he added, "Oh my. Is your sister mad? Is that why Mary never travels with your family when they come to visit at Oxford?"

Mary ignored the deep growl Thomas emitted. "My papa graciously allows me to remain in the country."

Swiveling his attention back to Mary, Gilbert asked, "Who were you talking to?"

She debated whether to tell him the truth. Her family had warned her never to admit to being able to see the dead.

With a smirk, Mary answered, "I was speaking to Lady Frances."

His frown deepened. "Who?" Gilbert looked about the field.

"Lady Frances." Mary pointed her thumb to her left. "The poor woman took her life after her beloved viscount disclosed that he had a wife and three children waiting for him in London. A fact he failed to share when he was naked and in Lady Frances's bed just the day before. The woman is now warning me against men such as yourself."

"Mary!" Phillip turned her to face him again.

At the fury in her brother's eyes, she bowed her head.

"Masterson, you fooled me into coming. You touted your sister as a great beauty. You claimed she was of extreme intellect and held high morals." Waterford snickered. "She is no diamond of the first water. She's a witch!"

Waterford turned his mount and headed back in the direction of the house.

Thomas gave Mary the Seaburn ducal glare he had recently mastered. "I'll go after him."

"Sister, mine. You have no idea what chaos you have just created. What the devil has got into you? You know better."

Mary teared at the disappointment in Phillip's voice. "I'm sorry. That man, he evokes strange reactions, and the others kept telling me to test him."

Phillip released a long sigh. "I guess in time, all will be, as it should."

With all the innocence of a girl, Mary asked, "What are you talking about?"

"Waterford. He is the one you will marry. One day."

Thump. Mary's book landed next to her booted foot and jerked her back to the present moment. She bent to retrieve the novel, and her aunt's note peeked out, taunting her.

Mary released a sigh and stared out the coach window. The scraggly hills of Scotland were no longer in view. Having been ignored by the man for over a decade, she could safely say her aunt and Phillip's predictions were wrong—Gilbert Elliot Talbot was not the man for her.

Even if he were, she would never agree to marry a man who thought her mad or a witch.

CHAPTER TWO

*G*ilbert rubbed his hands together, attempting to bring the feeling back into his frozen fingers. "Tell me, Hadfield. What are we doing on the docks in the middle of the night?"

The man whom Gilbert was assigned to protect, Landon Neale, the Earl of Hadfield, looked about the dimly lit dock before answering, "My cousin sent word that I am to pick up an asset who is aboard the *Quarter Moon*."

Without a cloud in the sky, the three-quarter moon provided sufficient light for Gilbert to scan their surroundings and confirm no one was within earshot. "To whom are you referring? Your newly acquired cousin, the home secretary, Lord Archbroke? Or the lovely lady he married, Lady Theodora?"

"The note was from Theo." Hadfield rubbed his upper arms. The man's flimsy French coat was no match for the sea breeze blowing in from the channel.

"Aghh— That explains why we are standing in the damp cold, waiting for— What is it again that we are to collect?" The Calais port was a hive of activity through which all sorts of goods were transported in and out of France.

"Theo's note merely indicated that I was to retrieve a critical asset. She's always been rather vague, but now that she is married to Archbroke, well, the tendency has exacerbated."

Gilbert was well aware of how ambiguous his superior, Archbroke, could be, especially since the last note he received from the man had consisted of two words— Protect Hadfield.

Six months ago, Gilbert had believed he was assigned to the Continent to retrieve crown jewels that had the misfortune of being misplaced. He hadn't anticipated Hadfield hunting him down, nor had he expected the traitorous Lady Cecilia to have followed Hadfield to the Continent. When Gilbert caught the pair stalking him through a remote French village, Hadfield informed him that his close friends, Matthew Stanford, Marquess Harrington, and Marcus Risley, the Earl of Hereford, were in need of rescue from a group of bandits.

But it was Lady Cecilia who had ensured their mission's success by offering critical intelligence in exchange for her brother's safety and allowing her to accompany them. The woman had a mean left hook and was able to deftly outmaneuver their hulking attackers.

Once they had located and freed Harrington, Hereford, and Lady Cecilia's brother, Lord Addington, Gilbert was resigned to return to England to fulfill his duties. The night before they were set to depart, Hadfield declared his wish to remain on the Continent. Gilbert's orders to protect Hadfield had mysteriously appeared upon his bed. He received no explanation as to why he was to remain with Hadfield or for what purpose. There was no mistaking the message. He was to ensure Hadfield's safety on the Continent.

And so Gilbert stood, freezing, waiting for the *Quarter Moon* to dock.

Unbidden, the image of Lady Mary filled his mind. "What are the chances of us boarding the *Quarter Moon* and returning home?"

Hadfield arched an eyebrow. "Why? Are you eager to become leg shackled?"

Did he know about Mary? "I'm no more ready to be married than you are."

Leaning closer, Hadfield inquired, "Why did you not return with Harrington and the others?"

Suspecting the man would be offended to learn Archbroke didn't believe he could take care of himself, Gilbert opted to openly share. "There are matters at home I'm not ready to deal with currently."

"Was it the prospect of hunting for a wife or returning to a damp, empty estate that had you content to remain on the Continent?"

A commotion of dockhands shouting directions and guiding the *Quarter Moon* to the dock drew Hadfield's attention. Thankfully, Gilbert didn't have to answer the former barrister turned earl.

Men scurried about, anchoring the vessel. As soon as the gangplank was in placc, the hairs on the back of Gilbert's neck stood on end, and the spot just below his left ear began to itch. Gilbert didn't have to lay eyes on the woman to know that Mary Eloise Masterson was aboard. The beloved sister of his fallen best friend had an acute physical effect on him. She merely had to be within a mile of him, and his body would react. Why had he made promises he could not keep?

Gilbert began to sweat. His shirt clung to his skin,

reminding him of the day he was covered with Phillip's blood. Mary's brother's last words rang clear as when he had first heard them. "Promise. Promise you will sign the papers and ensure her safety and well-being." There had been no question of who "her" was. Mary was always the sibling Phillip kept harping on about. The woman who haunted Gilbert's every thought each day since that disastrous summer when he first met her.

Upon his return from the war, Gilbert had made the obligatory visit to the ducal estate to give his condolences. The Duke and Duchess of Seaburn were devastated by the loss of their second son, while Mary appeared to be at peace with the news.

He had requested a private meeting with her, which her papa had granted. However, before he could sequester her away, Mary had marched right up to him and said, "I am in no need of another male guard. I release you from your promises to Phillip. He was delusional prior to his death. He will not haunt you for the rest of your living days as he claimed if you do not fulfill your pledge."

"It's a matter of honor, Lady Mary. I fully intend to keep my promise."

Mary had snorted. "Let me be clear. Stay. Away."

"I'm sorry, but I cannot oblige."

"Oh, you will." Her eyes had scanned the room. "You only have to endure my company for a short house party this Season."

"House party? I've no intention of attending such an event, nor have I received an invitation to one."

With a smug smile, Mary had said, "Lord Devonton will be holding one. But not to worry. You will not be obliged to stay the entire duration. You are bound for the Continent."

Involuntarily, he had flinched at the mention of the

Continent. "I'll not be returning to foreign lands anytime soon, I can assure you. In fact, Lady Mary, you can be certain that I shall remain in town, and I *will not* renege on my promises to your brother."

She had snorted again and left him standing in the middle of the room, staring at her retreating back.

He recalled thinking that the woman was mad or a witch. And maybe she was—for it wasn't long before every word she had uttered indeed unfolded as she had predicted.

Now here he was, about to face the woman he hadn't seen for near on six months. He didn't fear much in this world. After all, he had survived the war. But Lady Mary's effect on him was inexplicably intense and made him far too uncomfortable. He remained uncertain of her claim to be able to communicate with the dead.

Bright red slippers came into focus.

"Are you done daydreaming, Lord Waterford?" Mary's voice had a tinge of sultriness that Gilbert was loath to admit had his blood pumping harder. Faster.

"Lady Mary. A pleasure as always." He looked about, but there was no sign of Hadfield nor a chaperone.

"If you are looking for Lord Hadfield, he is kindly seeing to my trunks."

"Where is your chaperone?" Surely her papa hadn't allowed Mary to venture here on her own. "Who are you visiting?"

Her teeth grazed over her bottom lip, distracting him.

With a slight tilt of her head, she asked, "Did my aunt not arrange for Lord Hadfield and yourself to be here this eve?"

"Your aunt?" Gilbert scratched the back of his neck. "According to Hadfield, Lady Archbroke was the one who requested our presence here."

"Theo? But she couldn't have known about my travel plans." Mary's brow creased.

Hadfield approached and addressed Mary. "I've managed to arrange for your items to be loaded onto a travel coach. I wasn't sure where to instruct the coachmen to take you."

Mary smiled weakly. "My thanks, Lord Hadfield." She turned and said, "I shall be on my way, then."

Gilbert reached out to grab her by the elbow, successfully halting her progress.

Where the devil do you think you're going? Mere moments ago, she had given him the impression she was traveling sans chaperone and wasn't expected by anyone.

Mary looked down at his hand and then back up into his eyes. There was not an inkling of concern or fear in her gaze. He closed his eyes and counted to five. *This cannae be happening. The woman has no fear. She waltzes about as if not a thing bothers her.*

He opened one eye, and the heat in her stare made him release her—for now.

He cleared his dry throat. "Hadfield, I think it best I escort Lady Mary to her lodgings."

Hadfield's features visibly relaxed. "Yes, that is a fine idea. I still have to locate Theo's items. Captain Bane has them heavily guarded."

The odds were slight that it was pure coincidence Mary had traveled to France aboard the same ship as Lady Archbroke's treasured items. He had left Mary in the care of her family while he completed his mission. Her papa, His Grace, could not have misunderstood Gilbert's intentions and wishes for Mary. He again scratched the back of his neck. The woman should be safely tucked away in Scotland.

Mary bent to enter the travel coach. Her sweet derrière

momentarily scattered all his rational thoughts. What! She was leaving without him.

He scrambled to catch up.

Tarnation.

He was still in the midst of an assignment—to see to the protection and safe return of Hadfield. Overseeing the welfare of both Mary and Hadfield would be a challenge, yet he couldn't let Mary traipse about the Continent alone. The woman had the uncanny ability to attract the attention of the most unusual characters. What was he to do with her?

CHAPTER THREE

*G*ripping her shawl, Mary adjusted it about her shoulders as she placed her foot upon the coach steps. There were too many strangers pressed around her, not all of them alive. Living or not, they all spoke French. Linguistics was not one of her strong suits.

Stepping up into the coach, Mary spotted Greene huddled in the corner and grumbled, "Do *you* know where we are to reside?"

Greene wrung her hands and shook her head. "No, my lady. Perhaps Lord Waterford can assist."

"I'd rather sleep in a ditch than ask for his help."

A shiver ran through her at the thought of having to seek help from Gilbert. She tugged the collar of her coat up and over her nose and settled upon the coach bench. Greene sat across from her, head bowed and arms crossed.

A whisper echoed through her mind. *"Duc de Valois, ma chérie."*

Despite her maid's worried features, Mary was keenly aware that only she had heard the name and the endearment.

She leaned out the window to address the coach driver. Her French was rusty, and it took her a moment to construct the sentence she needed. *"S'il te plait emmène-moi voir le Duc de Valois."* The coachman's eyes widened, but he pulled up on the reins as if to set them off into motion. She hoped he understood her direction.

Gilbert strode over to her, his long legs eating up the ground between them faster than she cared. "Lady Mary, please allow me to escort you to town."

The coachman froze midmotion at Gilbert's arrival. She would have escaped if Gilbert had been a tad slower.

"No need, Waterford. I've arranged to visit the Duc de Valois."

Leaning against the coach, Gilbert's breathing was normal as if he had taken a stroll through the park rather than jogged a hundred yards or so. "Duc de Valois? The man may be a duke in name, but it is rumored he might very well be a pauper despite appearances and the land he was able to regain. How is it you came about the duke's name?"

Mary wasn't going to tell him anything, let alone the truth. She would prefer to never be called a witch again. No, Gilbert was not a man she could confide in. He had proven himself incapable of dealing with the truth.

Ready to be out of the cold, she withdrew to sit back upon the bench. How was she to get rid of the man? He was obviously not going to leave without her answer.

Stalling for time, Mary replied, "I'm well aware of what was reported to have occurred during the French revolution. I, for one, agree all should be treated as equals."

"You are avoiding my question." Waterford stuck his head in through the window. "Tell me. What do you know of Duc de Valois?"

Mary refused to let Gilbert bully her. She stared directly at him. His molten brown eyes still had her heart fluttering as they did the first time they met. Curse the man. She had yet to banish his image from her mind even after his disgraceful behavior and his obvious lack of interest in her over the years.

Gilbert crossed his arms. "I won't ask again. Explain how it is you are acquainted with one of the few aristocrats of old who continues to survive. Miraculously, Valois's lands emerged unscathed after the war."

She didn't know anything about the man whom she had boldly declared was expecting her. Yet again, Mary had placed blind faith in her guardian angels to direct her to safety. Reflecting on the voice, it had not been her most persistent and loyal angel, Lady Frances, who had supplied the name.

Had she made a terrible error?

Now was not the time to question her decision. She needed to rid herself of Gilbert before the unexplainable hypnotic effect he had upon her made her agree to anything he asked. "It was *so* nice to see you, my lord. But I'll have to provide you with a history lesson some other time."

His warm breath grazed her cheek as he leaned in farther. "Let me accompany you to your destination. Once I ensure you are safe, I shall leave you be."

She wanted to tell him to go to Hades, but the reality of the situation hit her—she was in a foreign country with no friends or contacts to rely upon.

Mary opened her mouth meaning to accept his offer, rationalizing that it would be the most prudent course of action. But instead, perversely, she said, "I do not require your escort. Shouldn't you be assisting Lord Hadfield? I believe your orders were to stay with *him* at all times."

Gilbert asked, "What do you know of my orders? How could you possibly—"

Boots pounded in the background, and Gilbert stepped back, withdrawing from the window. Who was approaching with such urgency? Mary stuck her head out of the opening. Lord Hadfield came bounding toward them, waving his hand above his head.

Ah. Perhaps Gilbert was needed after all.

Sneaking a glance at him, a tingling sensation ran up her spine. The man caused her body to respond in the most curious of ways. While pride prevented her from accepting his offer to accompany her, she had to admit the prospect of traveling alone at night to an unknown estate was rather daunting.

Lord Hadfield's gasps broke her train of thought. The poor man stood next to the coach, bent at the waist, panting for air. "Lady Mary!"

"Good gracious, Hadfield. You really ought to get more exercise." Gilbert was pounding on the man's back.

Wheezing, Hadfield waved Gilbert away and straightened. "I have a lung condition, you fool." He stood and reached into his coat pocket. "Lady Mary, I have a note from Theo for you. The captain conveyed it was to be read prior to your departure. Thank goodness Waterford slowed you down, or I'd never have caught you in time."

With the parchment in her possession, she sat back to read the note. Gilbert's rather large head appeared once more through the window and blocked most of the light. Mary shifted for the moonlight to fall upon the letter and reveal Theo's scrawling handwriting.

Dear Lady Mary,

I hope your journey across the channel wasn't too arduous.

Your aunt and I have been in correspondence, and we agree you are the only one capable of carrying out the next phase of Archbroke's scheme. My dear husband wants the stolen goods that we were able to retrieve from Lord Burke's stash returned to their rightful owners. You are to return the paintings to the Duc de Valois and the jewels to Comte Boucher.

Lady Agnes assures me that your family's connection to Valois should ensure you are received at his estate. However, returning the jewels belonging to the Boucher family will be challenging for you will need to procure an invitation to the comtesse's annual masquerade ball. We believe you are the best person to carry out this task.

If you are in need of anything, seek Landon's help. He will be your champion.

Be safe and use extreme caution. Archbroke believes Lord Burke will go to great lengths to ensure that the items are not returned.

Sincerely,
Your friend, Theo

Gilbert pulled back from the window, but Mary still heard him mumble, "I'm going to wring your aunt's neck the next time I see her. She's lost all sense of propriety involving you in such a dangerous mission."

She should be angry at him for reading her private correspondence. Weary from her travels, she hadn't the energy to reprimand Gilbert. Closing her eyes, she rested her head on the sidewall of the coach, needing a moment to process the content of the letter.

Mary must have misread the note. Lady Theo had

stated she had colluded with Aunt Agnes. Yet her aunt had made no mention of corresponding with the home secretary's wife or the prospect of assisting with a mission of import.

What had possessed Aunt Agnes to agree to involving her in such schemes?

Mary didn't possess any skills that were of value to the Home Office. Her close friend Lucy, Lady Devonton, was skilled at decoding. Lady Theo was extremely talented in devising schemes, as was her husband. Mary was no ninny, but she doubted that her ability to talk to and see the dead would position her as being the only one capable of this mission.

Her eyes remained closed as Gilbert's complaining continued outside. "Hadfield, a word. What the devil is your cousin up to, involving Mary?"

The coach rocked as someone leaned against it.

Gilbert continued his rant. "Let me be clear. While your cousin might have advised Mary to seek you out if she needs assistance, it will be *I* who sees to her needs."

Why did her lips curl into a smile at Gilbert's possessive tone?

Greene gently tapped her knee. "Lady Mary, are you ready for us to be on our way?"

"Yes." She crisply refolded the parchment and absently tapped it against her other hand. "But first, I'd like to speak to Lord Hadfield."

The man instantly appeared at the window. "Do you have a matter you wish to discuss with me?"

Lowering her voice so Gilbert couldn't hear, Mary asked, "Did you read this before giving it to me?"

Lord Hadfield's frame stiffened. "Why would I read your private correspondence?"

"Your reputation for expertly crafted arguments in

court precedes you, but I am not the one being questioned. Your answer, Lord Hadfield."

"No. My cousin supplied a separate note addressed to me. I'm assuming yours contains similar information and direction. Would you care to exchange so we can compare?"

"No need. Theo was clear in her wishes. Was Waterford supplied correspondence also?"

"He received orders from Archbroke. We will have to hope that the couple is in sync in their demands."

Pondering why Lord Hadfield's instructions had come from Theo and not Lord Archbroke, Mary said, "We shall have to wait and see."

She stuck her hand out, waiting for Hadfield to place the pouch of jewels in her possession. It was a test to see if Theo's notes really had shared the same information. A soft leather pouch landed in her palm. "I'm assuming you and Waterford will provide me with an escort to Duc de Valois's estate."

It was Gilbert who answered. "It would be our pleasure. If you require anything, please let *me* know. It's a fair journey, that is *if* Devonton's map is correct. We should arrive in no less than three days." In a barely audible grumble, he added, "A lesson well learned during the war, maps are never as reliable as one would hope."

Lord Hadfield straightened. "Are you ready to begin?"

Mary nodded as she mulled over Gilbert's odd statement. She had spied Lord Devonton sketching his now, wife Lucy on numerous occasions. Mary assumed it was merely a hobby. She searched her memory, pulling fragments of information on Lord Devonton together. Her theory that Lord Devonton was a cartographer for the British War Office was absolutely plausible. But to believe him unreliable was contrary to everything Mary knew of the man.

The coach jerked forward, and her thoughts snapped back to her current predicament – how to ignore Gilbert and focus on her assignment.

Finally, she was to be of assistance to others rather than wasting her days away in Scotland. Her dear friends, Lucy and Theo, had married men who valued their abilities. Neither were considered chattel by their husbands. Instead, they were revered, true life partners.

A tendril of hair grazed her ear as her trusted angel, Lady Frances, whispered, *If you married Waterford, you too could enjoy the same as your friends.*

Mary eyed her maid and muttered, "Bah. The man would never consider my abilities a talent. I'll not marry the fool."

Greene snuggled deeper into her cloak, oblivious to Mary's ramblings.

CHAPTER FOUR

*G*ilbert's heart hadn't settled from the shock of seeing Mary walk down the gangplank. What the devil was she doing here? He was on a blasted mission. His emotions mirrored the temper of his mount —unsteady.

He ran a hand down the beast's neck to soothe them both and looked at the man beside him. "Were you anticipating this shipment? Is this the reason you decided to remain behind?"

Hadfield kept his eyes trained forward. "I'm not at liberty to share with you my rationale for staying abroad."

Gilbert released a sigh. Hadfield had been a well-respected barrister before inheriting his title and could talk in circles if you allowed him. Confident that Hadfield had a particular agenda that even Archbroke and his wife were unaware of, Gilbert was determined to discover what it was.

"Archbroke has ordered that I am to remain with you even if that means parting ways with Mary. Why would he deem your safety a priority over—"

"I have no plans on leaving Mary's side. Not for *any* reason." Hadfield kicked his mount forward to catch up to the coach.

Hadfield's words replayed over in Gilbert's mind.

He straightened in his seat. The man couldn't possibly be considering marrying the lass.

Urging his mount forward, Gilbert came level with Hadfield. "Do *you* have a formal invitation from the Duc de Valois?"

"Apparently, Lady Mary does."

"I can assure you she does not. The woman arrived with no idea of her destination. This is a fool's errand."

"Lady Mary and I are bound for Duc de Valois's residence. You may choose to disobey orders and go your own way. I'm sure Archbroke will understand."

Gilbert snorted. "You know very well that I have no intention of crossing Archbroke."

"Come, Waterford, it is a long journey. No need to make it more strenuous than necessary." Hadfield slowed his mount so they fell behind the coach. "Let's take turns riding with Lady Mary. Would you like the first or second shift?"

"Neither. I'll remain in the saddle." He did not want to be confined with the woman. She always put a spell of sorts on him when she was near.

"You won't do much good against bandits if you can't keep your eyes open. Let's flip for it?" Hadfield retrieved a silver half crown from his pocket.

Relenting, Gilbert said, "Heads, you gain the pleasure of Lady Mary's company first."

Please let it be heads. Let Hadfield deal with the woman.

The coin flipped in the air. Hadfield deftly caught it in midair, and slowly he opened his palm. "Heads."

Finally, the universe was on Gilbert's side. Then why did his chest ache with disappointment?

Hadfield's lips curled at the corners into a remarkably symmetrical smile. "Excellent. After the next posting inn, I shall continue in the coach. I'm rather looking forward to becoming better acquainted with Lady Mary. Theo holds her in high regard."

The man's words and smirk had Gilbert tightening his grip on the reins. "Wouldn't you agree that Lady Archbroke tends to associate with some rather *unusual* females?"

The grin faded from Hadfield's features. "Good gracious, please don't refer to Theo as Lady Archbroke. I know she married the home secretary, but I try to forget the fact that I'm now related to the man. Call her Lady Theo or Theo, *please*."

Gilbert cracked a smile of his own as he recalled how the mysterious Lady Theo had challenged his superior's ideas on women. "I admit Lady Theo has been a rather positive influence on Archbroke. I have no doubt when we return he will be a changed man."

"One can hope." Hadfield slanted his head toward the coach. "It will be interesting to see which of us she will choose."

His smile vanished. "What are you babbling about now?"

"Lady Mary. I wonder which of us she will decide to marry."

Not following the man's logic, Gilbert asked, "Why would she marry either one of us?"

Hadfield's eyebrows snapped together. "She will *have to* marry one of us at the end of our journey. Otherwise, her reputation will be in tatters."

The curtain of the coach window shifted. Had Mary

been eavesdropping on their conversation? Gilbert agreed that Mary would have to marry before returning to England. However, there was no doubt in his mind who that would be.

"What makes you believe she would even consider marrying you?"

Phillip had been his best friend. It was he who had promised to honor her brother's dying wish.

"Lady Mary didn't appear overjoyed by your presence at the docks." Hadfield shrugged and then added, "I would say my chances are rather good at this point." The smirk reappeared on the man's face. "Yes, riding in the coach with the lady will provide the perfect opportunity for me to charm her."

Gilbert couldn't prevent the growl he emitted as he said, "There is no need to charm anyone, Hadfield."

Hadfield shot him a look. "Lady Mary is traveling with no male relative in sight. One of us will have to claim her at the end of this journey, or she will be ruined. I'm fairly certain her papa, the Duke of Seaburn, will see to it that one of us does the honorable thing."

The man was right. His Grace would employ whatever measures necessary to ensure Mary would not face disgrace. It was Gilbert's suspicion her papa would summon the entire family to journey to the Continent as soon as His Grace found out his wayward sister sent Mary to cross the channel with only a maid. Gilbert had yet to figure out why the old woman had placed Mary in such a position.

After years of avoiding the altar, he should be relieved that there was another willing to take Mary off his hands. What Gilbert couldn't deny was the deep ache in his chest every time Hadfield alluded to the possibility of Mary becoming the Countess of Hadfield.

"I've changed my mind. I'll take first shift riding in the coach."

Eyebrows furrowed, Hadfield asked, "Why the sudden change of heart?"

"After this ridiculous conversation, I'm weary, and as you pointed out, I'll be of no use to anyone if I don't get a few hours of sleep."

"Very well. I'll concede the first shift to you."

Hadfield, the trickster, had manipulated him into changing his mind. He'd have to remember the man had been a barrister and a wizard at twisting arguments. The problem was Hadfield was unassuming and appeared extremely comfortable with his lot in life, one often forgot he'd assumed the title merely a year ago.

Gilbert ran a hand over his heart. The deep-seated pain began to ease, replaced with a flutter of excitement. Alone for hours with the woman who could bring his blood to a boil within moments—How was he to ignore Mary's magnetic allure?

CHAPTER FIVE

*W*ith the sun barely peeking over the horizon, Mary stomped back to the dreaded coach.

Blasted titled gentlemen.

Having spent most of the night eavesdropping on Gilbert and Lord Hadfield's mundane male banter to fill in the time and remain awake, she had rested peacefully until they began discussing her future.

Her blood boiled as the men bandied about words of honor, ruin, and marriage. Deliberating over her future as if it were predetermined.

Men!

No—she would determine her fate. Marriage to a titled gentleman meant children— rearing offspring was not in Mary's future. The mere thought of bearing a child gave her hives. None of her mama's pregnancies were easy, and each one had drained the woman of every ounce of energy and life she possessed. The birth of Mary's youngest sibling had nearly cost her mama's life.

Despite her guides' reassurances that Gilbert was the man for her, he was titled. Marriage to a man as virile as

Gilbert would undoubtedly result in the Countess of Waterford bearing the future earl and a spare.

Mary rubbed her upper arms to ward off the chill of the brisk morning air and her dour thoughts. She would have to devise a plan to discourage Lord Hadfield. Marriage to Gilbert was simply out of the question. If he wanted to marry her, he would have done so already. Even her brother's dying wish had not prompted the man to prove himself worthy. Mary wanted a partner in life. A man to accept her for all her assets, including her ability to converse with those no longer living. She refused to accept she was destined for a marriage born out of some ill-conceived notion that she must marry in order to uphold her honor.

Picking up her clean skirts, she grinned as she recalled the ruckus Greene had caused demanding access to Mary's trunks. Greene had not only managed to obtain a clean change of clothes but had also convinced the men to allow Mary time to bathe and partake in a light repast. Mary was tempted to request that they remain at the inn for a few hours, for she sorely wished to lie upon a solid bed and sleep without being in motion.

After traveling days, upon days, in a coach from Scotland to Dover, then boarding the *Quarter Moon* to journey across the channel, Mary longed for a good long uninterrupted rest. Gilbert's gravelly voice boomed through the door, asking if all was well. When Mary envisioned the two of them together in her room—naked—she scrambled out to the courtyard, never looking back.

A footman assisted her into the coach, and she waited for Greene to follow. When she heard her maid instructing the footmen to rearrange the trunks, Mary settled back into the corner and closed her eyes in an attempt to gain some rest before they set off once more.

The coach dipped. Mary's eyes flew open as the scent of sandalwood filled the coach. The scent that set her senses on alert and belonged to the one man her body was inherently in tune with. "Gilbert, where is Greene?"

Drat. The man had changed and rid himself of all traces of horse and sweat. A scar ran from the corner of his lip down to his chin—it wasn't red or puffy, yet it hadn't been there six months ago. Oh, how she wished she hadn't memorized every inch of the man's features. She wanted to run her hand over his cleanly shaven square jaw and trace a finger along the healed wound. The war was over. He shouldn't incur such injuries.

Rather than take the seat opposite her, Gilbert sat next to her and removed his coat, with swift practiced movements.

Gilbert shifted, rocking the coach. "Your maid will join us shortly. I believe she is still unhappy about the placement of your items."

He lined up the shoulder seams, folded, tucked, and rolled up the coat material, creating a makeshift pillow. Deftly he placed it between the side of the coach and his head and closed his eyes. Just like that, he had simply shut her and the rest of the world out. To punctuate his lack of interest in her presence, Gilbert crossed his arms against his chiseled chest and yawned.

Inexplicably, Mary's gaze fell to the white linen material drawn tight over his muscled arms. Her chest tightened, and her pulse quickened. Blinking, her aunt's drawings flashed before her mind's eye. Mary inhaled and exhaled slowly. *Ignore him as he is ignoring you.* Not an easy task when the man smelled so good and her body instinctively sought his out.

Space. She needed a few inches of distance before she gave in to the temptation to lean against Gilbert. Mary shifted, but her skirts caught beneath his large muscular thigh. She tugged at the material. It refused to come loose. She continued to try to set herself free, except her efforts resulted in the back of her hand grazing alongside his leg. Heat radiated up her arm, and she quickly released her skirts. She glanced at Gilbert's face. Nothing—no reaction to the brief touch that had her heart beating rapidly.

Look away—pretend he doesn't exist.

Mary ogled the man's leg that slightly tensed and moved, releasing her skirts.

What was wrong with her?

Nothing. Lord Waterford is a handsome devil—sets the mind to wondering what those muscles would look like bare, doesn't it? Lady Frances's teasing words set Mary's thoughts down a wicked path.

For years whenever Gilbert was within fifty feet of her, she'd managed to ignore the tingling sensations, resisted the urge to move closer, and remained cool despite her rising body temperature. But today she struggled to summon the willpower to avoid the man's magnetic pull. Mary swallowed hard. She pried her eyes away from him and tried to huddle closer to the corner. Her leg brushed up against Gilbert, and every nerve in her body sparked. Blast the man.

She was about to move to the other bench when Greene entered the coach. Her maid promptly settled in. Greene angled herself to avoid Gilbert's long legs, which resulted in her occupying three-quarters of the rear-facing seat.

Greene asked, "Do you need anything before we set off, my lady?"

Mary shook her head. "No, go ahead and rest."

Her maid adjusted her cloak about her and was snoring within moments. It was preposterous how Greene could manage to fall asleep with such ease no matter what condition they found themselves in.

Mary, on the other hand, continued to wiggle and shift her weight. The crisp morning air had cooled the interior of the coach as Greene had entered, and Mary was now trying her best to avoid the alluring heat of Gilbert's body.

She uncrossed her legs. Gilbert's arm snaked about her waist and hauled her up off the seat. Gilbert quickly adjusted his position - one long muscular leg rested along the bench, slightly bent at the knee, while his other leg was planted firmly on the floor. Mary found herself wedged between his thighs. It was like being wrapped up in a warming blanket.

He cradled her against his chest. "Rest."

How was she to fall asleep in this rather indecent position he had put her in?

"Gilbert, release me at once." She wasn't a babe to be coddled. But the warmth of his body had her muscles betraying her need to relax.

"No. I tire of your wiggling about."

"And I of your—" Blast. Her brain couldn't fail her now. The harsh quips that normally rolled off her tongue when in his company evaded her.

Sneaking a look up at the man, his features were relaxed and composed. Mary released a sigh and gave in, resting her head against his chest. The steady beat of his heart lulled her to sleep.

ZOUNDS! He had finally confounded Mary long enough to escape her whip-like tongue, only to find she was a bundle of soft curves and delicious smells. Cinnamon. His favorite spice. Clearly, he had lost his mind. He tightened his hold around the woman snuggled in his arms. She had retracted her claws, and Gilbert found himself unable to resist his need for her. Burrowing his nose in her soft tresses, he inhaled. A calming warmth spread throughout his body. With her guard down, he pulled back slightly and took in her relaxed features.

Mary was beautiful awake, but in slumber, she was breathtaking. Her soft rosy lips, slightly parted. His traitorous hand ran up her arm, and his thumb couldn't resist tracing the slope of her pert little nose. His eyes rested upon her cherub lips, beckoning to him.

His mind wailed at him, *You promised her brother to take care of her, not ravish her while she slept.*

Mary rested her small hand upon his chest, and his heart skipped a beat. Phillip was right. Mary was a treasure —a woman to be protected and cherished, not placed in danger.

When Gilbert made his promises to Phillip, he hadn't hesitated in agreeing to sign the papers that would bind them for life. He also hadn't considered that his family's oath to protect others and his allegiance to the Crown might place Mary in harm's way. He had vowed to marry her as soon as he determined it safe. One more mission had turned into years at war, and then another critical mission arose, and he had no choice but to leave her in Scotland.

His heart tugged as Mary's fingers slid across his chest to come to rest under her chin. It was as if she were comfortably asleep, and he was her pillow. Suppressing a groan, Gilbert banished the image of Mary naked in his bed. Surely she would soon realize that his body was rudely protruding and prodding her side.

He bent closer as Mary began murmuring in her sleep. "Paintings. Madame Auclair."

Auclair. Could Mary be referring to the French modiste known for creating risqué costumes and elaborate masquerade masks on the Continent? Gilbert gasped as a vision of Mary in a glittering gown adorned with diamonds and pearls struck him, stealing his breath.

The scent of cinnamon filled his nose, again acting as a calming agent. Eyes closed, he rested his chin atop Mary's head. Her ramblings of the modiste reminded him of the many months he had spent away on the Continent. Perhaps Auclair's reputation had recently reached London. In any event, there was a reported yearlong wait to be seen by the woman. There was no reason for him to panic—these visions were mere figments of his imagination. The skin on the back of his neck prickled. Mary would never dare to wear such a gown, and while she was in his care, he would see to it that she didn't.

The coachman's "whoa" had him roughly shoving Mary off his lap and onto the seat beside him. Tarnation. What time was it?

Wide-eyed and confused, she stared at him. "Whatever is the matter? Are we under attack?"

His original intention had been to hold her until she fell asleep and then gently place her in the corner, but once she'd snuggled against him, he had not wanted to release her. No. He needed to hold her. Gilbert eyed her rumpled state. Instead of handling her with care, he had thoughtlessly jostled her about.

He crossed his legs and peeked out through the curtain. "We've arrived at the next coaching inn. Hadfield will be joining you soon."

He turned back to find Mary's lips turned down into a frown.

Shifting her gaze away from him, she said, "Wonderful. I expect Lord Hadfield's company to be livelier. But before we leave, I'd like to take a moment to stretch my legs."

Mary bent over, giving him the advantage of viewing her remarkable rump, and tapped her maid on the shoulder. "Greene. You must accompany me into the inn."

Gilbert uncrossed and recrossed his legs as her maid opened her eyes. There was an alertness in Greene's stare that had him on edge.

The door flung open, and Mary exited first. Greene eyed him as she rose to leave and, at the last moment, turned and gave him a wink. Good gracious. He was going to have to keep his hands off Mary.

Pacing about the courtyard, waiting for the women to return, Gilbert again resolved to act the gentleman that he was born and raised to be. What he needed was space from Mary who had the uncanny ability to unnerve him. A highly decorated soldier. A respected lord known for his skill handling any situation. Yet when he was around Mary, all common sense left him. He was on a mission. Now was not the time to deal with the woman who had plagued his thoughts and dreams for years. Gilbert rubbed the back of his neck, still ashamed of his nineteen-year-old self for calling her a witch.

Greene appeared, bringing him out of the recurring nightmare of the day he met Mary.

They both looked about for her mistress. There was no sign of Mary. Greene tugged on his coat sleeve. "My lord. I'll not be able to feign slumber every time you join us. You will have to behave— next time."

Not surprising, Mary would hire such an impertinent chit as a maid.

Straightening to his full height, he replied, "I'll try my best."

Greene scurried over to her mistress, who was exiting

the inn. He stood at attention under Mary's scrutiny. She never broke eye contact until her maid linked arms and ushered her to the traveling coach.

The sway of Mary's hips had him mesmerized until Hadfield's hand slapped him in the center of his back.

Hadfield chuckled. "You don't look well-rested, my friend. Did Lady Mary keep you awake all day with idle chatter?"

Deciding it best to ignore the man's queries, Gilbert said, "We have at least another day and a half's journey before we make it to our destination."

"Should we press on or stay at—" Hadfield squinted and read the sign. "Carrefour Auberge."

Crossroads Inn—a rather appropriate name that reflected Gilbert's own situation. Mentally debating the advantages and disadvantages of renting rooms for the night, Gilbert shrugged off Hadfield's hand. "We should continue on— unless you have a specific reason to dally here?"

"No. I'm rather looking forward to resting in the coach with Lady Mary."

"Be warned. The woman purrs like a small kitten when she sleeps."

Hadfield burst into laughter. "War hero I knew you to be, but a man of such literary prowess I would have never guessed."

Heat rose on Gilbert's cheeks, and he stomped over to his horse, leaving Hadfield behind. Where did that flowery nonsense come from? Mary. It was all her fault.

CHAPTER SIX

*A*fter having slept most of the previous day in Gilbert's arms and catnapping throughout the night, as Lord Hadfield was a rather quiet sleeper, Mary was well rested and eager to be outdoors. The jittery feeling in her stomach had nothing to do with the thought of spending another long day in the coach with Gilbert.

Having failed at bargaining for enough time for a bath, Mary hurriedly ran a cool wet washcloth across the back of her neck, down her chest, and over her arms, wiping away all the dust from a long night of travel. Dropping the washcloth into the murky basin water, Mary ducked her head as Greene assisted her with donning a clean lawn shirt and breeches beneath her riding habit. Thank the fates, the innkeeper only had one son to assist with the changing of the horse, buying Mary a little more time to refresh.

Greene wrung her hands. "My lady, I'm not certain His Lordship will be pleased to hear of your plan for today's journey." Despite her words, she fetched Mary's riding boots.

Mary sat to put them on while Greene tugged at her hair and skillfully arranged it into an intricate braid that would not come loose in the wind. "Oh, stop worrying and help me with my coat."

"Yes, Lady Mary." Greene never addressed her formally unless she was unhappy.

Mary raised her chin and buttoned up her coat. She was determined to ride. No one was going to stop her.

Striding up to Lord Hadfield, for he would be the lesser of two evils, Mary lightly tapped the man on the back to gain his attention. "I'd like to continue on horseback."

She didn't wait for a reply; instead, she walked over to size up the horses. Standing before a beautiful Arabian, Mary ran a hand along its neck and admired the animal.

Lady Frances's motherly warning rang clear. *That beast has to be at least fifteen hands, much too big for you, girlie.*

"Let me remind you I've been riding before I could walk. I know what I'm looking for, a steed of about eleven hands. Please be helpful and guide me before Gilbert arrives."

Too late—the scent of sandalwood and leather had Mary's pulse quickening.

Gilbert reached around her and ran a loving hand down the horse's neck. Bent, he whispered in her ear. "Who are you speaking to, Mary?"

It was as if he were embracing her, yet they remained slightly apart. A little breathless at being caged in by Gilbert, Mary quipped, "This beauty before me, of course."

She would ride the beast if she had to.

Lady Frances giggled. *Which beast are you referring to, my dear?*

Mary mumbled, "The horse."

Stroking the horse's mane, Gilbert said, "Hadfield

informed me you wish to ride rather than travel in the coach with me today." Gilbert patted the horse and stepped back. "We don't have a sidesaddle for you, so we will not be able to honor your request."

She straightened to her full height, not at all surprised that Gilbert would deny her wish. "I shall ride astride, Waterford. I wasn't seeking your permission, simply informing Lord Hadfield of my plans." She pivoted to face him. The bravado that normally fortified her nerves failed to flow through her veins, and her gaze fell short, landing on his simply knotted cravat.

Without long stretches of abstinence from Gilbert, her resolve to remain unaffected by the man began to wane. From the corner of her eye, Mary spotted Lady Frances waving her hand and pointing in the direction of a spirited young mare.

Mary made her way over to the horse that pranced about, full of energy. Lady Frances must have lost her mind. This mare would surely throw Mary to the ground. With Gilbert on her heels, she ran her palms down her skirts and then reached out to calm the horse, rubbing its nose.

Her guardian angel wouldn't put her in harm's way —would she?

Leaves crunched behind her. Of course, Gilbert wouldn't let the matter go.

A warm firm hand wrapped around her arm and turned her about. "Absolutely not. That animal is too spirited."

His normally gravelly voice was laced with concern. Instead of a flame of defiance burning her cheeks, a small flicker of rebellion prompted her to lift her chin and meet his heated glare. The man did not even blink. He simply stared back at her.

Releasing a sigh, Mary pointedly looked at his hand about her arm and shook off his hold. When he released her, she turned to face the horse again. It would be a challenge, but she was determined to ride this horse, even if it was the last thing she accomplished in this world.

As soon as Mary had a firm grasp of the reins, the mare settled. "Ah. You too are ready to be off then?"

Mary looked about for a mounting block.

Gilbert shook his head and bent down before her, cupping his hands to give her a boost. How peculiar for him to provide assistance. Before he could change his mind, she took advantage of his offer and took her seat upon the feisty beast. She made haste arranging her skirts before Gilbert could take issue with her attire.

One eyebrow cocked, he said, "Lass, if you fall off and break your neck, it'll be your own damn fault. I'll havnae any guilt, and an'aw not worry over me oath to your brother."

"You've never been in a rush to honor your promise before." Mary gave him a devilish wink and added in her best Scottish accent, "Dinnae fash yersel now!"

Her mare leaped forward with the barest of encouragement. Grinning, Mary glanced over her shoulder to find Gilbert sputtering as dust blurred her view of him.

As soon as she came level with the coach window, Greene's face appeared. "My lady, what took you so long? I was beginning to worry we would leave you behind."

Still smiling, Mary reassured her maid. "I'm here now. Why the long face?"

"His Lordship snores like a drunken sailor."

Mary tried to peer into the coach. She must have misheard Greene. "Lordship? Who is in the coach with you?"

Greene rolled her eyes. "Lord Hadfield."

"But he rode with us last night, and not once did he snore."

"That's because he sat awake, watching *you* all night."

"What utter nonsense. Lord Hadfield was fast asleep." Mary frowned.

Is that why the gentlemen had not traded off as Mary expected?

Lady Frances's voice laced with urgency broke all thought. *Lord Waterford is approaching, my dear. Now's the time to make haste.*

Taking heed of the warning, Mary said, "I'll see you at the next stop."

Kicking her mount forward, she managed to catch the eye of an outrider. *"Veux-tu m'accompagner?"* Apparently, her French needed improvement. At the man's blank expression, she repeated in English, "Will you accompany me?"

The man nodded. Mary didn't hesitate. She dug her heels into the mare's flanks, and it wasn't long before she was galloping down the well-worn path.

Mary inhaled the sharp scent of juniper. Exhilaration flowed as the wind whipped against her cheeks. The sense of freedom was short lived. Lady Frances warned, *Fallen log,* prompting Mary to narrow her gaze down the path.

A large tree trunk came into view. Mary yelled, "Jump."

Both she and the outrider bent low over their horses as they jumped the log and cleared it with ease. They needed to warn their traveling party, but the path was narrow, and there wasn't enough room to turn without the risk of being thrown. The outrider raised two fingers to his lips and let out a shrill whistle. What a handy skill. She'd have to ask him to teach her.

As they slowed their horses and were turning to warn the coach, Mary caught sight of Gilbert approaching the log at a breakneck pace. His Arabian was prepared, but Gilbert was not. He was solely focused on her. The Arabian jumped, and Gilbert uncharacteristically slipped from his seat midway.

Mary gripped the reins tight as her heart leaped to her throat. Her eyes glued to his form as he began to fall. "Gilbert!"

In crashing to the ground, Gilbert bashed his shoulder against the log. The horse, free of its rider, cleared the fallen tree with no issues.

For a moment, Mary remained frozen in her seat, blinking back the sudden wetness of a tear. Her heartbeat raced at the horror of his fall. Now was not the time to let her emotions rule. She needed a level head if Gilbert was in need of assistance.

Mary urged her horse forward and said, "See to His Lordship's mount. I'll check to make sure he hasn't incurred any severe injuries."

She found Gilbert lying flat on the ground, moaning.

Sliding down from her mount, Mary led her mare over to the tree line and secured the horse. Mary inhaled, taking a deep breath, to calm the jitters that had her hands shaking.

"Fweet. Fweet." The outrider's whistle brought her mind back into focus.

Looking down the lane, the coach wasn't within sight. Picking up her skirts, Mary rushed to Gilbert's side. She needed to assess him quickly and get him out of harm's way.

She knelt beside his prone form. For a moment, she hesitated—the idea of running her hands over him to check for injuries had her mind and heart at odds. Confound the man for making her thoughts a jumbled mess. Banishing her worries, Mary frantically examined the back of his head, checking for cuts and evidence of blood. Nothing but thick hair ran through her fingers. The pressure in her chest eased a tad at finding him uninjured. However, the brush of her hand against his cheek sent her pulse racing. Even in moments of distress, Gilbert had her body responding to him. Refocusing on evaluating his condition, Mary swept her palm down to his chest.

"I should have told Phillip to go to Hades. The woman will be the death of me."

Mary stalled at Gilbert's mention of her brother. Anger laced with grief banished her anxiety for Gilbert's well-being. She wanted to rail against his marvelous chest. Hades! That's exactly where Gilbert deserved to go, he who kept bedeviling her! She should leave him be and let the coach run over him—but then he would haunt her for the rest of her days.

Phillip scolded, *Sister mine, there is no time to waste.*

Fustian, her brother was right. She ran her hand over his ribs, gently probing. No broken bones.

Probing lower over his taut stomach, her own performed a flip, but for Gilbert's sake, she moved on, down over his hip and toward the top of his thigh.

Gilbert's hand grasped hers, halting her movements. As if in terrible pain, he growled, "Mary. Eloise. Masterson. You had best move away from me."

The coach would be upon them soon. No sense in risking her own well-being for the fool. "Release my hand, and I'll oblige you." As soon as Gilbert obeyed, Mary rose and stomped away, toward her mare.

She found herself sneaking another glance down the path and back to Gilbert, gauging how much time he would have to move out of the way. Why was she worrying over the obtuse man?

Phillip's even voice intruded. *Because he is the one.*

Mary crossed her arms and stomped her foot. "I don't know how many times I must say this—he can't be the one for me! Why won't you all listen?"

A vision of Lady Frances appeared before her. *Perhaps, Mary is right. It is time for us to stop interfering.*

Mary blinked, and her guardian angel was gone. Oddly, the constant hum of voices was also nonexistent.

She turned to look to her left. "Phillip?" Turning to her right, she searched for her constant companions, but none were about. "Lady Frances?"

Mary jumped as a hand grasped her by the upper arm, turning her about.

"Who are you looking for?" Gilbert gave her a slight shake.

Holding in a sob, Mary's shoulders crumpled. She shouldn't have spoken so harshly.

Looking around Gilbert, all that was before her were trees and the path they were traveling upon. Lady Frances, Phillip, the soldiers, and the ladies and gentlemen who typically surrounded her were gone.

"Lass. What is wrong? You look white as a ghost."

The irony of Gilbert's words were not lost on her. Releasing a sigh, she straightened and shrugged off his touch once more. "I'm well. We must warn the driver." She tried to step around him.

Gilbert blocked her way. "It's been taken care of." He took a small step closer.

Mary stood still, resisting the urge to lean her forehead against his solid chest. "Move, you big oaf."

When he didn't move, Mary raised her gaze to meet his.

A mistake.

Brow furrowed, he said, "Mary, please tell me." His brown eyes filled with such concern that she seriously contemplated telling him the truth. For a moment, he appeared open and unguarded. Her heart ached to share with him her despair at having lost contact with her guardian angels.

Did she dare try to make him understand that she was no witch?

She bowed her head. "You don't want to know the truth."

She attempted to sidestep around him once more, but the man was stubborn as he shifted in the same direction. Normally, she'd be irate at Gilbert's interference. Instead, bone-deep sorrow filled her at the realization that she could no longer see or hear her constant companions.

"Lass, I've never seen you like this." Cupping her face, Gilbert said, "I apologize."

Her usually perfect posture collapsed. "What exactly are you apologizing for?"

"For whatever it is that has you upset and distraught."

Stiffening, Mary muttered, "Not now. We need to move the log before anyone gets hurt."

Mary's eyes fell upon Gilbert's right hand. The man was right-handed, yet he had used his left to cup her cheek. Eyeing his shoulder, her fears were confirmed. It sat awkwardly, as if it were not actually in its socket. "Oh, Gilbert!"

She reached out, tentatively at first, but then more firmly as she ran her hand over the man's arm, making her way up to his shoulder, then examining his clavicle. It was definitely dislocated. He was too tall. She couldn't put it back into place at this angle.

Gilbert flinched. "Ooch. Careful."

"Kneel."

"What?"

Mary inhaled, then exhaled, and sent up a quick

45

prayer for patience. "I need you to kneel so I can set your shoulder back into place."

"You don't have the strength."

"It's not a matter of strength but a matter of technique. Stop arguing and do as I ask." When he remained standing, Mary added, "Please."

Gilbert lowered himself to his knees. Mary grabbed him by the wrist, and her other hand rested upon the joint. Carefully, she pulled his arm straight forward as her other hand gently pushed until the arm was back in its socket.

"Urghh." Gilbert let out a pained grunt.

Her hand quivered as she ran it over the well-defined muscles in his arm. "Leave your hand here, against your chest."

"How did you—"

"As you know, I have three brothers. Well, two now. They were a clumsy lot of rapscallions—constantly falling out of trees and such. To avoid our papa's attention, they sought out my assistance when they were in need of mending. It is quite remarkable what one can learn from books and a little practice." *And the advice of so many deceased healers competing to parade their skills.* Mary eyed his shoulder. "Might be a tad sore and tender for a few days. You'll have to keep it rested and in place in order for it to heal properly."

She looked down the path for any sign of the coach. "We need to fashion a sling out of one of my skirts for your arm. Where are Lord Hadfield and Greene? We couldn't have been that far ahead."

"Are you serious? You were riding like you were being chased by the devil himself."

With a grin, Mary confessed, "Oh. I do like to ride rather fast."

"Fast? Humph. Reckless is what I'd call it."

Why did he have to take the tone as if he were speaking to a child?

Mary marched over to the log blocking the path, muttering, "Now would be a good time for one of you to assist me."

No one appeared.

No one offered their advice.

For as long as she could remember, she'd never been left alone before. There had always been a lost, lonely soul at the ready. If they had all abandoned her, who would be there for her now?

Gilbert chuckled. "I'd assist you if you would allow me to."

What did the man find so amusing? She eyed his injured shoulder. "You are of no use."

Mary waited for Gilbert to reply with a quick-witted barb. Instead, he looked about and said, "Well, then how about we take a seat and wait for the rest of our party to arrive?"

Irritated that he had not acted as she anticipated, she snapped, "I'm not going to sit by idly."

"Would you like to hear my idea?"

"Very well. What is this brilliant thought you have?"

"Tie a rope about that protruding limb and then have your mare pull the trunk around. It will be slow, but I think it will work."

"I guess it is worth a try."

As Mary trudged past him, she readjusted his wrist and hand to lie flat once more against his chest rather than resting at waist level. Color flooded Gilbert's cheeks as if her caring for him in a miniscule way affected him. She smiled at having finally managed to evoke an emotion other than ire in the man.

"Fweet." The outrider's whistle caught Mary's attention.

"Gilbert, the coach will be here soon. Should we wait or proceed with your plan?"

"Are you actually asking me for advice? Normally, you go about without seeking others' opinions."

Mary paused mid-stride. How wrong he was. She never did anything without seeking the counsel of others. True, those she sought counsel from were no longer of this earth, but that did not mean their advice was not sound or greatly appreciated. Her angels often provided quality advice, regardless if she requested it or not.

Did others view her behavior as being too proud? She never considered how it might appear to those who saw her in this realm. Abandoned by her angels, she was left with only Gilbert to confer with.

His lopsided grin set her insides aflutter, as if she had swallowed butterflies. More accustomed to his prickly side, she said, "Currently, I'm stuck with you."

Instead of a biting reply, Gilbert said, "Lucky me. We should wait by the side."

He placed a hand on her lower back and ushered her to a spot slightly concealed by a tree. "You appear out of sorts. Are you sure there is nothing a matter?"

His intense gaze had her questioning her sanity. For a brief moment, her eyes locked on his lips and she envisioned him kissing her. The image was crystal clear, except their surroundings were different. Her pulse raced as the vividness sank in. They had been in a room full of paintings. Portraits. Shaking her head to clear her thoughts, Mary's gaze landed on his lips once more.

The corners of his lips raised into a smile. "Tell me, what is going through that head of yours?"

She certainly wasn't going to confess the truth—he'd laugh at her. The idea of kissing her had probably never even crossed his mind.

Mary shared her first logical thought. "You'll have to ride in the coach the rest of the way. You'll not be able to ride with your arm in a sling."

"Ah. I've ridden many a mile during the war in worse condition. This won't prevent me from being outdoors. But perhaps if you rode with me, it might be safer for all."

Confused, Mary asked, "Ride with you?"

"Yes, upon my Arabian. Would you not like that?"

She could not pass up the opportunity to ride such a magnificent animal. She could handle the reins, and she much preferred to ride than being cooped up in the coach.

"I'd love to, and you know it."

"Perfect. It is settled then, and I won't have to risk my neck chasing after you again."

CHAPTER SEVEN

*I*t had been miles since Mary had last uttered a word. Three thousand one hundred and sixty-two heartbeats ago. Gilbert had resorted to counting in an attempt to distract his thoughts from the luscious form that rode in front of him. He had successfully used the trick many times during the war to divert his mind from the images of Mary that plagued him. Today, the tactic was failing miserably as his eyes feasted on the creamy skin above her coat collar, and he inhaled the faint scent of cinnamon.

How long would it be before she spoke again?

Mary seemed rather content to take in the scenery. It also provided him with glimpses of her extraordinary profile. His hypothesis that being in her company for long would make it extremely difficult to focus on anything but her was proving to be accurate. Far too accurate. The smattering of faint freckles that graced Mary's neck taunted him as he adjusted his seat once more.

Heavens above, what was the count—three thousand two hundred and sixty-eight or nine?

For years he had purposely ensured they would rarely cross paths. On the rare occasions they found themselves in each other's company, he acted like a churl, vowing to redeem himself as soon as he had devised a scheme to ensure her safety if they married. He never expected it to take more than a few years to formulate a feasible plan. Over a decade later, he was no closer to determining how to best honor all his promises than he was when he was a green lad of nineteen calling her names. The memory had him releasing a groan.

Mary twisted at the waist, peering back at him. "Are you in pain?" Her brow crinkled, and her smile vanished.

A simple "No" was all he could manage.

She turned back around to face forward. "It will be late by the time we reach the next posting inn. Perhaps we should have Hadfield look into renting rooms."

"Absolutely not. Hadfield and I reviewed the map and calculated that if we maintain our pace, we should make it to Valois's estate by nightfall."

At the last coaching inn, he had gone rounds and rounds with Hadfield, debating the advantages and difficulties of pressing on for the day. Though Hadfield was a trained barrister, Gilbert won the battle by utilizing the man's softness toward Mary.

He pointed out that Mary would spend the rest of the journey riding in front of him with her back straight as an arrow to avoid leaning into his shoulder and causing further injury or dislodging his arm, now securely held in place by a sling fashioned out of one of Mary's own skirts. Gilbert rounded out his arguments stating de Valois's estate would more likely accommodate her need for a nice warm bath to ease her stiff muscles than a sit bath at some local inn.

Never one to share his deepest desires, Gilbert ensured

none of his reasons hinted at his need for her to be close or his wish to continue eyeing those tempting freckles, begging to be kissed.

He sighed as he banished from his mind the image of him running his tongue along the bare skin of her neck.

Mary's head swiveled toward him. Eyes narrowed, she stared at him once more.

He really needed to rein in his thoughts.

Gilbert stared back, searching Mary's face for any indication she too might be suffering from wayward ideas of ignoring proprietary and succumbing to the desire to explore the powerful attraction that had him wanting to taste her. Her honey-brown eyes widened. He smiled at the telltale sign. She most definitely was not immune to his closeness. Mary quickly turned back around.

Disappointed at no longer being able to see her features, he attempted to engage her in conversation. "I wasn't aware that you were such an accomplished rider."

It was no exaggeration. Mary managed his Arabian with impressive skill. The silly beast even seemed more at ease with her handling the reins.

Glancing behind her once more, she asked, "Was that a compliment?"

Gilbert grinned. "I do believe it was."

She loosened her hold on the reins, swiveled, and placed the back of her hand on his forehead. "What ails you?"

"I'm perfectly well." His smile remained plastered to his face.

"Are you certain you didn't hit your head? You've been acting rather peculiar toward me ever since your fall."

If his smile only garnered questions, he had better change tactics. Raising one eyebrow, he asked, "Have I?"

His Arabian shook its head, rattling the reins. Mary

regained her seat and leaned forward to stroke the horse's neck.

Blasted beast.

He wanted Mary's attention. "Pray tell, how have I been acting strangely?"

Remaining faced forward, Mary answered, "Well—For starters, you are not ignoring me." Placing the reins in one hand, she combed the horse's mane with the finger of her free hand. Gilbert's scalp tingled, as it had when she ran her fingers over his head, searching for injuries.

He couldn't tear his eyes away from her slender fingers. An involuntary groan escaped his throat. Gilbert waited to see if she would turn around once more. When she remained forward facing, he asked, "Would you prefer I ignore you?"

"No. But perhaps you could go back to counting."

A giggle escaped her lips. The chit was laughing at him.

Better than silence.

Had he lowered his guard over the hours they traveled inches apart?

Yes—he had allowed the woman to invade his every thought. He should be panicked. Instead, he gave in to his need to touch her and placed his good hand upon her waist.

Mary ceased her giggling, and her head bent forward. The freckle that had tempted him all day was in clear view and mere inches from his lips.

Leaning forward, Gilbert whispered in her ear, "Shall I start from the very beginning or from—" He stopped midsentence, his heart pounding against his chest as Mary place a hand over his.

Mary laced her fingers through his. "From the beginning, please."

Cinnamon tickled his nose as he inhaled deeply before he began. "One——"

His Arabian nickered, sending Mary's weight slightly to the side, brushing her ear up against his lip. The tip of his tongue instantly peeked out. Gilbert resisted the temptation to nip at her ear. Instead, he bit his bottom lip.

Mary rotated. Her eyes focused on his lips.

Gilbert prayed Hadfield's calculations as to the timing of their arrival was accurate, for he wasn't sure how much longer he would be able to resist his urge to taste the woman.

Breathing heavily, Gilbert swallowed before he resumed counting. "Two. Three. Four."

Mary raised her gaze to meet his. Desire blazed in her eyes.

Gilbert blinked. In that split second, an image of Mary lying naked beneath him appeared before his mind's eye. Then his mind went blank. The palm of his hand tingled as if her lush breast filled it.

Mary's sweet voice brought him back to the present. "Gilbert?"

Her eyes were wide open, concern replacing the desire he'd seen mere moments before.

Gilbert shook his head to clear the lurid images. "Sorry lass, say again?"

"Are you certain your fall hasn't befuddled that brain of yours?"

No, it was not the fall that had him discombobulated. It was the inviting woman that sat before him. He wanted Mary to turn back into the prickly lady of the ballroom.

Lights flickered in the distance. "Ah— finally. Valois's estate is in sight."

"Oh, it's like a French version of Seaburn Manor. Isn't it beautiful?"

The mansion before them was as enormous as the ducal home Mary grew up in. Three large buildings surrounded the circular drive. Both square and dome-shaped rooftops housed a multitude of chimneys, and the two extensive rows of windows blazed with candlelight. Yes, it was a lovely sight, but Gilbert's attention wasn't upon the French duke's estate.

Hadfield had dropped back and now rode alongside them. "Lady Mary, we shall arrive soon. Might I suggest you retire from riding for this last leg of the journey?"

Mary withdrew her hand from Gilbert's and pulled back on the reins. "I'd rather not, but I agree with you that it would be wise for me to arrive in the coach rather than seated upon Lord Waterford's Arabian."

Hadfield's dimple appeared as he said, "You handled the beast extremely well. Wouldn't you agree, Waterford?"

With his thoughts distracted, Gilbert blurted, "Adequate."

Every muscle in Mary's body stiffened. "Lord Hadfield, would you mind assisting me?"

Hadfield quickly dismounted and reached up as Mary deftly swung her leg over the horse and jumped into the man's arms.

Mary let out a giggle as he caught her and twirled her about like a little girl.

Hadfield said, "Give your legs a moment to adjust."

Anger blazed through Gilbert like a wildfire. "Let her go. She's quite capable of standing on her own two feet."

Hadfield slowly lowered Mary to the ground and promptly winged his arm. "I'm sure she is."

After spending the entire day in her company, Gilbert's aversion to their predestined union was diminishing. The thought of Mary belonging to another did not sit well with him. Not well at all.

After Mary was safely tucked away in the coach, Hadfield remounted and turned to face him.

"You could have at least had the decency to give her a compliment after she nursed your arm."

"I'm not one to exaggerate or lie."

Hadfield chuckled as he turned his steed about. "It will make my courting her easier if you continue to behave as you have."

Gathering up the reins in his good hand, Gilbert urged his horse forward to catch up to Hadfield. "You'll not be able to sway Mary in your direction."

"Is that so?"

Grumbling, Gilbert said, "She was happily residing in Scotland. Archbroke and his wife should have left matters be and not involved Mary in their schemes."

Hadfield placed a hand on his good arm. "Please tell me you didn't have something to do with her banishment."

"I promised Phillip I'd look after the chit. I sent a note to her papa informing him of my extended stay here on the Continent. I did pen the suggestion he might send her to live with her aunt while I was away and unable to keep an eye on her."

Gilbert eyed the curtains. They fluttered unnaturally. Tarnation! If Mary had heard his confession, then she would be livid with his actions. An ache at his temple had him rubbing the side of his head. Perhaps it was best if she were angry with him.

"Waterford, you are a fool." Hadfield shook his head and then motioned to the coach. "Inside that vehicle is a brilliant, kind, and not to mention beautiful young woman who needs a husband who can provide more than food and shelter. Mary shares the same thirst for adventure as Theo and Lucy." Hadfield kicked his horse and paced slightly ahead. Over his shoulder, he said, "Mary should not settle for any man who is not willing to embrace and foster her desires."

Gilbert closed his mouth, which had hung wide open at Hadfield's words.

What did Mary desire?

If anyone were to find out, it would be him. There was no way he was going to leave Mary alone with Hadfield ever again.

CHAPTER EIGHT

*A*s the coach rolled to a stop, Mary inhaled deeply. She could only hope a footman or Lord Hadfield would be there to assist her down, for she could not face Gilbert. His words had torn apart every kind sentiment she had conjured while riding alone with him. He was the one responsible for her banishment to Scotland. Not that she had hated it, but it was beyond comprehension as to why her family had listened to Gilbert's suggestions. He wasn't her betrothed. He had no claim over her. Oh, why had she let her guard down with the man? Gilbert obviously wanted nothing to do with her.

Mary longed for Lady Frances's reassurances. Her guardian angel would have told her that all would be well and to have faith. Never in her life had silence been her companion. The loneliness was suffocating.

The coach door swung open, and a liveried footman appeared. Mary sighed in relief. She took the young man's gloved hand and descended from the coach.

A man with near-black hair, without a trace of silver, descended the ornate staircase before her. Mary took in a breath. The man's features were stunning. Eagle-like nose. A face graced with lines from years of laughter. But it was his striking eyes that had Mary questioning her vision. They were the same shade of blue that all Mary's male relatives were blessed with.

Up close it was clear he was of a similar age to Gilbert. How surprising—she was expecting Duc de Valois to be older, nearer in age to her papa.

"Ahh. Mademoiselle Mary." He bent and kissed both her cheeks that were now flushed red. "Welcome."

"*Merci beaucoup*. I appreciate the warm greeting."

He bent low to whisper, "Our ancestors alerted me to your arrival, but they did not provide me with the reason for your visit. But first, go inside." He waved his hand toward the enormous front doors.

Mary could not help but ask. "They speak to you also?"

"*Oui*. All the time. But let's discuss your stay in private. Here are your men."

"My men?"

"*Soupirants? Comment les appelez-vous en anglais?*" Her cousin wasn't speaking to her, but those that others could not see, which now included Mary. "Ahh. *Oui*—suitors."

"Oh no," Mary shook her head. "They're more like bodyguards, not suitors."

"Not what I was told." He looked her over, and when their eyes met, there was a distinct glimmer of interest. "I can't wait to talk."

The skin on the back of her neck prickled. What caused it, the look from her cousin or brush of Gilbert's hand across the small of her back?

Stepping out of Gilbert's hold, Mary grabbed the skirts of her dress and began marching up the stairs.

Without Lady Frances to guide her, she slowed as she reached the top and waited for the men to catch up.

Valois reached her first. "Meet me in the library tonight." He continued toward the elegantly carved doors and waved their party in. "*Bienvenu*—Welcome."

The foyer was magnificent. The marbled floors were accented with deep blue glass that mirrored the color of Valois's eyes. A deep rich mahogany wood staircase wound around and up to the second and third floors. Mary tilted her head all the way back to view a ceiling covered in the most beautiful garden scene. How had the painter achieved such a feat?

"*Mademoiselle Mary*—"

"Oh, please call me Mary. We are cousins, after all, are we not?"

"Distant. Very distant cousin, *ma chérie*."

A young maid scurried to Valois's side. "Louisa will take you and your maid to your rooms."

"My thanks, cousin. I look forward to joining you later—"

"Yes, you all must join me for *souper*."

Mary's foot had barely touched the riser when a hand on her elbow stopped her. Without the immediate spark of heat from the contact, she knew it must not be Gilbert.

Turning, her gaze fell upon Lord Hadfield. "Do not meet with Valois alone for any reason."

Had the warning come from Gilbert, she would have probably dismissed it in its entirety. But since it came from Lord Hadfield, she didn't hesitate to agree, with a slight dip of her chin. Lord Hadfield released his hold on her.

Mary was accustomed to having Lady Frances caution her whenever danger lurked.

Without her guardian angel, who should she trust?

Those with whom Mary interacted within this realm

often disappointed. She would have to use extreme caution.

GILBERT FOLLOWED Hadfield to the north wing of the expansive estate. As they entered his luxuriously decorated chamber, he asked, "What did you say to Mary on the stairs?"

"I warned her not to meet with Valois alone."

"Good. I didn't care for the way the man raked his eyes over Mary earlier. Like a wolf who had spotted his next meal."

"Interesting. I sensed something was amiss, but it wasn't Valois's interest in Lady Mary." Hadfield walked the perimeter of the room, running a finger along the walls. "What I found curious was the fact that he was expecting us."

Gilbert offered the most logical explanation he could come up with. "Perhaps the foreign secretary sent word prior to our arrival."

"Mayhap, but there is something of Valois' character that leaves me unsettled. I cautioned Lady Mary, but I think it might be wise if one of us is with her at all times during our visit."

"You can't be serious. We can't be in Mary's chambers at night."

Hadfield pulled back the curtains and peered out the window. "Not we, only one of us. The other will have to keep an eye on Valois."

"Mary's reputation is already at risk, if not already ruined. She's a lady! We are not at liberty to do as we please. Good gracious. Mary is the daughter of a duke, and we should treat her with due respect."

Hadfield simply arched an eyebrow.

Tarnation, the man was right. Mary needed their protection more than their gentlemanly regard. With a sigh, Gilbert fished out his lucky coin from his breast pocket. "Heads or tails?"

"Tails."

Placing the well-worn coin on his thumb, he flipped the coin in the air, caught it.

Again he made a wish. *Please let it be heads.*

As he placed the shilling upon the backside of his other hand, he slowly revealed the coin and released a deep breath. "Heads."

Hadfield peered at the coin. "Very well. You shall be in charge of Lady Mary's welfare for tonight."

Mary was his responsibility. He should have married the woman and settled her in his country estate. Instead, here he was traipsing about the Continent with limited resources, with two other gentlemen panting after Mary. "Let me be clear. I promised her brother to look after her, and I will."

"Waterford. Theo was clear. She did not mince words. I am not to return home until I see to Lady Mary's welfare. The woman gets to decide."

"Humph."

Hadfield chuckled. "From the looks she gave you this eve, I'm of the opinion that my chances are better than fair."

Gilbert walked over to the door and opened it wide. "Seek out your own chambers, and I'll meet you later."

As he shut the door, Gilbert began to mentally make a list of all the tasks he wished to accomplish before supper. He would start with a nice long soak in a bath, then investigate as to where Mary's chambers were located and the best way to reach her without detection.

A scratch at the door had Gilbert swiveling toward the door. "Enter."

A footman dragged in a hip bath followed by more footmen carrying buckets of steaming water. Lastly, a petite maid entered, her arms ladened with linens and soap. Working efficiently, the footmen poured the water and exited, leaving him alone with the maid.

Gilbert looked around for a bench or a table for the poor lass to set her items upon. When his gaze returned to the bath, the maid had laid the linen upon the floor and was kneeling before the bath with her head bowed down.

While at war, Gilbert had grown accustomed to traveling with a batman. However, both he and Hadfield had opted to travel without a valet during their time on the Continent, preferring the freedom and flexibility to change direction at any time. Gilbert had become rather adept at dressing and bathing without assistance.

Making his way to the bath, he said, "*Vous pouvez partir.* You may leave."

The maid shook her head. *"Non, je suis à votre commande pour répondre à vos besoins."*

The poor lass had been sent to tend to his every need. He reached down to assist the maid to her feet. *"Mademoiselle, je peux me laver sans votre aide."* He could bathe himself without her assistance and said as much.

The maid rose, her voice barely above a whisper. "You prefer another?"

Gilbert was relieved to find the lass spoke English. "No."

Eyeing his sling, she reached for the buttons of his falls.

"Thank you, but I do not need your help this evening." He grabbed her wrists with his good hand and shook his head.

Mimicking his head shake, the maid said, "I've been

told I must assist you. I cannot leave without performing my duties."

"We can't have that. Why don't you go sit by the fire while I bathe? When I'm done, you can leave, and no one will know."

He turned her about and gave her a gentle shove in the back toward the fireplace. He wanted to get into the water that was growing cool. It was taking an extraordinary amount of time to unbutton his clothing with one hand.

The maid appeared before him once more, and her small hand slapped his away. "The water will be cold. I'll help you undress. *Oui?*"

"*Oui.*"

She spun him about, and it was her turn to push him in the back toward the bed.

"No, no, no."

"Monsieur, I need you to sit so I can remove your boots."

What a dullard. He needed to get his mind out of the gutter.

Bracing himself against the sleigh bed, the maid knelt before him and began tugging at his boot.

With the maid's back toward the door and her slight form bobbing, he looked up as the door to his chamber opened.

A wide-eyed Mary appeared at the entrance. She gasped and began to back up.

Gilbert jumped up and ran toward the closing door. Risking his fingers, he grabbed the side of the door before it shut. Whisking it back open, he pulled a white-faced Mary inside. "What the devil are you doing here?"

"I was— I wanted to tell you—" She covered her face with her hands.

He reached out and pried her fingers away from her honey-brown eyes. "What did you need to tell me?"

The maid scurried to Mary's side, grabbing her wrists away from Gilbert. "Oh *non*. My master will be most unhappy. He must not hear of this. Let me take you back to your room."

Mary regained her voice as she slipped out of the maid's grasp. "I will certainly not inform my cousin."

"*Non*. He plans to visit you tonight. You cannot be here with *him*."

Gilbert's fists clenched. "Over my dead body will Mary be left alone with Duc de Valois."

The maid nodded. "Mademoiselle Seaburn, you pretend to be ill. I am going to— I will say your monthly has arrived. *Oui?* He will not pursue you."

Mary blushed at the mention of her cycle, but it was a good strategy. As Gilbert nodded his approval, the brash maid pushed him aside to peek out the door. She looked from side to side, then turned and shook her head at his feet, one boot on and the other off. "Can you manage without me, monsieur?"

"Make sure you don't leave her alone until I arrive." There was no soaking in the tub in his future. He would have to make quick work of bathing.

"*Oui*, Monsieur Waterford." The maid again grabbed Mary by the wrist and tugged her out of his room.

"Oh!"

It was apparent "Mademoiselle Seaburn" was not enthralled with the idea of being escorted back to her rooms, but Gilbert couldn't help thinking her outrage was adorable. Pressed up against the cracked door, he peered out into the hallway and watched until they both disappeared out of sight.

"Arghh." Gilbert winced as he removed his arm from

the sling and carefully placed Mary's skirt upon his bed. His injury slowed his progress, but he reeked of horse and sweat. He needed to get clean and update Hadfield.

Then he'd find out what was so crucial that Mary would risk coming to his room to tell him.

CHAPTER NINE

*M*ary rubbed her shoulder as the bossy little maid shoved her into her chamber. The girl had tugged and pulled her arm so hard it ached.

"Mademoiselle. Come."

She followed the girl around to the dressing chamber, where Greene looked up. "Tsk-tsk."

Mary narrowed her gaze at her maid. "Not a single word from you."

"My lady, it is so unlike you to get caught. What happened?"

Sneaking about without Lady Frances to guide her was extremely challenging. She had entered Gilbert's room like a bumbling fool. Having grown up with three brothers who had no qualms boasting about their activities during some rather formative years, Mary was fully aware of what a man and woman could engage in behind closed doors.

Cool air hit her skin as the French maid stripped her of her dress.

Greene jumped up. "Oh no, you don't. She is my mistress."

Thank the heavens Mary's maid slipped a plain nightgown over her head.

The French maid approached Mary with a face brush covered in powder. "Come."

Greene reached for the brush. "What are you doing? She is for bed, not a ball!"

Within seconds, the two were battling for control.

The feisty little French girl spat out, "My master wants your mistress. Tonight. We must make her look white."

Greene froze. "What?"

Mary grabbed the brush and held it above her head. "What is your name?"

"Aimée."

"How did you hear of your master's plans?"

"Sometimes my master, he talks to himself. *Mon frère* is a footman. He overheard Monsieur le Duc say he would come to your room."

"Greene, step aside and let Aimée make me look like I'm on my death bed."

Her maid sneezed as she was surrounded by a plume of powder. Her entire body and nightgown were covered with the white substance. Each maid grabbed a hand and pulled Mary over to the large canopy bed. She crawled between the sheets and lay flat on her back.

Her mind swirled. Why would her cousin wish to seek her out in her chambers? She let out a loud sneeze. This was foolishness. There must be some misunderstanding.

Mary sat up to share her thoughts, but she found herself being pushed back down by Aimée, who tucked the sheet under Mary's chin and said, "Stay. I will bring you your dinner."

Aimée hopped down from the bed and turned to Greene. "Do not allow her to move. If my master comes, you go"—the French maid pointed to the adjoining chamber and pretended to stomp as she continued —"trample on the floor three times and three times again. One of us will come."

Mary called out as the maid turned to leave, "Wait. I want to ask you a question."

"*Oui.*"

"Has your master ever mentioned a Lord Burke?"

The maid screwed up her face. "*Oui.* Lord Burke. He comes and takes the *peintures.*" The girl put her thumbs and forefingers together to form a square.

"Can you arrange for a message to be delivered to Lord Waterford?"

"*Oui.*"

Greene frowned and turned toward the door. Mary's maid had impeccable hearing. Seconds later, the door swung open to reveal Valois himself, elegantly dressed for dinner. With his broad shoulders and narrow waist, the man could definitely attract a woman's attention.

He leaned casually against the doorframe. "*Ma chérie,* I heard you were ill and shall not be joining us for dinner."

"Ah— Yes— I've— Well, it's—"

"You do look pale. Make sure Aimée takes good care of you." Pushing away from the door, he scanned the room before saying, "I shall see you at breakfast."

He didn't wait for a response but simply turned and left.

Aimée shook her head. "I do not think he believes you are ill."

Mary smiled. After seeing her cousin's relaxed manner, she believed there had been an enormous misunderstanding. She didn't think he posed a threat. "My brothers taught me how to defend myself. I'm not afraid of your master should he return later this evening."

Twisting her skirts with her hands, Aimée said, "His

fortune was gone before he inherited. All traded for security during the revolution. He needs to marry a rich woman."

Was Duc de Valois really a villain?

She needed to find out more information. Many times she had been cast aside for her peculiar behavior. She didn't want to assume anything. Hadfield had warned her to be wary. Oh, how she wished to confer with Lady Frances. Her head began to ache.

Rubbing her temples, she peeked through half-closed eyelids to see a concerned Aimée leaning over her. "Shall I get a tray?"

Mary murmured, "Please."

"I won't be long." Aimée's worried features were gone, quickly replaced by Greene's sweet familiar face.

"All will be well, my lady. I'll not let anything happen to you." Greene placed a cool hand on Mary's forehead. "You do feel rather warm."

"It's because you have me under a mountain of blankets."

Greene grabbed a handful of the covers and pulled them lower. "You have been rather quiet. No mumblings for hours." Her maid froze and looked back at her. "Now I think of it, you haven't been yourself for near on a day or so. What is the matter, my lady?"

"Do you find it hard to work for me with my eccentricities?"

"Oh, not at all. You are kind and generous. You never yell at my mistakes or my absentmindedness." Greene tilted her head and reached to rearrange the covers once more. "I was worried. You seem out of sorts. Forgive me for asking."

"Stop fidgeting with the sheets. You're not in trouble. I

was curious as to how another might view my sometimes-odd behavior."

"My lady, you are unique, not odd. It is what makes you special, and I wouldn't want to serve a boring lady who had no mind nor interesting thoughts."

"Greene, you can stop with the compliments. I'm fully aware of my shortcomings."

Greene rolled her eyes. "My lady, you are an extraordinary lady, and I believe Lord Hadfield would appreciate all you have to offer."

"And what of Lord Waterford?"

Greene tapped a finger upon her lips, deep in thought. "He's a tortoise. Slow on the uptake. Wise with a hard exterior. *But* soft and kind on the inside."

Mary chuckled. Greene straightened, and her nose twitched. Her maid slowly turned to peer at the darkened entrance of the dressing chamber.

Appearing out of thin air, Gilbert stood in the door casing of the adjoining enclosed chamber. Mary's jaw fell, but she quickly closed her mouth. She peered past the man, now striding across the room. Gilbert was of flesh and blood; he was not one of her guides who could walk through walls.

Greene moved away from the bed and curtsied.

"Where is the little French maid? I told her not to leave until I arrived." Gilbert's eyes scanned the room and settled upon Mary's face. "What have you done to your mistress?"

He bent closer and sneezed. Shaking his head, he said, "Never mind. I can see she is merely covered in powder. You may leave. I shall tend to your lady."

"Yes, my lord." Greene scurried to the room he had just entered from.

"Tell me, are there secret servants' entrances to all the rooms?"

Gilbert brushed his hand over her forehead and down her cheek. "It would appear so. I can't stay long. I'm due to appear in the dining room, but I wanted to check on you first."

More likely, he wanted to ensure she hadn't absconded off somewhere.

Mary batted his hand away, though her traitorous body ached to seek out more of his touches. "The maid informed me that Lord Burke is a frequent visitor, and he often leaves with paintings."

"Does he, now? How very interesting."

Why was Gilbert still staring at her? He didn't appear in the least surprised by the intelligence she had gained and shared. "Theo mentioned in her letter that we are to restore items to their rightful owners, but I'm questioning the assumption that they might have been stolen in the first place."

"Hmmm—Perhaps before we hand over the paintings, we should investigate further. Do you know if Valois is aware that the paintings are in our possession?"

The bed dipped as Gilbert leaned against it. Cleanly shaven, the man had her pulse racing once more.

Overheated, she pushed back the covers. "I have not informed Valois about the paintings. Perhaps over your meal, you can assess the man's character and what type of dealings he might have with Lord Burke."

At the mention of Lord Burke's name, Gilbert scowled. "The man is the devil. Burke only associates with those who can benefit his cause."

"Or those he can manipulate or blackmail." Mary closed her eyes as soon as Gilbert's piercing gaze settled upon her. She had spoken too quickly and revealed too much.

"What do you know of Burke and his dealings?"

How was she to explain? Lady Frances had been exceptionally well-connected during her reign on earth but even more so in the spiritual plane and was a constant source of information on the ton and their dealings.

"My lord, they are ringing the dinner bell." Greene's hurried words had Mary opening her eyes.

Gilbert bent down closer. "We will finish this discussion later."

His lips hovered above hers. Mary held her breath. The rapid staccato of her heartbeat in her ears drowned out every coherent thought.

Gilbert lifted his hand to her face and ran his thumb along the top of her cheekbone. "I prefer you without the powder. Get some rest and keep Greene close by." He stood and left the room the same way he entered.

Mary puffed out the breath she had been holding and pulled the covers over her head.

Where had she seen that tender look in Gilbert's eyes before?

Ugh. Her aunt's sketches.

CHAPTER TEN

*M*esmerized by the rainbow of colors flickering off his crystal glass, Gilbert waited for the next course to be served.

With a sigh, he rubbed the back of his neck, his thoughts preoccupied with the strange conversation he had overheard in the hall on his way to the dining room. Valois had loomed over the petite maid, asking her if she had seen a mark. The maid's frenzied claims that she saw no mark repeated over and over in Gilbert's mind. Had Valois sent her to determine if he was a PORF—Protector of the Royal Family? How peculiar that Valois would even know of such matters.

Gilbert continued to swirl the wine in his glass. He had barely touched the previous three courses, which included heavily peppered onion soup, a turbot with caper sauce, and salmon with spring onions. Silently he prayed for a course devoid of onions.

He stifled a groan as a footman placed a plate of sole fillet with truffle sauce before him. His host knew they were English. He could have ordered the chef to prepare at least one meat dish—beef sirloin or a braised leg of lamb.

Valois asked, "Lord Waterford, something not to your liking?"

Pushing the fish about his plate, Gilbert answered, "No. The meal is more than satisfactory."

"Ah, then perhaps it is the company you dislike?"

Hadfield interjected. "Don't mind him. His palate is more accustomed to eating from a tin marching the lines than fine dining. I, on the other hand, appreciate the fine flavors your chief has prepared for us tonight."

"Benton—best in France. You will not experience food finer than his." The arrogant French duke placed a petite bite upon his fork and slowly raised it to his mouth.

"It is a shame we must depart early in the morn." Hadfield had timed his response just as Gilbert closed his lips about an overstuffed forkful of fish.

Valois released his fork, letting it fall to the table. "Why not enjoy my estate for a few days? Let Lady Mary rest and gather her strength before your journey." Picking up the fork, he twirled it about as if he were considering the matter of their departure. "I wish to get to know my cousin better."

Gilbert's grasp on his fork tightened. His knuckles turned white.

"We only stopped at Mary's request. We are expected by the Boucher family." Hadfield's reply had been directed at Valois's objections, but his attention was on Gilbert.

Gilbert had no recollection of Mary making such a request. What was Hadfield up to?

Gilbert swallowed. "We appreciate your hospitality, Valois, but we really must be leaving in the morn."

Eyes wide, Valois said, "Ah, you are attending Boucher's annual masquerade, *non*? I too received an invitation.

Comte Boucher's estate is no more than a three-day journey. Why don't you reside here while Mary recoups, and I shall accompany you to the party."

Hadfield waved off the suggestion. "I believe Lady Mary has an appointment with a modiste—"

"*Madame Auclair*." Gilbert supplied the name that Mary had murmured in her sleep.

"*Oui.* My cousin has excellent taste. *Auclair* produces the finest masks for such festivities. She, along with the most renowned modistes, resides on Boucher's estate for the event, which is considered the most wanted invitation of our little season." Valois clapped his hands together and stood. "Settled, I shall accompany your party. I'll arrange our departure tomorrow. After breakfast. *Oui?*"

The duke left the room mumbling and waving his hands about. Gilbert had seen Mary behave similarly, but not in recent days. His hand automatically went to rub the back of his neck.

He turned to confront Hadfield. "What the devil just happened? When were you going to tell me about the blasted masquerade party?" Pushing his plate away, he continued to rant. "Those events are notorious for couples engaging in scandalous behavior, and the one held by Comtesse Boucher has the worst reputation of them all."

"When did you become so overmodest? Relax. I'll take care of Lady Mary, and you deal with the villains."

"I don't trust Valois."

"I don't trust anyone." Hadfield rose from the table. "I'd better find where Valois has nicked off to, and you— Well, you know where you should be."

Gilbert hastened his steps down the dark stairwell.

Valois's estate was riddled with what appeared to be old but frequently used passages. Why the servants would use pathways that scarcely accommodated his shoulders didn't make any sense. As he approached Mary's chambers, a muffled male voice wafted through the walls.

Heart pounding, he burst into the dressing chamber and came face-to-face with Mary's maid. The woman quickly placed her small hand over his mouth and motioned him to remain still and quiet. As soon as he nodded his assent, she turned and placed an ear close to the curtain divider.

Valois's voice boomed. "And what happened next, *ma chérie?*"

Bollocks. Why was Valois in Mary's rooms?

Fists clenched, Gilbert shifted to remove their host, but Greene placed a hand up in front of his face.

Mary's voice filtered through the curtain. "They refused to play hide-and-seek with me and ran off."

Her tone held a twinge of sadness that he had never heard her use before. Anger roared through him as he pictured a young Mary being abandoned, with no one to play with. Being an only child and heir on a remote estate, Gilbert knew all too well what it was like to be alone.

With a self-deprecating chuckle, Valois said, "*Moi aussi.* I learned when I was young that it is not wise to share my gift with others."

"You consider it a gift and not a curse?"

The incredulity in Mary's voice had Gilbert frowning. What were the pair discussing?

"*Ma chérie*, I was not blessed with siblings. I would have been lonely had I not had their company."

Gilbert moved closer to the curtain only to have the maid swat him behind her. That was twice now that Valois had used the French endearment, and neither time had

Mary objected. She was not now and never would be Valois's sweetheart. Stepping back, he rubbed his temples. He should have shared with Mary his true feelings. Now was not the time to deal with his unrelenting attraction to the woman he had carefully avoided for years.

Leaning down, Gilbert whispered, "Whose company is Duc de Valois referring to?"

Greene turned to meet his gaze and steadily answered, "The dead, my lord."

"What?"

"Shh— Listen." Greene moved so that he was now in front of her.

Unable to resist, he peered around the fabric. Valois was leaning against the wall, his arm bent and resting along the fireplace mantle. The man's intense gaze solely focused upon the chair facing the roaring fire. The white cotton of a shift or nightgown caught Gilbert's attention.

If Mary was only dressed in a chemise, no wonder the man's eyes hadn't strayed from her.

Gripping the material, he was about to charge into the room until the sadness in Mary's usually even voice filtered through his anger-filled brain.

"My brothers did not inherit the ability, and while they love me, they never quite understood."

"But he did." Valois pointed to the chair next to Mary.

"Who?" Mary asked.

"Your Phillip." Valois scowled. His attention darted between the empty chair and Mary. Ignoring her, he addressed the vacant chair. "Why would you do it?"

Who was the man speaking to?

The duke straightened and placed his hands behind his back. Clearly agitated, he began to pace in front of the fireplace. The man's incoherent mutterings of unreasonable requests, utter madness, and family ties had Gilbert wondering if he was, in fact, engaged in some sort of discussion with another rather than himself.

Barely above a whisper, Mary asked, "Is he with us now?"

Absently, Valois nodded.

"Why can I no longer see him or the others?"

What was the man up to? Why did he not answer her?

Valois abruptly stopped and came to stand in front of Mary. He held out his hand, ready to assist her to rise. "It's late. To bed, *ma chérie*."

From his viewpoint, Mary took Valois's offered hand and began to stand. Gilbert couldn't believe his eyes. No wonder Valois couldn't tear his gaze away from her. With the glow from the fire, Mary looked like an angel in a soft white linen robe.

The cad pulled Mary into his arms, wrapping his arm tightly about her tiny waist.

Before Gilbert could push back the curtain, Greene placed a hand on his arm. "Wait, my lord."

Gilbert's whole body tensed as Valois lowered his head. Instead of the man's lips meeting with Mary's, his head snapped to the side.

Mary's fist connected solidly with his cheek. "Fustian! Cousin, what do you think you are about?"

A burst of pride at Mary's actions replaced the anxiety that had swept through Gilbert. With a wide smile, he turned and was confronted by Mary's maid, who had a deep scowl on her normally pleasant face.

Greene sighed. "Why did she not give it to him?"

"Whatever do you mean? The blighter will certainly wake up with a black eye in the morn."

"Oh, she can wail upon another with much more force than that. My lady knows all too well how to fight. She grew up with those rapscallions she calls brothers."

Gilbert would have to keep that in mind for the future, for he definitely did not want to be the recipient of Mary's wrath.

Peeking into the room once more, Gilbert caught Valois rubbing his face.

Valois stared at Mary. "Tomorrow you will ride with me." He shook his head and strode out of the room without a backward glance.

Mary stood, staring at the empty chair that Valois had pointed to earlier. As soon as the latch fell into place with a click, Gilbert rushed to Mary's side.

Wide-eyed, she took a step back. He'd never before caught her unawares. Just as his body was attuned to Mary's presence, the woman always had the uncanny ability to predict when he was to appear, even when he approached from behind. Only this time, he had caught her off guard. Something was amiss, but how to convince her to open up to him after he had spent so many years putting barriers up between them?

He glanced down at Mary, who was absently rubbing her ruby-red knuckles. Needing to soothe her ache, he reached for her hand and carefully prodded, checking to make sure she hadn't broken her thumb or any other bones.

She looked up at him in bewilderment. "I have no idea what came over him. One minute we were conversing like old friends, and the next, he tried to kiss me."

Gilbert grumbled. "I do not trust the man." Keeping ahold of her injured hand, Gilbert placed his other hand on her lower back and gently guided her over to the bed. "He's definitely hiding something. I don't know what it is, but I intend to find out."

Pulling out of his hold, Mary untied her wrap's sash

and let the garment fall to the ground before crawling up onto the bed. "Are *you* relying on your intuition?"

Shifting his weight and redirecting his gaze away from Mary's bottom, he answered, "I don't care for the way he looks at you either."

"How does he look at me?"

She must know that Valois's penetrating looks were not at all innocent. Gilbert took in her perfectly symmetrical heart-shaped face, sparkling brown eyes and cute pert nose. A man would have to be an idiot not to appreciate her beauty.

He was an idiot. Or he had been.

Swallowing hard, his eyes latched onto the simple pink ribbon tied into a bow at the base of her throat. "With fondness and not in a brotherly way."

Mary abruptly sat up, and the covers dropped to her lap. Through the sheer material, her nipples were taut, and he couldn't draw his eyes away. *Are they rose or russet in color?*

Thankfully, Mary's gaze cast downward as she fidgeted with the turned edge of the linen. "I can assure you his kind looks are of a unique understanding we share. His actions were simply a mistake."

"You are wrong."

At his stern declaration, she popped her head up. "And what if it is *you* who are wrong?"

The sparkle of defiance in Mary's eyes that regularly brought about his ire now created a twitch in his loins and an itch in his hands to pull her closer.

"While I admit you have a mighty impressive right hook, I'm never wrong about such matters."

"Is that so?"

"I have a talent for assessing another's character."

"Ah. Yes. I recall you calling me a witch upon our first meeting."

Mary would have to bring up his folly. He took the barb that caused his chest to ache. With a resigned sigh, he said, "And I was correct, for you have obviously cast some type of spell over Hadfield and Valois."

She slid back under the covers and pulled them over her head. Mary grumbled, "I'm tired. Please leave."

He wasn't going anywhere, and it was about time she realized it. "Hadfield and I agreed, I will oversee your safety tonight."

Mary threw the covers back and peered up at him. "Safety? Who would cause me harm?"

"We do not know what business Valois has with Lord Burke nor anything of his character. I'll make a pallet and sleep upon the floor."

"Don't be ridiculous. There is enough room in this bed for three or more." Mary shifted closer to the edge and then proceeded to build a wall between him and her with pillows.

Weary from traveling, he was in no mood to argue, and the idea of the hard floor terrified him. If he was reminded of the cold hard nights he spent sleeping upon the ground, nightmares of his days killing and maiming others would surely return.

"Do you not trust me?"

She shouldn't, not after the way he had manhandled her in the carriage and his treatment of her in the past, but for some reason, her answer was important to him.

"I've been told I sleep like a pinwheel."

"How would anyone know?"

"Well, when your maid comes in to wake you and your feet are in the top corner and your head at the bottom opposite corner, I'm sure it is not a hard conclusion to come upon. It's for your own safety."

Gilbert grabbed the pillows and rearranged them. "I

think I'll take my chances and use these as they are intended, to rest my head upon."

After repositioning the pillows to his liking, he stood to remove his clothing. He preferred to sleep in his smalls, but that would not be appropriate. Removing his jacket and waistcoat, he paused and debated whether to remove his breeches. From the corner of his eye, he caught Mary staring. Best not to scare the woman. He pulled his tails from his breeches but left them on as he sank back into the mattress. He turned to lie on his right side, the position he preferred, but it put Mary in his direct line of sight.

Without a thought, he reached out with his left hand and pushed back a tendril of hair behind her ear. "Close your eyes. It's time to sleep."

As he withdrew his hand, Mary turned her cheek into his palm. Her soft skin was like a balm beneath his toughened skin.

Unable to resist, he cupped her face while his thumb stroked down the bridge of her nose before resting upon her lips that were full and lush when not pulled into a tight line.

Mary's eyes fluttered closed. His mind screamed at him to remove his hand, but the devil in him wanted to know how Mary would react if he ran his thumb over her lips. Before he could decide, she opened her mouth as if to speak, and simultaneously his thumb met her tongue, and her lips closed around him. It was the most erotic image he had experienced in years. A deep guttural growl escaped him. He pulled his hand away. "I'm sorry."

Why wasn't she yelling at him?

He pulled his eyes from her lips, and the chit still had her eyes closed.

"Gilbert."

"Yes."

"Don't be sorry." She tucked her hands between her cheek and pillow. "Good night."

"Good night, lass."

He waited until her breathing slowed and steadied before he closed his own eyes, but the images of Mary's honey-brown eyes and rose-pink lips continued to haunt his dreams as they had every night since he promised Phillip to take care of her. At first, he had believed her brother had placed a curse upon him to ensure he carried out his vow. But tonight, he was overwhelmed with the reality that she was mere inches away, and all he could think of was protecting and cherishing her. Cherish. Where in the world did that thought come from?

CHAPTER ELEVEN

*T*here was a bear in her bed.

Mary tried to kick off the blankets, but her leg was trapped. Her eyes popped open. This was not her cozy bedroom. She glanced down at the arm wrapped about her waist. There was that sound again. Much more accustomed to waking to the chatter of a few dozen voices, she was confused by the lack of conversation; instead, all she heard was the sound of birds chirping and the occasional growl from the man who was wrapped about her like a vine.

Gilbert.

She should be ashamed of the rather intimate position they were in. But since Lady Frances wasn't present to harp on etiquette, perhaps it was time Mary had a little fun. Admittedly, it was nice to wake up in a warm bed for a change. She closed her eyes once more and wiggled until her back was flush against Gilbert. The man generated a vast amount of heat.

"Lass. I suggest you quit moving."

Was he accustomed to waking with a woman in his

arms? Bile rose in her throat. She shifted, attempting to move out of his grasp.

"Mary, please. I beg of you. If you dinnae cease—"

As soon as she heard her name, she stopped trying to pry his arm away from her waist. His raspy plea had her snuggling back into his embrace.

"You were right; you are a restless sleeper. The only way to prevent you from kicking me was to hold you. Do you object?"

"No. You are better than a warming pan."

Gilbert chuckled and rubbed his foot against hers. Yes, definitely better than any warming devices she had tried in the past.

It had to be close to dawn. "You will have to leave soon."

"Umm— I still have a while yet. Unless you want me to go now."

"Oh, no." She placed a hand over his, securing it against her stomach. Threading her fingers through his, Mary said, "I'd like it if you would stay. I don't think I've slept this soundly since I was—well, ever."

He grunted as she moved again, this time to try to look over her shoulder at him.

"Are you well?"

"If I'm to leave with any dignity, either you stop rubbing against me, or I'll need to roll over."

The urge to wiggle and press herself farther back against him was overwhelming. After years of restraint and moderating her behavior, she gave in to temptation. Bringing his hand up to her breast and undulating her hips, she asked, "Are you telling me to refrain from this type of movement?"

"Lass, are you trying to kill me?"

She stilled her movements and shook her head. Over

the years, Mary could count on one hand the number of times Gilbert had used the Scottish word. Yet on this trip, it rolled off his tongue as if it were a special endearment, solely meant for her.

Head tilted to one side, she said, "I don't believe I know the full extent of your Scottish lineage."

"And what do you know of me?"

Hmm. Everything Mary knew of the man was passed down from her brother. "Phillip spoke and wrote about you often before and after your visit to Seaburn Manor."

"Is that a fact?"

She was glad they were not face-to-face, certain her cheeks were beet red. She had partly fallen in love with the man Phillip had portrayed in his letters to her. But the boy she had met in the field was a rude, judgmental fellow who had called her names. After the disastrous visit, Phillip had continued to harp on about Gilbert's strengths.

How noble he was.

How intelligent he was.

How courageous he was on the battlefield.

She hadn't laid eyes on the man again until he had returned to visit Seaburn Manor to pay his condolences. She recalled Gilbert's stifled features as he tried to inform her of his promise to Phillip and how mortified she had been that it had taken her brother's death to secure a marriage proposal from the man. While Mary loved Phillip dearly and wished she could willingly fulfill his dying wish, she could not marry a man who considered her a witch.

From their brief interactions, Mary witnessed all the qualities that Phillip had harped upon, but she was also cognizant of the fact that Gilbert questioned her honesty. While she did not believe love was required for a successful marriage, she most certainly believed trust essential.

Gilbert began to caress the underside of her breast

with his thumb, bringing her thoughts back to the present. "Yes. But I realize now that my brother's portrayal of you was not exactly accurate."

His movements stilled, and his whole body tensed.

Mary hadn't meant to offend him. Her brain wasn't quite fully functioning. Distracted by his gentle caresses and the distinct hardening length against her bottom, her thoughts were becoming erratic along with her breathing.

"How did Phillip depict me?"

She selected her words carefully. "In the early years while you two were away at Cambridge, he used words like *reliable*, *solid fellow*, *even temperament*, *good with his fists*, *grows broader and stronger*—which he appreciated by his scrawny side."

Gilbert began to relax with each word she uttered, but his hand remained unmoving. Her skin prickled. She wanted to move and shift against him, seeking the friction her body ached for. Wanting to be done with their discussion, she quickly added, "And while you were away at war, he referenced *fearless*, *brilliant*—*often outsmarting the enemy with little to no loss of life*. Claimed he would follow you to the end of the earth if need be."

Phillip had been her closet sibling and fierce protector. Sad at his passing, she was at first relieved he had chosen to remain on this earth but recently wondered why. Had she been the reason for him not moving on? Phillip had up until two days ago been a constant companion along with Lady Frances. She couldn't prevent the shudder that rolled through her.

Gilbert lowered his hand to rest upon her hip. "I'm sorry. I shouldn't have brought up Phillip. You must miss him."

She rolled to face Gilbert, wanting to tell him that Phillip didn't harbor any ill will against him and that it wasn't his fault that Phillip died during the battle. But he would ask her how she knew, and he wouldn't want to hear the truth. With a sigh, she said, "Not until recently."

Gilbert's eyes were still half-closed. "I believe his fondest wish will be fulfilled."

"Which wish is that?"

Eyes now wide open, Gilbert stated, "For us to marry."

Grabbing him by the chin, she tilted his head down until he met her gaze. "Beg pardon?"

With a slight frown, Gilbert answered, "As soon as I can have it arranged, we will be married."

He was serious.

Narrowing her gaze, she asked, "Why?"

"Because I'm in your bed, and I promised Phillip."

He was daft if he thought she would agree. "I refuse your offer."

She would rather be a boring old maid than be married to someone who held no regard for her.

He merely grinned. "You are bonny even when angry."

"Gilbert, I've never known you to be a liar. Don't—"

"Your beauty was never in question."

"Then what was? Oh yes, I remember now, it was my sanity."

She tried to roll over, but his arm curved about her, pulling her closer to him.

Gilbert asked, "Why did you allow me to stay?"

She wanted adventure, and she believed he would provide it.

She refrained from snuggling back into his warm body. "Obviously, I'm not right in the mind. And neither are you if you think I'll marry you."

"I can't take back words already spoken. But I promise you if you agree to marry me, I'll never abuse or hurt you—"

"Oh, I know you won't. Because you'll lock me away in the country like you told my papa to do until you were ready to fulfill your promise to my brother." He closed his eyes. It was an admission of guilt. This time it was he who rolled away. "I will write to your papa, and we will be married within a fortnight."

Jumping down from the bed, she raced to the other side so he faced her. She put her hands on her hips. "Gilbert Elliot Talbot."

The man had the nerve to smile.

His eyes lowered to where her nightgown was stretched taut across her chest. "Yes?"

"I won't marry you."

At her rejection, he finally raised his dark brown eyes to hers.

Mary said, "I want—" Gilbert's intense stare had her mind going blank.

"Tell me, what is it you require?" His jaw clenched as he waited, and his eyes remained trained on her. "Don't tell me you are hoping for a union fostered out of love. They do not exist."

She was fully aware of the fact. Her own parents were a prime example. No, it wasn't a love match she sought.

Lady Frances had always advised, *If you don't ask, you will never know*.

Mary rolled her shoulders back. Gilbert's gaze lowered to fall upon her chest. Ah, so she could distract the man.

Refocusing her thoughts, she said, "Love can grow. This is not what I seek from my husband. I want a man who can provide me with adventure. Trust in me and my abilities to assist him in whatever challenges arise in our life and marriage together. Someone to believe in me."

Gilbert's mouth fell open, but no words emerged. She turned and began stomping over to the adjoining chamber.

Footfalls sounded behind her. She suppressed a squeal as Gilbert's arm snaked about her waist. He picked her up and carried her back to the bed. Falling unceremoniously upon the soft mattress, Mary scuttled backward until her shoulders hit the headboard. Gilbert climbed up on the bed, and loomed over her. "Do you believe in me?"

Did she? Mary stared into his eyes. She honestly couldn't say one way or the other.

She said, "I trust you."

Gilbert's lips began to move, drawing her gaze away from the warm brown eyes that had her mesmerized. "Ah, but that is not the same, is it? You ask something of me that you, yourself, are unable to return."

Short of breath, her brain was struggling to devise a quick retort. His lips curled into a smirk. The truth of his statement struck her—believing in and trusting another were indeed two different matters. Flustered, she conceded, "Very well. You have a point."

Leaning in an inch closer, he whispered, "Grant me permission to court you."

Hmm. What would Lady Frances advise?

No longer able to converse with her angel, Mary would have to decide on her own. Only it was hard to consider all the arguments for or against a courtship when he was so near.

She wanted adventure.

He was an agent of the Home Office.

She needed to feel his lips on hers.

As if he could read her thoughts, Gilbert tilted his head slightly and bent near until his lips were a hairbreadth away from her own.

Grazing her front teeth over her lower lip, Mary swallowed hard. She was about to experience her first kiss.

Tearing her eyes away from his mouth, she said, "Permission granted."

A gentle force pushed her from behind. Her lips found his.

Gilbert's kiss was light and feathered, not at all what she had imagined. The Gilbert Elliot Talbot she knew was a man of great emotion beneath his cool exterior.

Passionate.

Without her guides, she had interpreted the flickers of excitement in Gilbert's eyes as desire—had she been wrong?

Overcome by the need to be closer to him, Mary wound her arms around his neck and threaded her fingers through his hair. Gilbert pushed her back against the wood and deepened the pressure of the kiss. A moan escaped her. The force of his kiss eased as his tongue peeked out to touch her lower lip. Her own lips parted. Glorious heat seeped through her body. Pulling him closer, she mimicked his actions. The scandalous feel of Gilbert's tongue in her mouth banished all thoughts from her mind. Devoid of the constant voices and concerned eyes of those who had passed, she was free to indulge. Her heart soared.

Sounds emerged from the changing chamber. Gilbert pulled back with a groan. Greene must be awake and getting ready for the day.

Gilbert rolled to stand next to the bed. "I must go. I'll ride with you and Valois today." He ran a hand through his hair that mere moments ago had been in her grip.

Without his warmth, the cool air reinvigorated her mind. This was her chance to test her mettle against Gilbert. "You said we need more information on my cousin's motives and his dealings with Lord Burke. Let me ride alone with him, and I'll try to gather the information."

A deep crease appeared on Gilbert's forehead. Mary

gripped the sheets and pulled them up to her chin as she waited Gilbert's answer. Was it his trust or his belief in her to gain the intel necessary that she sought?

She slowly released the breath she held as he said, "For today only."

Mary stared at Gilbert. She had won. He bent and gave her a quick kiss before turning to leave. Uncertain if the patter in her heart was from his kiss or her victory, she slid farther down under the covers.

Now to figure out how to carry out the enormous task without the assistance of Lady Frances and the others.

CHAPTER TWELVE

 $\mathcal{M}$ ary cringed as her cousin entered the coach. The dark shadow at the corner of Valois's eye and the awful blue-purple discoloring on his cheek marred his otherwise handsome features. After the age of thirteen, she hadn't had cause to actually hit a person. Her brothers had ceased agreeing to spar with her as soon as she developed buds on her chest. It was obvious that despite her lack of practice she was still extremely proficient at defending herself.

Covering her slightly swollen knuckles with her left hand, Mary focused on not fidgeting and blurting the question that plagued her. What had prompted him to attempt to kiss her? She had tossed the early-morning hours away trying to deduce a logical explanation for his behavior. Except her thoughts were preoccupied with Gilbert and *his* kisses.

"*Bonjour, ma chérie.*"

Mary jumped at Valois's greeting. "Good morning to you, *cousin*." She quickly turned her gaze out the window.

The coach was surrounded by a large contingent of men on horseback. Scanning the group, her pulse raced.

At the sharp rap of Valois's hand against the coach, Mary started. Breath hitched, she swiveled to sit back against the plush squabs of the coach bench.

Valois chuckled. "I am surprised your lords allowed you to accompany me alone."

"They both prefer to be out of doors and ride."

"And you?"

At the teasing tone of Valois's question, Mary raised her gaze to his. Her cousin's smile was back to that of a friend. If she wanted him to be open, honest, and forthright with her, she would have to treat him the same. "I too prefer to travel by horse, but that would not allow me the opportunity to get to know you."

Wide-eyed, Valois asked, "Ah. But for what purpose? Is a proposal what you seek from me?"

Mary blinked twice. "Proposal? Of marriage?"

"*Oui.*"

She studied her cousin's features. There was no hint of amusement or teasing. "Do you find me attractive?"

Valois's gaze roamed over her features. "*Mais oui.* You are very beautiful, *ma chérie.*"

The man needed his sight checked. She was no beauty. Unlike her brothers, who were blessed with blond hair and striking blue eyes, she had been born with dull brown eyes and hair. "Is that all you require of your duchess? To be easy on the eyes?"

"Better for me to produce heirs." His stare did not waiver. "But you do not look at me like a husband, *oui?*"

The mention of heirs had Mary panicking. "No. Yes."

Her cousin's English was, at times, a little confusing. She needed to turn the conversation to safer topics, or at least to topics that would allow her to gain the information she'd promised Gilbert she would obtain. She fidgeted with the tassels on her cloak while she calmed her nerves and realigned her thoughts.

Ready to take on the task of extracting as much information as she could, she lifted her gaze back to Valois. The muscles in her neck relaxed. Valois had once again adopted the features of a confidant and friend. If she were to ask now, would he answer her questions regarding his dealings with the evil Lord Burke, or should she wait?

Valois rested the back of his head against the plush squabs of the coach and closed his eyes. "Plenty of time, *ma chérie*. It will take us a little over two days to reach our destination."

Had he read her mind?

Eyes remaining shut, he answered her unspoken question. "They are afraid you will remain stubborn."

"Who are you referring to?"

"You know who. The ones you choose to ignore."

He couldn't possibly be referring to Phillip, Lady Frances, and the others. It hadn't been her choice. "Ignore. They left me! Poof. Disappeared. I've tried to contact them."

"That is not how it works. They *never* leave. You are the one who silenced them."

Mary released the tassel, which she had managed to reduce to a mangled piece of material, and clasped her hands tight in her lap. Valois spoke the truth. Her aunt Agnes had mentioned the same thing—she was the only one capable of banishing the spirits.

Tapping her cousin on the knee, Mary asked, "How do I get them back?"

Unmoved, Valois only asked a question of his own. "Do you really want to see your brother again?"

"Of course!"

As Mary sat back, she reflected that the truth was she had enjoyed the night devoid of voices. Free of guilt, snuggled warmly in Gilbert's arms.

"I don't believe you, and neither does he."

"Can you see Phillip, now?" She whisked her head to the empty space beside her.

"*Ma chérie*, I have my eyes closed, I see no one."

The man was being obtuse. "But you can *hear* them."

"*Oui.* Of course." Valois's head rolled slightly from side to side. "The silence— would be strange, *non*?"

"I admit it was at first." Mary smiled as she explained. "To hear only the sound of the carriage wheels along the path. The snorts from the horses. Knowing the only voices I could hear were those of the physical plane. It is rather refreshing."

Valois popped his head up. "Interesting. Those sounds you are talking about; I cannot hear them.

"That is because it is near impossible to hear anything but their voices. I admit I do miss the advice of a few."

"I am afraid I listen too much despite my suspicions."

Recalling the advice of Aunt Agnes, Mary said, "They can only advise. It is you who acts."

"Wise woman." He tugged on his elegantly designed coat sleeves before crossing his arms across his chest. Letting his head fall back to rest against the cushioned seat, he closed his eyes once more. "Time to rest. I am told you did not get much rest last night. We shall discuss matters after luncheon."

His advisors were mistaken. She was, in fact, well-rested. Mary had slumbered like a babe in Gilbert's secure arms. Without all the racket in her mind, she had drifted to sleep relatively fast.

She stared at Valois, intrigued by his relaxed appearance. Her cousin's carriage was well sprung and a comfortable temperature with the carriage windows open, but how was he able to relax and banish the voices so quickly?

Valois's head bobbed about without care until it came to rest against the coach wall. Mary studied his features. Relaxed, he easily could have been mistaken for Phillip. She blinked. Were her eyes playing a trick on her?

While Valois's skin was a slightly darker shade, his hair color, the angle of his nose, and the slight protrusion of his ears were remarkably similar to Phillip's.

Thank goodness she had reacted as she had last eve. Kissing him now would be like kissing her brother. She closed her eyes, attempting to dispel the image and the queasy feeling in her stomach. Focusing only on the drum of horse hooves rhythmically hitting the ground, she smiled and relaxed her head against the coach sidewall.

GILBERT RODE CLOSE to the open window, but no voices emerged. They were still an hour or so from the coaching inn where they had planned to stop for luncheon. It was too quiet in the coach. He wanted to lean over and pull back the drapes.

Hadfield came up alongside him. "Let them be."

"It is too quiet in there. Mary promised to obtain information."

"Give her time. She has to build trust. It wouldn't do to just come out and accuse the man of consorting with the enemy. We have at least another day and a half to ride."

"What are they doing then?"

"Resting would be my guess. By the looks of those dark circles under your eyes, Lady Mary needs to get some sleep."

Irritated by the man's statement, Gilbert snapped, "*She* slept fine."

Hadfield had the annoying habit of simply arching a single eyebrow when he sought out specifics. Gilbert wasn't going to supply more details than necessary.

He returned the nonverbal question with a shrug.

When Hadfield remained obstinately quiet, Gilbert declared, "I'll need your assistance in arranging a ceremony once we have completed our assignment."

"Are you telling me Lady Mary has agreed to marry you?"

Gilbert wanted to bow his head in defeat. His deep-seated distaste of arranged marriages surfaced again. "Not exactly. Mary has agreed to my courting her for the duration of our trip." He sat straighter in his seat to dispel the unwanted nervousness that had him doubting if Mary would eventually choose him for a husband. "She will be my wife by the end of our journey."

"We shall have to wait and see. I will only assist you if the woman willingly agrees to the union. Why the change of heart?"

"Not so much a change of heart. Rather, I have finally accepted the decision that had been made for me a long time ago." Heaving a sigh, Gilbert continued, "Wasn't it you who said Mary's reputation would be in tatters? I won't let that happen to her, and— the woman has always intrigued me."

Slowing his mount, Hadfield turned to face Gilbert. "What are you talking about?"

"Years ago, Mary's brother invited me to their home during a holiday while we were at Cambridge. Phillip had been ranting on about his sister since the very first day I met him at Eton. For years I had heard how Mary had not only inherited her mama's good looks but was also highly intelligent and even tempered—qualities Phillip was aware I was seeking in a wife. My own family has a reputation for making rather rash decisions out of pride or stupidity."

"Yet, you are not at all temperamental."

Gilbert shrugged. "I must hide it well then."

For years Gilbert had worked hard to eradicate any and all similarity to his papa. The man who sired him had neglected both his mama and him for years. A stabbing pain hit him right in the middle of his chest. *Tarnation!* Gilbert paused for a breath. He had acted as sinfully careless toward Mary as his papa had toward his strong, intelligent mama.

"Extremely." Hadfield's singular response hung in the air.

Gilbert inhaled deeply through his nose before continued with his story. "From the very first moment I stepped onto the ducal estate, I was plagued by a heavy weight upon my shoulders. It was if my future would be dictated by the events of that visit. Strange thoughts of meeting my future spouse consumed my mind. I was only nineteen at the time. I wasn't ready to be tied down. I wanted to choose the lady who would become the next Countess Waterford. But the old hag, their aunt Agnes, declared me to be the one, and that was that. Ever since she placed that curse on me, the Masterson family treated me as one of their own. At first, I was delighted, not having any siblings, to be welcomed into such a warm, loving family. Mary was not simply pretty. The chit literally took my breath away. But it felt like someone else had deemed it so, and I, in my youthful stupidity, rebelled. I used her confession of talking to and seeing the dead as a lame excuse to refuse the hand that had been given to me."

"Lady Mary is a— what is it called?"

"I'm not sure there is a name." He looked at Hadfield. "Don't tell me you believe in such nonsense."

"There are things in this world that cannot be simply explained. Lady Mary never struck me as the sort to lie or make up stories. If she says she can, then I believe her."

Then I believe her. Gilbert's blood pressure rose. It was what Mary said she wanted—someone to believe in her. He would not let Hadfield take her away from him. After having Mary in his arms and savoring her peaceful effect on his rioting thoughts and emotions, he knew with all his heart that she was meant for him. Him and no one else. Especially not Hadfield.

Gilbert would have to convince Mary he was worthy of her hand. But could he give her what she most desired—an unwavering belief in her?

CHAPTER THIRTEEN

*A*fter a brief respite at an inn, Mary entered the traveling coach and adjusted her skirts. She settled back into the corner of the coach as Valois reclaimed his seat opposite her.

Blasted skirts.

Normally she was unaffected by the weather, but with the combination of the afternoon heat and her reaction to Gilbert, a bead of sweat trickled down the back of her neck.

Confounded man. Mary released a sigh as she readjusted the layers of material about her legs once more.

"*Ma chérie*, do you feel ill?"

The concern in her cousin's blue eyes reminded her once more of Phillip. She missed the ability to consult her brother. She pasted a smile on her face. "I'm well. Why do you ask?"

"You barely ate anything at the inn. Although with Waterford looking at you the way he did, I do not blame you."

Relief washed over her. "So it wasn't my imagination—Gilbert was being a bear."

"Hard to say what the man thinks, but I am sure he did not like it that you chose to sit next to Hadfield and me and not him.

"I don't understand the man. I already agreed to his request to court me."

What logic was there in sitting next to Gilbert? She had purposely chosen to sit directly opposite so she could have a better view of him. She'd anticipated charming looks and lively conversation, all designed to make her favorable to his proposal, but instead she'd been the recipient of surly grunts and dark scowls. She'd spent most of the meal pushing her food about her plate.

Valois clapped his hands. "Ah. Excellent news."

"Is it?"

"*Bien sûr*. Now, what other issues do we need to discuss?" He tapped the side of his head with a forefinger. "Ah. *Oui*. Lord Burke."

It was apparent that while she no longer had the assistance of the angels about, Valois was still communicating with them. Jealousy roiled her. Her cousin made no effort to disguise his odd mannerisms, while she had spent her whole life hiding in the shadows and corners to prevent others from detecting her ability to converse with the dead.

How had Valois managed to go about with such ease without being deemed mad? His title and gender would have protected him. Daughter of a duke herself, she knew all too well how much power a peer could wield. Her own papa had used his title to protect her for years, but even threats of financial ruin made by the Duke of Seaburn couldn't prevent the horrible gossip that still managed to reach her ears.

Frowning, Valois reached out for her hand. Had she

mumbled her thoughts? It was one of the many terrible habits she had acquired over the years.

Mary snatched her hand back. She didn't want his sympathy.

She cleared her throat. "Why do you allow Lord Burke to remove valuable paintings from your possession?"

"How do you know he takes these paintings?"

Mary was a terrible liar, and she didn't want to get the young maid in trouble. Avoiding the question, she said, "They were recovered from him."

"Magnificent. How did you come to have them? Lord Burke stated I'd never lay eyes upon them again unless I ventured to the Orient."

The Orient! Lord Burke was the devil to make such threats. Mary never understood how it was that Lord Burke, notorious for his dishonesty, had been appointed a personal advisor to the Crown. "I intended to return them to you, but first, I must know. Did you give them to him willingly?"

"What? Never! They have been in my family for generations. Lord Burke demanded the paintings as payment for the safe return of my nephew, Victor."

Mary asked, "Safe return from where?"

"England. About a year ago, Lord Burke arranged for Victor to be taken to England while I attended to matters of his guardianship. There were others who sought to take the boy from me. Until I sire my own children, Victor is the heir to the dukedom."

"Heir? Where are Victor's parents?"

"Gone from this earth, but until he returns home safe to me, I believe they travel with the boy."

Poor boy. He must be scared and confused. "Does Victor share the gift?"

Valois shook his head. "He inherited our family's

unmistakable blue eyes but not the ability that we share. I've been reassured that he is safe. Victor has been residing in a well-respected household with children of similar age. What were their names—" He tapped the side of his head once more. "Ah. Maxwell and Clare."

"Lord Archbroke's nephew and niece?"

"I do not know of this Archbroke, you mention, but I met the children's papa, Lord Beckham, and his lady at court. I was advised they are trustworthy."

Mary nodded. "Yes, Lord Beckham is, himself, heir to a dukedom. His wife is sister to Lord Archbroke, a very powerful man in Britain. But what do you know of Lord Burke?"

Leaning forward to rest his elbows upon his knees, Valois steepled his hands together. "In addition to being dangerous, Burke is very well connected. He extorted every penny from my coffers."

Lord Burke was primary counsel to the king and Prince Regent. If the man had abandoned all sense of loyalty and morality, it was no wonder Archbroke, the home secretary, along with the foreign secretary, was interested in Lord Burke's activities.

Valois's gaze shifted to a spot to her right. "*Oui.* I shall tell her." Redirecting his attention back to Mary, he continued. "I introduced Burke to the Boucher family and the others. At the time, I thought it was a favor, but it turns out I'm not the only one who Burke assisted for extremely high prices."

Mary had never before met him, but Lord Burke was renowned for his wealth. The blackguard filled his coffers with funds from vulnerable families.

Curious, she asked, "Do your peers hold you accountable for Lord Burke's actions?"

"*Ma chérie.* For years it has been difficult for those of us whose blood flows from lines of old. I fear without the assistance of my advisors, I would have failed." Valois paused and reached for her hand. "You do not understand. I would do anything to protect Victor, my family— *anything*."

He squeezed her hand. It appeared the motto *Family First* ran strong in all branches of her bloodline. Her own family lived by the creed, and it had been drilled into Mary from birth.

She asked, "Besides the paintings, coin, and connections, did you provide Lord Burke with anything else?"

He released her hand and turned to face the coach window. "Besides women, food, and drink? *Non*." Valois turned back to face the space next to her and mumbled, "She should not know of such things."

With his brow creased, Valois said, "There was one time Burke asked for information about the supply of opium. This I refused to assist him with."

"Opium?" The London papers had reports of the substance crossing the channel and the terrible effects it had on a man and his behavior.

"*Oui*. Many soldiers seek it out constantly. To alleviate the pain of body or soul." Valois's gaze took on a glassy look. Were the voices of soldiers past becoming too much?

Mary leaned forward and placed a hand upon his knee. The physical contact would help Valois focus on the conversation. In soft tones, she asked, "Please explain. I don't understand how knowledge of opium would help Lord Burke?"

With his gaze clear, Valois answered, "A man who has been in battle, a skilled killer, and addicted, would do anything to obtain more of this drug. Burke could command a small army fully under his control."

"What would he need with a band of ex-soldiers?"

Valois lowered his gaze. "Burke once had vast dealings, but it is rumored he now survives on blackmail money. Burke has lost the ear of the Prince Regent in recent months and is desperate to regain it, and his power within the court. Who knows what the devil has in mind?" Tapping the side of his head, her cousin said, "*Oui. Oui.* I will warn her. Burke is a very dangerous man and has many working for him. Be very careful with the information that you now possess."

"No one will ever suspect me of knowing anything. I'm but a spinster upon whom her French cousin has taken pity and decided to show her how to live a little by inviting her to accompany him to a scandalous masquerade ball."

Mary's smile radiated from within. She was proud of herself, managing to come up with a plausible story all on her own without the assistance of Lady Frances or Phillip.

Raising his gaze to meet hers, and with a twinkle of mischief, he said, "A wonderful story indeed. One we shall use upon our arrival. I suspect it will be a surprise to Boucher that I have brought with me such a large English entourage."

"I suspect you are correct. But it is one of the finer lessons I learned, having to live with the gift—the ability to adapt and accept things as they come along."

"Ah, the best is the knowledge of what is to come, even if it is only mere moments before."

Mary laughed. It felt good to speak of her ability without shame or embarrassment.

CHAPTER FOURTEEN

*T*wo days!

Torture beyond what Gilbert had endured during the war was what the past few days had been. Over forty-eight hours of watching Mary and Valois laugh and conspire in hushed tones. He was supposed to be the one courting her, the one responsible for placing a smile on her face. Not the handsome blue-eyed frog.

How was he to court her when she paid him no mind?

Valois was now the recipient of those impish grins she used to bestow upon him when she would win a verbal argument. Starved of her attention, Gilbert craved the occasional sideways glance. Like the one Mary was currently giving him as she and Valois made their way back to the luxurious travel coach for the final leg of their journey.

Pride prevented him from seeking her out. No, it was envy. The French man could make Mary's face light up like fireworks—eyes bright and full of exploding energy. While all he had ever managed to evoke from her was ire.

What a fool he had been all these years. All because

he had perceived his match to Mary as a forced arrangement when the fact of the matter was she was the only
woman for him. Inwardly groaning, he finally admitted
that there had only ever been one woman who captured
his attention for longer than a moment. Her physical
beauty aside, it was her rapier-like wit and breadth of
knowledge on topics that were exceedingly more interesting than the latest fashion plate that had him
constantly pondering what Mary was about for near on a
decade.

How was he to ensure that she would not become a
French duchess but instead his countess? He wouldn't lose
her to a Frenchman.

Left alone to stew in his thoughts, Gilbert was surprised
to see the gates of the Boucher family estate before him.
His Arabian pranced about, reflecting Gilbert's unease. A
long line of horses, carriages, and luggage crowded the
main entrance to the mansion. The throng of guests
waiting to disembark was far worse than the crowd at
Almack's doors during the height of the Season.

Anticipation filled the air. The frenzied energy that
flowed about them set every cell in his body on alert. All
too familiar with the unnerving sensations Gilbert was
certain deception and danger lurked nearby. He needed to
be closer to Mary.

Curiously, the cluster of guests before them parted to
allow them through. Gilbert maneuvered his way to the
side of the coach. Mary's smiling face peeked out from
behind the curtain, her eyes wide as she gazed upon the
enormous mansion. At the sight of her slight grimace,
Gilbert turned to find out what had caused the woman's
delight to disappear.

Upon the expansive stairs, stood the Comte and
Comtesse Boucher, flanked by boys and girls of various

ages. All but the eldest boy's features were similar to that of the comtesse.

What was amiss?

The coach rolled to a stop. Gilbert dismounted to assist Mary, but Valois already had her in hand and was escorting her up the stairs to greet their hosts. Hadfield appeared on his right, and together they made their way to Mary, each taking a post on either side of her.

Next to Mary, Valois smiled and said, "Boucher, *ma cousine Anglaise*, Lady Mary."

Mary sank into a graceful curtsy, then placed her gloved hand in their host's as she rose. Boucher brought Mary's hand to his lips, while Gilbert's hands balled into fists.

The comte said, "Welcome, Lady Mary, welcome."

Mary's head remained cast downward. Odd. The woman never refrained from meeting another's gaze head-on. What was it about their host that made her behave so strangely?

Instead of introducing Hadfield and Gilbert next, Valois continued to converse and laugh in French until Hadfield coughed loudly. Rotating on one heel and with a wave of a hand in their direction, Valois quickly said, "*Excusez-moi*. Lady Mary's *copains*, Lord Hadfield and Lord Waterford."

Boucher finally relinquished Mary's hand. How peculiar? She had remained mute the entire time. The heated gaze of the comte distracted Gilbert. Boucher took in both Hadfield's and his measure and grumbled in French about having more handsome men under his roof. Valois slapped the man on the back and steered their host off in the direction of the house.

Meanwhile, it was the Comtesse Boucher's turn to give

them a once-over. The comtesse's assessing gaze made Gilbert's skin crawl.

The woman's lips curved in a smile as she turned to lead them into the mansion. "We did not expect Valois to bring such a large party with him. I will make arrangements, but it will take some time with the number of guests arriving today."

She spoke with a strong French accent, but her grammar and word choice were those of a native English speaker. Eyes focused on the woman in front of him Gilbert mentally debated whether the lady was English-born.

A sharp elbow to his side brought his attention back to Mary.

With a scowl, he leaned down to ear level and said, "I thought you had obtained an invitation."

"I never declared such a thing. You merely assumed." Mary's impish grin appeared. She had transformed back into the unflappable woman he was accustomed to. His muscles relaxed as she hooked her arm through his. "Stop worrying, Gilbert. All is as it should be."

Coming to a halt, Comtesse Boucher turned to face them. "Lady Mary, come." The woman's mouth slashed into a frown as she noted Mary and Gilbert were connected. "You too, Lord Waterford."

Gilbert turned to address Hadfield, but the man was nowhere in sight. The clever fellow must have followed Valois and Boucher.

Trailing their hostess and surrounded by strangers, Gilbert's pulse began to race. Large groups milled about, filling the halls and entrances to a variety of rooms. He peered into each room as they walked past, noting a number of them were set up with card tables. Others had billiard tables, but most were crammed with guests. Some dressed casually, others in what he would consider evening wear, and then some appeared to be already in masquerade costumes.

Mary stroked his arm. The simple glide of her hand up and down his forearm settled him and solidified their connection. She was in tune with him and he with her. Cursing his years of foolishness once more, Gilbert placed a hand over hers and squeezed. She rewarded him with one of those marvelous smiles that he had been so envious of for their entire journey to the Boucher estate. Wrapped up in the vision of Mary smiling up at him, he nearly guided them directly into Comtesse Boucher.

The lady of the house had slowed in front of a long line of guests. "Duc de Valois mentioned you are to see Madame Auclair."

Mary demurely nodded.

Where was his brazen Mary, the woman who walked about with certainty wherever she went? It had always appeared to him that she knew precisely where to go and when. He had been extraordinarily pleased by her touch, but what caused her to seek him out now? She was so typically independent; the air of uncertainty that surrounded her now was somewhat shocking.

Grinning like a fool, he patted her hand once more, pleased that she had turned to him in her time of distress.

Mary straightened and stood taller as Comtesse Boucher said, "Come see me when you are ready. Otherwise, you will be milling about like these peasants."

The chatter surrounding them continued as if no one heard the lady's offensive statement. The French were an odd lot.

Mary nodded once more and sidled an inch closer to him as they followed Comtesse Boucher weaving her way through the throng of guests.

Gilbert searched the crowd about them, looking for signs of a threat, but all he saw was harmless party revelry. He shouldn't complain; he liked Mary's lush form pushed up against him. But something was definitely amiss.

They made their way through the grand estate full of twists and turns, like a maze. Gilbert made a mental note each time they took a turn, identifying a piece of furniture as a marker. He had no wish to become lost among all these strangers. He would have to caution Mary not to venture about without him. No, he wouldn't have to. Mary's grip had steadily tightened as they continued to make their way through the estate. She was fully aware and smart enough to know the inherent risks.

Finally, Comtesse Boucher stopped in front of elegantly carved double doors and opened them with a flourish. "This is to be your chamber, Lady Mary."

He stopped and waited for Mary to enter. When she didn't release her hold, he leaned down and asked, "What is the matter?"

"I'm not sure, but I do not trust the woman," whispered Mary. "My skin crawls every time she speaks. It's not a good sign. Please don't leave."

It was inappropriate for him to enter with their host present. But the worry in Mary's eyes convinced him to ignore propriety.

Striding in with Mary still securely latched to his arm, he said, "Lady Mary, this is an exquisite room."

Not only did it house a bed, a writing desk, and a chair, but there was also an entire sitting area cozily arranged in front of a fireplace. Books were stacked strategically about the room; an easel sat near the window. This was the perfect room for Mary. The worry in her eyes was quickly replaced by excitement as she took in the room. If they weren't on a mission, he would have suggested they spend their entire time right here in her bedchamber. Alone.

"Dine as you wish. Food is served throughout the day. As a family, we observe the traditional times, and I welcome you to join us if you prefer, but we shall not wait upon anyone." Comtesse Boucher restacked a pile of books that were scattered upon the bed and dropped them to the floor without care.

Mary's gasp had Gilbert turning to face her. Her gaze was trained upon the books that lay in disarray upon the floor.

Their host's skirts swooshed as she turned and approached, pulling his gaze away from Mary. Comtesse Boucher's gaze took in his form from head to toe. Boldly she ran a finger across his chest and then down his arm.

"Lord Waterford, follow me. I'll show you to your room."

Mary's cheeks flushed, and her luscious lips thinned into a straight line.

"I shall return to escort you to dinner." Gilbert pulled his hand out of his hostess's petite fingers and leaned in to whisper, "Don't leave the room without me."

He wanted to look into her eyes, but she would not meet his gaze. Mary simply nodded. To his relief, Greene appeared along with footmen in tow with Mary's luggage.

He swooped a hand in front of him and said, "After you, my lady."

Comtesse Boucher's practiced smile unnerved him. "Yes, my lord."

She exited the room, and he obediently followed.

It wasn't until they had gone down several hallways that she turned to face him. At her abrupt stop, he nearly bowled the woman over, grasping her by the arms so that they didn't end up in a heap upon the floor. Comtesse

Boucher giggled, and Gilbert released her immediately. The she-devil knew precisely what she was up to.

"Lord Waterford, would you care to join me for tea?" She glanced at a set of double-wide doors, with handles that appeared to be carved from ivory.

"I'm weary and dusty from our travels. I should wish to refresh before joining you."

She ran her palm down his chest and continued until her hand rested upon his family jewels. Her thumb rubbed along his length. Usually, the bold attention of a gorgeous female neatly packaged in an exquisite gown would require his mind to override the physical stimulation. However, after spending days with Mary, or perhaps because she was under the same roof, he had absolutely no interest in another, and his body was in agreement.

Comtesse Boucher, purred, "Perhaps later." She snapped her fingers, and a footman appeared. "Escort Lord Waterford to the Green Room."

She turned and left without another glance, trailed by two very eager footmen.

The footman assigned to him only sighed and led the way to a room that was but a few doors down from Comtesse Boucher's chambers.

He entered, and after releasing the footman, who looked anxious to return to his mistress, Gilbert leaned back against the door. His own chamber was not quite as grand as Mary's, but it did house a very inviting bed, large enough to accommodate himself and another.

Removing his jacket and waistcoat, he eyed the massive bed. A whiff of his own scent had him striding directly to the changing chamber. A quick wash and a fresh set of clothes were a necessity.

Clean and refreshed, he lay upon the bed and closed his weary eyes. Recalling the way Mary had eased him with her gentle caresses had his body waking in ways Comtesse Boucher had hoped to invoke.

Placing his hands behind his head, he began to list the tasks he should complete.

Assess the security of the estate.

Ensure Hadfield had not gotten himself into trouble.

Find out from Mary what information she had managed to extract from the French duke.

The image of Mary's hand stroking his arm distracted him once more. There was only one way to banish his scandalous thoughts. He donned his coat, opened his door, and looked out into the hallway. Ensuring no one of import was about, Gilbert crept out and sought the one room his body desired to be in.

CHAPTER FIFTEEN

*M*ary leaned her head back against the towel that was placed on the edge of the enormous tub that engulfed her tired and stiff body. Despite Duc de Valois's coach being well sprung and luxuriously padded, it didn't change the fact that she had been sitting for two solid days and her muscles were stiff from lack of use. Relaxing in the warm water, Mary let her thoughts roam freely. A luxury she had never experienced before. Baths weren't particularly enjoyable when surrounded by the constant racket of voices and prying eyes, even if the "angels" swore they weren't looking.

"My lady, you will turn into a prune if you remain any longer."

Water splashed as she raised a hand to inspect her skin. Wiggling her wrinkled fingers, she grinned as she replied, "Greene, you might be correct, but the water has yet to cool."

"I've never known you to lounge in the tub this long."

A twinge pulled at her heart. She worried how long it would be before she would see Phillip and Lady Frances again, but the solitude was enough to make her forget her worries. Now that she couldn't see or hear them, she could convince herself she was entirely alone except for Greene.

"Just a few more minutes."

Greene lifted a bottle to her nose. "How kind of Duc de Valois to send along the jasmine-scented oil."

"Yes, my cousin recalls the most unremarkable things I care for."

"Don't you find it peculiar that he knows so much about your likes and dislikes after only such a short period of acquaintance?"

"No. He is a great listener."

The creases on Greene's forehead deepened. "And when was it you mentioned your love for jasmine?"

Water sloshed as Mary stood abruptly. "Please assist me out."

Greene placed a warmed linen cloth about her as Mary's feet landed upon a thick rug. She missed such luxuries.

Tucking the ends of the material in the valley between her breasts, she swiveled to follow Greene into the changing chamber. Only she came to an abrupt halt as she came face-to-face with bronzed skin.

Mary leaned back to see whose neck tempted her lips. "Gilbert!" She stumbled backward, but his warm hands wrapped about her arms and pulled her to his chest.

"Shh. Greene will hear you."

"What are you doing here?"

"I needed to see you."

"Why?"

Confusion flickered in his eyes. What had prompted Gilbert to risk coming into her chambers?

His hands rubbed her arms. "I need to know what you and Valois discussed these past two days."

Mary pulled back and searched his eyes. There was a vulnerability she'd never seen before. She was about to reassure him that Valois posed no danger when he bent and his lips lightly brushed against hers. She reached up and wrapped her hands behind his neck and rose on her tiptoes, following him and preventing him from achieving a full retreat.

Gilbert closed his eyes. "I apologize, but all I've been thinking of is you."

She rubbed her thumb along his neck. When he opened his eyes to meet her gaze, she demanded, "Kiss me."

Like the dutiful soldier he was, he obeyed her command. But unlike before, there was an urgency as his lips glided over hers and down her neck. When his mouth returned to hers, he didn't relent until she gave him access, and his tongue swept inside. Her head spun at having a part of him inside her, and she tentatively returned the gesture. It was like they were mating with only their tongues. If his tongue could evoke such delicious feelings, what would it be like to have him fill her in the most intimate ways? His kisses were dizzying. Gilbert began to lift her, but her legs were tangled in the sheet, and she wasn't able to wrap them about him. Bending, he scooped her up into his arms and strode over to the bed.

Mary looked over his shoulder to where Greene was peering around the curtain from the changing chamber and gave a slight head shake. The partition material fell back into place as Greene retreated back into the chamber.

Gilbert wanted her. She didn't need anyone else to tell her it was so. She had seen it in his eyes. For years Lady Frances had told her he did deep down inside. But for years, he had never shown any such interest. Oh, he had shown care but like that of a guardian or caretaker. But now the heat in his gaze told her he wanted her in the most carnal of ways, and she wanted to experience whatever it was he was offering while the voices remained silent.

As he laid her on the bed, the knot in the linen came undone. Bent over her, Gilbert's gaze lowered to her chest briefly before it flickered back to land on her lips.

She reached for him. Gilbert turned toward the adjoining chamber. Oh, she wasn't about to lose this opportunity. She sat up, letting the material fall to her waist. Reaching for his hand, she placed it upon the swollen globe that now ached to be touched.

Gilbert withdrew his hand from her breast and cupped her cheek. "Mary. You have yet to agree to marry me."

"I'm agreeing now."

"Are you certain? I've not had a chance to properly court you, and I thought that is what you wanted most."

"What I want most is for you to believe in me, to trust me. You not interfering these past two days proved more to me than showering me with compliments, poems, or flowers."

"Poems?"

"Isn't that what young bucks do to gain a lady's hand?"

"I'm no young buck."

Mary shifted closer to the edge and pulled his shirttails from his breeches. "Then you know what it is I'm asking for."

"But do you?"

Did she? Having grown up with brothers that were not at all shy, she believed she had a relatively good idea of what intimate relations would entail. She might not have seen, but she had undoubtedly heard enough bragging from her brothers. There was also the matter of the possibility of conceiving. Her gaze roamed over the man before her.

Her mind decided, she scrambled to her knees and reached under his shirt to place her hands upon his waist. With a groan, Gilbert grabbed the back of his shirt and pulled it over his head. Mary inhaled a deep breath. His sculpted muscles were marked with scars, no doubt incurred while he was on the battlefield. It wasn't the markings upon his skin that held her interest, it was the trail of hair that led down into his breeches. She traced the line of hair with her finger as she hooked a finger along the edge of the material that prevented her from exploring further.

Gilbert's hand covered hers. "Lass, you promise to become Lady Waterford?"

Is that what she wanted? She had known for years this was to be her destiny, but ultimately, it was still her choice. Did she want to marry the Adonis before her?

She had prolonged the inevitable for long enough, and the gravitational pull was undeniable. She had no fears of Gilbert being unfaithful, unlike her own papa. Once Gilbert made a vow, there would be no question as to his loyalty. He was stable, reliable, and oh the warmth that radiated from him. She wanted to press herself against him and soak it up like when she lifted her face to the summer sun.

She nodded and tugged on his waistband.

He let out a long breath and crawled upon the bed, forcing her to lie back. As he loomed over her, she ran her hands up over his chest shoulders and back down his arms. She was about to retrace her movements when he bent and said, "I love your hands upon me, but I want to see to your pleasure first."

What did he mean? She didn't recall her brothers mentioning such a thing. Mary withdrew her hands from his arms. "You would prefer I not touch you?"

Staring into her eyes, he said, "You can do as you please." Gilbert lowered his head and placed soft kisses along her jaw.

Remaining undecided as to where she wanted to place her hands, Mary lay unmoving until Gilbert ran his tongue along her collar bone. The glorious awakening of her skin had her running her hands through his hair. When his tongue continued to make a trail to her nipple, she inhaled with anticipation. Flicking his tongue on her hardened nipple twice, she wasn't sure if it had been her to pull his mouth down to suckle upon her or if she had arched up, pushing her breast into his eager mouth. Either way, she didn't want him to stop.

She moaned as Gilbert teased and pinched a nipple with one hand as he laved and suckled the other. Glorious sensations filled her. Mary's core contracted and ached for attention. Without thought, she ran a hand down Gilbert's back and slid it between them to touch herself.

Gilbert lifted his head and flicked her nipple once more as he shook his head. Eyeing her hand, he growled, "Lass, it is my duty to see to your needs."

Mary quickly removed her hand. "Of course." Unsure of where to place her hands, she rested them upon his shoulders. With a smirk, she added, "I've never known you to fail in carrying out your duties, but—"

She couldn't finish her thought as Gilbert shifted backward and placed his tongue where her hand been moments ago. The man knew exactly the right amount of pressure to apply. Mary hitched a breath as he raised her hips and began to lick and tease every inch of her center. Sparks flew before her tightly closed eyes. On her own she had not managed to invoke such intense sensations. Gilbert's warm breath and the feel of his skin beneath her hands added a different element to the experience.

Unable to remain still, Mary squirmed, pressing back onto the bed. Gilbert was no novice. The man was adeptly building up the tension within her. His hands shifted to her sides, and he ran them up along her body, stretching out his arms until each rough palm finally rested upon a breast. While his tongue continued to flick and circle the sensitive flesh at her core, Gilbert's fingers circled and pinched her erect nipples.

Mary's heart thudded hard against her chest. She wanted him to taste her again. She wanted his fingers to continue their teasing, pinching, and pulling upon her now engorged nipples. When Gilbert acquiesced and gave her all she wished for simultaneously, she melted against the bed and allowed the pleasure to build.

At the loss of heat against her left breast, Mary opened her eyes to catch Gilbert gliding his palm down to her core, where his skillful tongue continued to circle, around and around. He pressed his hand against her, and she lifted her hips off the bed. This sensation, this experience engulfed every sense in her body. Gilbert slid a finger deep into her center until she felt his knuckles brushed up against her. Her inner muscles contracted as he began to withdraw his hand.

Concerned he was about to stop, Mary reached out, grabbing his biceps that was flexed taut, halting his movements. "Gilbert— don't—"

"Shhh. Not to worry, lass. I always finish what I start. Lie back, and I'll take care of you."

Ignoring the condescending words he chose to use, she did as he bid. Moments later, she was writhing against the bed as Gilbert took her to heights she had never known before.

It was a release she had never achieved by herself, and as soon as she floated back to reality, she realized Gilbert hadn't taken his own pleasure. He lay next to her, skimming his hand over her side, with a very smug look upon his face.

"But what about you?" Mary sulked. Did he not want her?

"Lass, once I have you, I'll not want to let you out of bed for days. I'll have to wait until you have scrawled your name in the register."

Blood was returning to her head, but all her brain could manage was, "Oh."

Chuckling, he tucked her under the covers and stood to put his shirt back on. Mary's eyes were glued to the bulge in his breeches. Surely he had to be in discomfort.

Gilbert looked to the adjoining chamber and back down to his obvious state of arousal. "I'll have to take the service exit. I can't wander the halls in this condition."

Mary couldn't help but giggle. He gave her a wink and strode over to the dressing chamber.

From behind the curtain, she heard Gilbert say, "Make sure your mistress is ready for dinner."

Mary closed her eyes. If Gilbert had spoken the truth about not letting her leave the marriage bed for days, she had been a ninny not to have convinced him sooner to make her Countess Waterford. But—if she was like her mama, who became enceinte every time she lay with her husband, then she was right to have avoided the man all these years.

CHAPTER SIXTEEN

*B*ent at the waist, palms planted on his bed, Gilbert took in another deep breath. What had just occurred? He shook his head to clear it of the images of Mary naked. Never in his life had he wanted so badly to sink deep into a woman. Blast! He needed to regain control over his thoughts, or he would never make it to dinner.

When he left his room a little over an hour ago, he had convinced himself that he was seeking Mary out to confront her, to find out what information she had gained from Valois. When he entered and found her wet and naked from her bath, all rational thoughts had fled from his mind. He should be unsettled at not knowing all the pertinent details.

Gilbert straightened from the bed and tugged off his coat. A warm, satisfying feeling settled in his chest as he recalled Mary's enthusiastic responses to his touch. Proud of his achievements, he had extracted from Mary the words most critical to his future—a promise to marry him. His knees nearly buckled as a vision of a baby in his arms with striking blue eyes—the same shade that ran strong in Mary's family—appeared in his mind's eye.

A scratch at the door had Gilbert blinking to banish the image of the child. "Enter."

Hadfield meandered in and stopped short as he took in Gilbert's appearance. "Good Lord, man, what have you been about? You're all rumpled." Glancing about the room, Hadfield walked over to the window.

"Why is it every time you enter a room, you head straight for the window and peer out?"

"Accessing the best possible escape route, of course."

Gilbert would have expected no less from a fellow agent, but from a former barrister? Perhaps he had underestimated the man before him.

Slapping his gloves idly against his leg, Hadfield said, "Well, don't just stand there. Be quick about things, or we will be late for dinner."

Gilbert ducked into the changing chamber and ran a hand along his jaw. He needed a shave. *Had he left marks on Mary's thighs?* The wayward thought had him tugging at his breeches.

"Waterford, hurry up! We don't have all evening. We barely have enough time as is, assuming we don't get lost. This bloody estate is like a maze."

Gilbert slipped the last button in place. It was statements like the last one Hadfield had uttered that made Gilbert question the man's capabilities. An agent would know how to navigate the vast estate.

Exiting the smaller room, Gilbert strode straight past the man to leave.

A footman approached as the door swung open. "My lord, follow me."

Oddly, skin on the back of Gilbert's neck prickled.

Hadfield was right on his heels. Interesting. The man could move without a sound.

At the sight of Hadfield, the footman shook his head and stepped to the side. It was clear the footman was to only escort Gilbert alone. He suspected Comtesse Boucher had sent the servant to fetch him.

What games was the lady up to?

Gilbert would have to be mindful of his interactions with the woman.

Oblivious, Hadfield said. "Oh, good! A footman at the ready."

Eyeing the footman, Gilbert said, "Please take us directly to Lady Mary's chambers. We would like to escort her to dinner."

The footman lowered his gaze to the floor.

"Perhaps you should speak French."

Shaking his head, the footman replied, "*Non*. Duc de Valois declared he was to escort the lady."

Gilbert's hands clenched at his sides. "That will be all."

The footman scurried down the hall.

Placing his hands behind his back, Hadfield turned and said, "Lead the way."

When they entered an empty corridor, Hadfield leaned closer and asked, "Did you ensure Lady Mary was settled in?"

"Yes."

"Any update?"

Gilbert was loath to admit he hadn't managed to get a full accounting from Mary. "Not yet. Where did you nick off to?"

"It doesn't appear that the lord of the manor is a fan of Valois. They heartily disagree on how to deal with our friend Burke."

"Is that so?" Gilbert was glad that at least one of them

had made progress and was focused on the mission at hand.

"Boucher wants the man dead and is willing to see to it the next time Burke sets foot on French soil. Valois wants to let the Crown handle the matter."

"And who would you support?"

"The Crown, of course."

"Of course."

Gilbert found their way to the dining room with little difficulty.

As they entered, his gaze fell directly upon the back of Mary's beautiful swan-like neck. A string of pearls covered the skin he had nibbled upon earlier in the day. Mary was standing next to Valois with their backs to the entrance. Valois was fingering the end of the bow at the small of her back. Gilbert wanted to grab the man's wrist and snap it like a twig.

Leaving Hadfield's side, he strode toward the group that was intently listening to whatever Mary had to say. Comtesse Boucher's eyes widened as he approached, and the glimmer of interest was evident. Mary turned, and Valois's hand dropped to his side.

The blush that rose on Mary's cheeks had his lips curling into a smile. The grin fell away as Gilbert's gaze fell to Valois, giving him a hard stare. The man understood his meaning and quickly stepped to the side.

Gilbert slipped in to stand next to Mary. "Good evening, Lady Mary." She was his, and he would make sure everyone was aware of the fact.

The duke's eyes darted between Comtesse Boucher and Mary, and then he said, "I'm famished. Let's dine." Valois led their small group along with Hadfield and Boucher's son, André, who had joined them.

Gilbert sat at the table, and to his chagrin the comtesse

sat to his left and Mary across from him between Hadfield and Valois. Genteel conversation filtered throughout the room, and Valois pointedly kept the topics light—the weather and their journey.

Sometime between the onion soup and leek-encrusted fish, a hand slithered under Gilbert's napkin. He glanced toward Mary, who was deep in conversation with Hadfield, and reached for his glass of water as he lowered his other hand to remove the comtesse's fingers that were creeping along his thigh. Her hand tightened before he could remove it, and he almost knocked his glass over. He pulled at her hand—the woman had a damned strong grip for a lady. He finally pried her fingers from his person, dropping her hand back into her lap. He looked up, victorious, only to find all eyes on him and Comtesse Boucher.

Comte Boucher and his son simply returned their attention to their meals, while Hadfield glared at him. Valois had a wide smirk plastered to his features, boastful like he had won a prizefight.

Gilbert shifted his gaze to Mary, who raised her nose a smidgeon higher in the air before resuming her discussion with Hadfield.

Heat rose on Gilbert's cheeks, a combination of anger and embarrassment. He glared at Hadfield, stuffing another forkful of fish into his mouth.

Comte Boucher raised his glass to his lips and paused. With a frown, the man asked, "When is Victor to arrive?"

"Within the month."

"Humph. We shall see."

Gilbert sneaked a glance at Hadfield, who gave a slight shake of the head.

With her eyes focused on Hadfield across the table, Mary said, "Victor is Valois's heir and nephew."

What other information had she obtained but had yet to share with them?

Comtesse Boucher leaned forward, giving him full sight of her assets. "Lady Mary, perhaps you would care to join me in the cardroom this eve."

"It would be my pleasure."

The ladies rose, and so did the gentlemen.

Comtesse Boucher led Mary away from Gilbert—like a lamb being taken to the slaughter.

CHAPTER SEVENTEEN

*M*ary trailed behind her host. The lady of the house yielded much power, and the comtesse was fully aware of her authority and charms. Nor did she hesitate to use them. Comtesse Boucher swayed her hips, flashed an occasional sensual smile to guests, and issued the most nerve-racking glares when displeased.

The comtesse was definitely not a friend.

How to convince the woman to assist in Mary's investigations? She needed to know how the Boucher jewels had ended up in Lord Burke's possession. Without the assistance of Lady Frances, Mary had no choice but to try to outwit the wily woman before her.

As her hostess continued to make her way through the room, Mary caught the attention of more than one handsome young male guest. She lifted her chin. *I'm the daughter of a duke.* From childhood, she had endured endless lectures and lessons on deportment and etiquette. She knew how to conduct herself with elegance and grace, which would have to compensate for her lack of beauty. She followed in the wake of the comtesse, executing the Seaburn ducal nod to those who had managed to tear their gaze away from their hostess and come upon Mary.

Comtesse Boucher stopped in front of a table with cards neatly arranged in two rows. "Do you know how to play faro?"

"I'm not familiar with the game, but I am a fast learner."

One corner of the comtesse's lips rose in a smirk. "Faro is complicated and not for the faint of heart. Do you have the coin to play?"

"Why, of course." Coin. Mary had plenty. For the past six months, she'd had no reason to spend her generous monthly pin allotment her papa sent. It was safely tucked away in Scotland with her aunt, but Gilbert would spot her the blunt if need be. Wouldn't he?

"Perhaps we should play a game with less risk."

"Oh, no." Mary sat at the table. A footman took the chair across from her.

"Jean will be our banker for tonight." Comtesse Boucher arranged her skirts and sat in the chair next to Mary and pushed a stack of red-colored coins in front of her.

Counting out the coins, Mary asked, "How much do each of these represent?"

"Five francs."

Mary's hand paused. The stack before her represented one hundred francs. That was more than all her savings. Her palms began to sweat.

Comtesse Boucher arranged her own coins into four even stacks. "Jean, let us use hearts this eve."

The footman fanned out the cards. Selecting those marked with a heart, he arranged them in descending order, starting with the king, to form a singular line in front of them.

"Each round, you place a wager on which card will be the winner. Jean will turn two cards over. The first will determine the losers and the second the winners, and then they will be placed to the side." There was a devilish sparkle in the comtesse's eyes. "You may bet as much or little as you wish. Wager on as many cards as you choose, *oui*?"

The rules seemed simple enough. Mary nodded.

The trick was to calculate both the odds of the remaining cards appearing and how much to wager. Having never played before, would she be capable of such mathematical enumerations?

Jean shuffled what appeared to be a full deck and turned over the ace of clubs.

"Ready?" The smirk on Comtesse Boucher's features solidified Mary's determination to win.

Figuring the odds of another ace appearing, Mary placed a single chip upon the six of hearts. "I am ready."

Comtesse Boucher tilted her head. Grabbing a stack of coins, the woman placed two on either side of Mary's wager, on the five and seven of hearts.

The comtesse nodded.

Jean slid two cards off the top of the deck.

Mary's heart pounded with anticipation. She inhaled, steeling her nerves, and laced her fingers in her lap.

The footman turned over the first card, the one that would determine who the loser was. The six of diamonds.

Mary blinked hard—she had lost.

Comtesse Boucher smirked as the footman retrieved Mary's bet, moved the card over next to the ace of spades, and flipped over the second card, all with deft hands. The seven of spades.

Giggling, the comtesse retrieved her winnings, leaving her original wagers on the six and seven of hearts.

Mary glanced at the discarded cards and then stared at the row of hearts before them. Her hand hovered over a stack of coins.

Comtesse Boucher laughed. "Ready to quit so soon?"

"No. I just need a moment to decide." Mary stared at the cards laid out and recounted her pile of coins once more.

Her host had placed wagers on two cards on the previous round, increasing her chances of winning. Glancing at the discarded cards, Mary counted out three coins this time.

Comtesse Boucher's lips curled into a smirk as Mary placed her wager upon the six of hearts. It was certainly a daring bet.

Eyes remaining trained on Mary, the comtesse gave the nod to go ahead.

Smiling at her host, Mary couldn't bear to watch as the footman slid another two cards onto the table. Phillip was brilliant at cards and mathematical calculations. How she wished she could consult with her brother. Mary glanced about. But his familiar features were nowhere to be seen among the small group of young bucks surrounding their game.

The losing card was a three, and the winning card a king. Neither of them had lost nor won this round.

Retrieving her coins from the board, Comtesse Boucher said, "It doesn't appear to be your night for winning. Perhaps instead of coin, we should play for something else."

This could be Mary's chance to barter for information. Mary turned to face her host. "What would you suggest?"

"Whoever accumulates the most coin wins Lord Waterford."

Gilbert? Mary answered, "I don't understand."

"If I win, you will assist me in having a private moment alone with the man whom I wish to warm my bed tonight. If you win, I shall not pursue him this evening."

The woman was after the man Mary had promised to marry. After the wonderful experiences Gilbert had shown her that afternoon, there was absolutely no way she would relinquish him to the she-devil who sat next to her. Her brother's gambling advice rang loud and clear—never let your opponent know your true intent. "I do not see how you *not* pursuing Waterford is a win for me."

The comtesse tapped her forefinger against her pursed lips. After a moment of contemplation, she said, "Name your winnings."

"Complete and honest answers to three questions of my choosing."

"I'm always frank. But if it is information you seek, I agree to your terms."

Mary nodded, and the footman carried out his duties, turning cards over two at a time. Comtesse Boucher's stack steadily grew while hers volleyed up and down.

If she had counted correctly, only two rounds remained.

You know the odds. Do not doubt yourself.

Mary glanced about, but there was no sign of Lady Frances. She must be going mad—she was beginning to hear voices.

Her hand shook, but she counted out half her stack and placed it upon the king of hearts.

Comtesse Boucher assessed Mary's stack and then her own and proceeded to count out precisely enough coins that, should she lose the round, she would have Mary beat by one chip, assuming Mary didn't win the round.

Pushing her stack, Comtesse Boucher placed it upon the four of hearts.

Swallowing hard, Mary stared at the two cards before them, willing the first to be a four. Jean flipped over the card—the four of diamonds. Mary had won.

"Ah, but we still have one more hand, my dear. If the next card is not a king, I still have enough to win."

"But it will be a king, and there will be no need to play further."

"Let us see."

The sweat on the footman's brow was clear for all to see. Surely the comtesse wouldn't retaliate against the poor man, for he had no control over which card was next. Did he?

The card landed on the table—the king of clubs. Mary bounced in her seat while the comtesse leveled her gaze upon the footman.

"No need to count it out, Jean. Lady Mary is the victor tonight. You are dismissed."

"Madame la Co—"

Comtesse Boucher cut off the stuttering footman. "For now. Report to my chambers later, and we will discuss your future then." She turned her direct stare to Mary. "I assume your inquiries will require privacy. Come, let's retire to my library."

The woman had her own library? The comtesse, a bluestocking? Mary shook her head. Libraries were used for all sorts of purposes, not only for reading.

Mary stopped midstride; she had entered the most magnificent room. The smell of paper and flowers was heaven. There were three walls lined with bookcases and filled with volumes. She twirled about, glancing at all the titles that surrounded her.

Comtesse Boucher chuckled. "You covet this room as I long for your Waterford."

"I do not own Waterford. While a wife may be considered chattel, I do not believe that is reciprocal."

"You silly girl. One look and anyone can tell that man is an excellent lover. The rare type of male who seeks to give his partner pleasure before his own. Oh, what I'd give to run my hands over his body." The lady shivered right before her eyes.

Mary's hands itched as she recalled the delicious feeling of Gilbert's muscles moving beneath them.

She followed Comtesse Boucher and took a seat next to the fire that blazed.

"You know what I speak of. Your cheeks are aflame. But let's not dally. What is it that you want to know?"

"What do you know of your husband's dealings with Lord Burke?"

"Ah, Lord Burke. He is the devil. My husband manages many trading lines across the Continent and has the connections allowing certain items to cross international borders without question."

"What type of items?"

"Artifacts, drugs— and individuals."

"People? Who?"

"That would be four questions, but I'll be generous and answer. The last lot, I believe, were Englishmen Burke wanted gone. Hmm— what were their names again?"

Mary recalled Lucy mentioning her brother being on the Continent, but there also had been rumors of him being missing. "Harrington?"

"Ah yes. Harrington, Hereford, and Addington. Three fine-looking men. They did not stay long enough for me to —. Well, my husband assisted Burke in transporting them, but rumor has it that one fled to the colonies, and the other two returned to your homeland."

"When? How did they manage to leave the Continent?"

"You are all out of questions— unless you want to bargain for more?"

The jewels.

"I have something I believe belongs to you." The locket contained a picture of a young lady and what looked to be her mama. On the opposite side, a portrait of a man Mary guessed to be the young lady's papa.

"There is only one thing that currently interests me." The woman waggled her eyebrows.

"Waterford is not for me to give."

"Here in France, it is rude not to garner the other woman's permission."

"Or badger her into agreement?"

Comtesse Boucher laughed. "I see why Waterford remains loyal to you. You are unique. What is it that you have that you believe worthy of more intelligence regarding my husband's dealings?"

"A locket."

Eyes wide, the comtesse asked, "You have my missing jewels?"

"I thought they were your husband's."

A fierce scowl appeared on the woman's face. "He doesn't even know about them. Burke took them after I refused him."

"Would you be interested in a trade?"

Eyes narrowed, the comtesse asked, "What do you want to know?"

"Everything you know of Burke's plans."

"Burke has run out of favors here and throughout the Continent. The man worries that his time as a loyal servant to the Crown is limited. Burke wanted my husband to assist him in carrying out some plan to remove those in his way. I believe he specifically mentioned a Lady Grace and a Lord Archbroke. Burke appeared desperate and even a little afraid of the pair."

Fear rolled down Mary's back. She needed to tell Waterford. They needed to get word back to England. "Who should I have deliver your jewels?"

The comtesse stood and shook out her skirts. "I'll send Jean to collect them on his way to my chambers." Before she crossed the threshold into the hall, she said, "I shall find you in the morn for the fittings."

The wicked twinkle in Comtesse Boucher's eyes had the hair on Mary's arms standing on end. She would have to deal with the woman tomorrow. Tonight she would draft the necessary missives to alert her friends of the danger Burke posed. Would Gilbert return to her chambers again tonight? The tingling sensation that ran through to her core had nothing to do with fear and everything to do with the thought of sharing a bed with him again.

CHAPTER EIGHTEEN

A figure loomed over Mary in her semi-darkened bedchamber. Had Gilbert finally come to see her?

"My lady." Greene's small hand tapped Mary's arm. "Wake up. You've not slept like the dead before." Her maid scowled and placed a cool hand to her forehead. "You don't appear to be unwell. What is the matter with you?"

Nothing was amiss with her physically. She simply no longer had Lady Frances waking her as soon as dawn broke and the voices of others chattering to keep her awake all night. Mary had slept soundly once she had finally given up on Gilbert appearing.

Sitting up, she stretched her arms and hands above her head. It was peaceful to wake to not a sound but that of Greene's mumblings. "What time is it?"

Greene pulled back the curtains. Bright sunlight streamed into her room. It was well past dawn. Lady Frances believed it sinful to lie about all morning. Mary released a sigh as she lowered her hands to her lap. She missed Lady Frances.

Her eyes fell upon the pile of discarded missives. How

many times had she begun to draft the critical messages only to be disheartened to find her mind unable to produce the appropriate words? Lady Frances was never at a loss for a quick retort or nice turn of phrase. After hours laboring over the correspondence, Mary had been quite pleased with the end result and was certain Lady Frances would have approved of her efforts.

Greene clucked her tongue. "Out of bed, my lady. It is time for us to meet that nasty Comtesse Boucher and get you fitted for a gown for tomorrow's masquerade party."

Swiveling her legs over the side of the bed, Mary eased herself down until the balls of her feet touched the plush carpet upon the floor. "Tomorrow? I thought it wasn't until the end of the week."

Shaking out a day dress of light green muslin, Greene said, "Rumor below stairs is that the lady of the house changed her mind late last night. Everyone is in a scurry to have all readied for tomorrow."

Mary stretched her arms out, allowing Greene to quickly dress her, and then she retrieved the mound of discarded paper by the bed and added it to the fire that blazed in her chambers. She prayed the missives that she had dispatched late the prior eve would reach Lord Archbroke in time—before any harm could come to Lady Grace or himself.

Absently, Mary padded over to the washbasin to perform her morning routine. The empty feeling in her chest that had plagued her all night remained. Why had Gilbert not sought her out? Her hand stilled—her toothbrush jammed against her back teeth. Had the comtesse lied and sought out Gilbert despite their agreement?

There was a scratch at the door. Mary promptly placed the toothbrush next to the basin and raised a cup of clean water to her mouth to rinse. Humph. Gilbert and the comtesse. Mary spat, ridding herself of the water in her mouth and the horrid image her mind had conjured up of the pair.

Mary swiveled to face Greene and nodded. Her maid turned the door handle and swung the door open wide. Gilbert and Hadfield stood shoulder to shoulder in the doorway. It was as if they were battling over who would enter first.

Gilbert won. "Good morn, Mary. Did you sleep well?"

With a mischievous smirk upon his face, Lord Hadfield closed the door and leaned back against it.

Mary turned her gaze back to Gilbert. "Good morning to you and Lord Hadfield. Why are you both here?"

Lord Hadfield cleared his throat. "We have a rather important matter to discuss with you."

Mary took a step toward Gilbert. "I have information that I was able to garner from our hostess last eve that is of import."

Gilbert tilted his head and nonchalantly said, "Ladies, first."

"Burke utilizes Comte Boucher for transportation schemes."

Gilbert's features visibly relaxed and his lips curved into a smug smile. "We are well aware of Boucher's dealings with Burke."

Mary wanted to box Gilbert's ears for employing an all-too-familiar condescending tone with her. "Oh, so you know he assisted Burke to transport three of your fellow peers."

"Beg pardon?"

Good. She had wiped the all-knowing grin from his features. "Yes. Comtesse Boucher informed me that her husband at times transports individuals, and when I pressed her, she recalled Lord Harrington, Lord Hereford and Lord Addington's names being mentioned. All peers of the realm. The comtesse also informed me that it is rumored the men have escaped Burke's clutches."

Gilbert turned to face Lord Hadfield. "We should tell her."

Hadfield nodded. "Lady Mary, Waterford and I came to the Continent to track down some misplaced crown jewels. It was Lady Cecilia, under the instruction of Lady Grace, who followed me and informed us that Harrington and Hereford, along with her brother, Lord Addington, had been captured and were being held prisoner in some remote location in Spain."

"Did you know it was Lord Burke who had orchestrated their detention?"

Gilbert shook his head. "We did not. Not until Lady Cecilia produced the note from the foreign secretary, which she only shared with us after she had been reunited with her brother."

Mary's forehead wrinkled. The number of members of the ton involved with the Home Office was astounding. It was apparent not all titled gentlemen lead lives of idleness and decadence.

She assessed the men before her. No, they were certainly not men of leisure.

Facing Gilbert, she said, "I was led to believe that Lucy's brother, Lord Harrington, was an agent of the Home Office, like you."

"It would be hard for one to define Harrington's role."

Placing her hands on her hips, Mary asked, "Does he or does he not report to the home secretary, Lord Archbroke?"

"He does." Gilbert glanced over at Hadfield, who shrugged.

Mary wasn't done with her questions. "And what of Lord Hereford and Lord Addington?"

Gilbert ran a hand over the back of his neck. "Hereford and Addington are agents of the Foreign Office. Like me, Addington spent most of the war here upon French soil but in a vastly different role—he was not enlisted by the military."

Half the gentlemen Mary was acquainted with led rather complicated lives. Here she had thought the men of her circle were preoccupied with attending the House of Lords, running their estates, and producing offspring.

How did the two governmental bodies determine who of the ton was worthy to be involved with such covert activities?

Mary leveled her gaze at Gilbert. "If Lord Archbroke is the home secretary, who is the foreign secretary?"

"That is of no import to the current matter at hand." Gilbert reached for her, but she backed away and his hands fell to his sides. "Valois and Boucher are at odds as to how to end their association with Burke. If Boucher has his way, the man will be dead by the end of the Season. But simultaneously, that will place many of our own agents and innocents in jeopardy."

"Is Comte Boucher really capable of such a scheme?"

Gilbert answered, "Yes."

Mary looked between the two men and said, "Then we must stop the comte."

Lord Hadfield opened the door and peered out into the hall.

Gilbert whispered, "Boucher has accumulated many supporters. Apparently, Burke has either blackmailed or double-crossed many who live on both sides of the channel. Hadfield and I need to obtain the list of his supporters and the details of Boucher's scheme."

Lord Hadfield waved his hand in a circle as if telling them to wrap up the conversation.

Gilbert reached out for her hand and clasped it tight. "We need you to distract Boucher so we can search his study."

"*Me?*" They needed her. Mary's pulse began to race.

She caught Gilbert's gaze and asked, "Are you certain *you* want me to assist?"

Hadfield interjected, "You are the only one we can trust."

Lord Hadfield's words extinguished the jolt of excitement that flowed through Mary. "Oh, I understand."

Gilbert squeezed her hand once more. "I believe you can do it. Please Mary, assist us."

She had asked him to believe in her, and he had stated he did. She would prove to him she was worthy. "Very well. I shall entertain the comte."

Gilbert pulled her close and kissed her forehead. "You will do well."

Without another glance, the men promptly left her chambers. Mary crossed the room and fell back upon her bed. How was she to hold Comte Boucher's attention for an entire evening?

CHAPTER NINETEEN

$\mathcal{T}$he weight of Hadfield's hand upon his shoulder slowed Gilbert's pace as they strode down one of the many hallways. "Do you really believe Mary will be able to create a distraction?"

"She is a clever lady."

Hadfield stared at him. "It's unlike you to evade a question." The man cocked his eyebrow and said, "Tomorrow's ball is our best chance."

Gilbert stopped and debated whether to voice his worries. Up until a year ago, Hadfield had occupied his days arguing the finer points of law. Why Archbroke trusted him to execute highly complex missions such as locating the missing crown jewels, rescuing captured British agents, and now obtaining crucial evidence against Burke, the Crown's advisor, was still a mystery to Gilbert. Never had he ever questioned a direct order from Archbroke, but his intuition needled him to discover how Hadfield had gained his superior's unwavering confidence so quickly.

Hadfield met his gaze straight on. "Ah, it's not Lady

Mary's performance that worries you. It's I whom you question."

"Do you even know how to be stealthy? I've yet to see you exhibit the skill. Do you know how to pick a lock? I'm sure Boucher won't leave the list simply lying about."

"Archbroke saw to my training prior to my departure. While I've little actual experience, I do recall his long-winded lectures. You are to be the lookout, and I'm to retrieve the information. We must act before it is too late."

"I agree. With our limited resources, it's the best plan. However, I've got a bad feeling about all this."

"Now is not the time for you to become superstitious."

Hadfield began to make his way down the hall. "I'm going to check out Boucher's stables. I need to be outdoors."

Gilbert remained rooted to the spot. He wanted to join Hadfield, but he needed to keep an eye on Mary.

Walking backward, Hadfield said, "No need to worry over Lady Mary. She will be tied up with fittings and whatnot today."

Gilbert did not agree. "May I suggest you find Valois and keep him out of trouble?"

"Very well. I'll play nanny to Valois."

Hadfield strode down the hall, boots clacking loudly, and when the man missed the turn to the main hall, Gilbert released a groan and shook his head, but to his surprise, Hadfield grinned and waved like a fool, indicating that he was aware of his mistake and was now headed in the correct direction.

It was no wonder Gilbert had qualms about the man carrying out his duties tomorrow eve.

AFTER A FEW DISCREET INQUIRIES, Gilbert located the room that was purported to house the famous Madame Auclair. He had expected a long line of women waiting to see the modiste. Instead, the hall was devoid of activity, with only two footmen guarding the entrance to the chamber. Fortunate for him, a cardroom fairly empty of guests had been established on the opposite side of the hall. He walked the perimeter and assessed the various vacant chairs. Decided, Gilbert settled into a seat that not only provided him an unobstructed view of Madame Auclair's chambers but also placed him in full view of its occupants should the door open.

He played a few hands of *vingt-et-un*. On a losing streak, he was about to take his leave when, from his vantage point, Gilbert spied Mary and Comtesse Boucher entering the chamber across the hall. Mary looked her usual calm, confident self, while their hostess had an eagerness about her that worried him. With the door closed, he wasn't able to ascertain what exactly was occurring, so he collected his winnings and made the excuse he was heading off to dine. He needed entrance into the chamber where Mary was sequestered.

Gilbert looked down the hall and spotted the servants' entrance. Edging closer to the door, he paused as a group of young maids exited and then another cluster entered. Blast. There were too many people scurrying about. With no alternative way to enter, Gilbert turned on his heel and returned to the cardroom.

There was only one seat in the entire room Gilbert wanted, and it was currently occupied. Biding his time, he milled about, cataloging the various guests. Finally, when the young buck had lost his entire stack, Gilbert was at the ready to take the seat that afforded him a peek into the room Mary remained trapped in.

Luck was on his side, he captured a glimpse of her standing upon a platform, arms outstretched, as the modiste took her waist measurement. His gaze fixated upon her lips shaped like a heart, her eyes aglow with moonlight. Blast Robert Burns and his poems. Reality was he wanted to be the reason she grinned like that. He'd do anything in his power to make her happy every day they remained on this earth, for Mary was absolutely stunning when she genuinely smiled.

A procession of footmen carrying bolts of material made their way into the room.

Comtesse Boucher sashayed into sight. Standing directly in front of Mary, the woman blocked his view as she directed the men about. The comtesse looked up and caught his gaze. Her lips curved into a slow, seductive smile, and his host waived her petite index finger side to side at him like his nanny had when he was a boy caught doing something he shouldn't.

Returning his attention to the cards, he refocused on the game before him.

Two dark figures appeared at the entrance.

Valois's voice reached Gilbert first. "Let us join Waterford."

Gilbert faced the men. "Valois. Hadfield. Returned so soon?"

Hadfield shrugged, and Valois answered, "It is raining, dear Waterford. I wouldn't want to catch a cold and miss all the festivities tomorrow."

Gilbert sneaked a look at the closed door. What material would Mary choose? The dark blue velvet would look gorgeous against her buttercream skin. Ugh. Gilbert swore —no more reading works by Burns, Byron, or the lot.

"Well, we wouldn't want that now. Would we, Waterford?" Hadfield took the seat between Valois and himself.

Capturing Valois's gaze, Gilbert said, "It would be a shame to miss all the lovely ladies in their glory."

Valois played with the coins before him. "I wasn't talking about those activities. Although I will be sad to miss this year."

Gilbert looked at Hadfield, who merely gave him a shrug.

Valois confessed, "I know what you are up to. And no, Waterford. Hadfield was not the one who revealed your plans."

"Then who?"

"You would not believe me if I told you." Valois smirked. "What are you going to do with Comtesse Boucher?"

Hadn't Mary used that particular phrase with him before? "What do you mean?"

Valois's smirk turned into a snarl. "The woman is in heat for you. Mary had to play and win for your honor last night."

Gilbert raised both eyebrows in question, "Mary did what?"

Valois looked at Hadfield. "He does not know?"

Hadfield chuckled, "You will have to excuse the man for his slowness. He has only recently fallen in love with your cousin."

"Ah, *oui*. Love confuses the brain. But what have you planned for the lady of the house? Otherwise, she will be a handful."

"Love? I'm not in love, you fools. I'm—"

Valois and Hadfield both stared directly at him, wide-eyed. Then simultaneously the pair burst into laughter. Humph. He admired Mary. He definitely felt desire for the woman, but love—what a ridiculous notion.

Gilbert tapped his finger on the table and waited until

the pair had ceased chuckling and regained their composure.

Addressing Valois, Gilbert growled, "Hadfield and I were not aware the comtesse would be a problem."

Tugging on his coat sleeves, Valois straightened. "Very well. I shall take care of the lady."

"If you feel the need to." Hadfield raked in his winnings from the table. "Waterford, you don't have any objections, do you?"

Both sets of eyes narrowed upon him. His only concern was Mary's welfare, and she was still trapped in the chamber across the hall with the comtesse.

Hadfield and Valois shared a sideways glance. The pair promptly burst into fits of laughter again.

At the swoosh of a door opening, Gilbert swiveled in his chair. Footmen carried bolts of material out of the room this time. He shifted to afford himself a better view of the procession. Mary stood frozen as a footman held a tall looking glass in front of her. The extravagant blue gown was pinned with strings of pearls and diamonds sparkling like her eyes.

A column of lace bows that started at mid-chest drew his eyes to her décolletage. The swell of her breasts had him shifting in his chair once more. Greene tied the ribbons of an elegant red mask that complimented the gown, but it did nothing to conceal the delight in Mary's eyes.

She would be the most beautiful lady at tomorrow's ball. All Gilbert could think of was how to get the woman out of that extravagant dress and corset and into his bed—but no, he and Hadfield would be tied up obtaining the intelligence they desperately needed before dawn.

Valois leaned over, all traces of laughter gone. Admiration shone in the man's eyes. "She looks delightful. It will not be hard for her to retain Comte Boucher's attention in *that* dress."

Gilbert's hand balled into a fist. Deuce.

How had Valois come to find out about Mary's assignment? She wouldn't have been foolish enough to confide in her cousin. Narrowing his gaze upon Valois, the man's lips moved as if he were conversing with another. Peculiar yet familiar. Over the years, Gilbert had observed Mary's mumblings as she stood alone in secluded alcoves.

Comtesse Boucher's musical laughter wafted through the hall, drawing his gaze back to the woman his mind was preoccupied with.

Mary stood smiling as she fingered a bow.

"That gown is gorgeous, Madame Auclair." The comtesse circled Mary. "I would love to have one also." The woman's voice was tinged with jealousy. Perhaps Valois was correct. Comtesse Boucher could pose a problem at the ball.

CHAPTER TWENTY

*C*ursing her mama for inheriting the tendency of sweaty palms, Mary ran her hands down her sides and let them settle on her hips as she twisted. She smiled at the swish of her skirts. Never had a gown made her feel so wonton and beautiful at the same time. Her décolletage cut lower than she ever dared to wear before. "Thank goodness Papa is not here to see."

Greene placed a hand on Mary's back and tugged on her laces once more. "Yes, it's an excellent thing His Grace is not here to see the activities you have chosen to partake of in this trip."

Wagering large sums. Sharing a bed with another—she hadn't done anything her own papa wasn't guilty of.

Breaking Mary out of her thoughts, Greene said, "My lady, you look splendid." She stepped back to inspect her handiwork. "I don't know what has brought about the change in you, but I'm grateful for it. The gown is stunning, but it is your inner self shining through that makes you incomparable tonight."

"Why, thank you, Greene. That is by far the nicest thing you have ever shared with me."

Greene's cheeks turned a rosy red. "Where is Lord Waterford? Wasn't he to come and escort you to the ball?"

Yes, where was the man? Mary had forgotten to share the most critical piece of information she had garnered from Comtesse Boucher—the threat to her friend Lady Grace and Lord Archbroke. Mary had deliberated all day whether to seek Gilbert out. But the comtesse had invited her to break her fast and steadfastly refused to let her go for the rest of the day.

Twirling in front of the looking glass, Mary said, "Gilbert is never late. I'm sure he will be here soon."

She inhaled a deep breath. It had been only a few hours since she had left Comtesse Boucher's company. Impossible. There was no way the she-devil could have succeeded in her plans to corner Gilbert. Yet the woman had boasted of her scheme yesterday during Mary's long and arduous costume fitting and again today at tea.

Mary jumped at the sound of Gilbert's voice at the doorway. "I'm sorry I'm late."

She turned to greet him, and Greene mumbled loud enough for all to hear, "And so you should be," before she scurried into the adjoining chamber.

Gilbert strode into the room, his eyes never leaving Mary's.

Mary gasped for air. Blasted corset. It had to be the cause of her inability to breathe— and not the man before her. "Gilbert, how did you manage to obtain such a magnificent coat?"

The coat was crafted from dark navy-blue velvet. It almost looked black. Elegant silver embroidery scrolled across the shoulder line, highlighting Gilbert's broad chest. The metallic design flowed down the front all the way to his narrowed waist. Mary's eyes continued to follow the front seam of the coat to its pointed ends that fell slightly above Gilbert's knees.

"I'm not sure where the ensemble magically appeared from. However, both Hadfield and I were relieved to find that they were not too ostentatious. Although Hadfield claimed the forest-green cravat left for him brought images of Archbroke to mind in his role as a dandy."

Images of the home secretary and the various outfits she had seen the man in over the years flittered through Mary's memory. She raised her hand to her lips as a croak of a laugh escaped her. "Now that Lord Archbroke is married, I believe Theo will have a positive influence over his wardrobe, and perhaps we shall never see another gamboge waistcoat again."

Gilbert chuckled. "You didn't care for the color?" He pulled out a mask made of the same material as his coat with ribbons that were orange in color.

They both burst into laughter.

Greene shook her head as she approached with Mary's domino in hand. "My lady, please remain still."

Mary straightened and turned to allow her maid to affix her mask. Instead of Greene's cool fingers, it was Gilbert's warm touch she felt along her temples.

Gilbert whispered, "Lass, you look bonny tonight."

"You never answered me the other night. Was it your mama who was Scottish?"

"Aren't ye a clever lass. Aye, me ma was Scottish. And t'was me nana who shared stories of hobgoblins and wraiths with me as a bairn."

Mary's heart skipped a beat when he slipped into his Scottish brogue. This was a part of him she had never known him to share with another. It filled her heart with joy that he had shared it with her.

Gilbert's hand rested on the edge of her shoulders and then spun her around to face him. "My parents' marriage was arranged." His eyes were clear and intense as he gazed down at her. "All my papa cared for was my mama's dowry. My papa didn't care for my mother's Scottish accent and was determined I'd not adopt the heathen language she spoke."

Had he refused her all these years because of her vast dowry, not wanting to appear the fortune hunter his papa had been?

Mary began to say, "But how—"

"Oh, my mama was a clever woman and a proud Scot at that. When I was a lad, each year my papa would leave for town to attend to his duties at the House of Lords. Mama would arrange for us to journey to Scotland to visit her family. That was until the year he came down with the influenza and returned early to our country seat. When he was informed we had left, he came to Scotland to retrieve his wayward wife and son." Gilbert's eyes became glassy, as if he were no longer in the present. "Upon arriving, my papa was deathly sick and ordered that only Mama was to tend to him; neither of them survived that trip."

"How old were you?"

"Ten. I was to attend Harrow's come spring, but my grandmama on my papa's side insisted I attend Eton, and she saw to it that I never returned to Scotland again."

"Is your nana still alive?"

"No, my grandmama outlived her. I wasn't allowed to attend my nana's funeral, and I refused to attend my grandmama's."

Lowering her gaze, Mary said, "I understand now."

"Beg pardon?" Gilbert blinked. The mistiness gone, clear-eyed once more, he stared down at her.

"I realize now why you were opposed to the idea of

marrying me. You wanted the freedom to choose your wife. Perhaps it felt like you were being forced into an arrangement without your say."

He leaned down and said, "I'm relieved you comprehend my youthful stupidity. But Mary, I know you are truly the only woman for me. I'm sorry it took me these many years to finally grasp that our union would be in no way the same as that of my parents."

Mary wrapped her arms about his waist and leaned her cheek against his chest. "No need to apologize. Lady Frances always said men were slow."

At the mention of Lady Frances, Gilbert's whole body tensed.

Mary leaned back and asked, "Is something the matter?"

"Do you really see and talk to the dead?"

The look of incredibility shouldn't have hurt; she had seen it too many times. "You will be happy to hear as of a week ago I ceased to have the ability."

"Can you resume or desist at will?"

"Unfortunately, that is not how it works." Mary tried to pull out of his arms, but Gilbert tightened his hold, and his gaze intensified.

"You miss them."

She crumpled, and he pulled her in tight. "At first I didn't, but as each day passes, I worry I'll never regain what my cousin calls a gift."

"Valois shares this ability?"

"Yes."

Gilbert chuckled. "Ah, well, that does explain his odd behavior at times."

It was her turn to stiffen at his use of the word "odd." Mary bowed her head. She didn't want to be viewed as one with peculiar habits. Gilbert placed a finger under her chin, forcing her to lift her face to his. The flare of concern in his eyes had her muscles relaxing slightly.

He removed his hand from her face and returned it to her waist. "I'm sorry. I meant no offense. Valois does go about in a way—"

Mary waited for Gilbert to finish his sentence.

His brow creased. As he was clearly at a loss for the correct words, she took pity on him and said, "My cousin doesn't attempt to hide the fact he is able to converse with others. He appears to care naught about what others deem normal or appropriate."

Gilbert abruptly released her and took a large step back.

What the devil?

Greene emerged from the adjoining chamber and calmly padded over to door. Her maid's hand hovered over the door handle. Absorbed in her conversation with Gilbert, Mary hadn't heard anyone approach or scratch at her door. Greene had incredible hearing.

Had her maid overheard their entire conversation?

Mary trusted Greene, but she had never shared the full truth about her abilities.

Greene asked, "Well, my lady, should I let the gentleman in or not?"

Mary said, "Please."

A stunningly handsome Hadfield waltzed into the room along with her cousin. The dark charcoal of Hadfield's coat complimented his gem-green cravat. Gilbert had referred to it as forest green but she would disagree. The cravat highlighted the green specks in Lord Hadfield's hazel eyes, causing them to sparkle like emeralds. Coupled with the dimple he rarely shared, Mary was taken aback at Lord Hadfield's charming appearance.

Lord Hadfield reached for her hand and brought it up

to his lips to place upon it a chaste kiss. "Lady Mary, you look delightful."

Valois stole her hand away and lifted it out wide to the side. *"Magnifique."* Her cousin tugged on her hand, toppling her closer. Instead of falling, Valois guided Mary into a full spin.

Mary released a giggle. Blood rushed to her cheeks as all three gentlemen leveled a gaze upon her as she came to a stop. Her eyes fell to the center of Valois's black coat. It was also made out of velvet and of a similar cut to the other two gentlemen's coats.

Hmm. Mary frowned. It would be challenging to tell the three men apart as they were all of similar height, and with dominos affixed, their features would be masked. One would have to be close to see the different hair color— Valois's blond, Hadfield's medium brown, while Waterford's looked near-black.

"Waterford, we need to be off. Let me assist you with your mask." Hadfield took the forgotten mask from Gilbert's hands and lifted it up. As he caught sight of the color of the ribbons, he said, "Good Lord, I'm plagued by constant reminders of Archbroke."

Mary hesitated to vocalize her thoughts, but for his safety, she said, "Lord Hadfield, perhaps these occurrences mean something."

After tying a rather intricate knot securing Gilbert's mask, Lord Hadfield turned to face her. "Beg pardon?"

"Could it be your subconscious is trying to tell you something?"

"That I made a mistake in letting my dear cousin, Theo, marry a dandy?"

"No. Everyone knows it was no mistake. Could it be that for you to be successful tonight, you need to recall something of import related to Lord Archbroke?"

Talk of Lord Archbroke, was a reminder that she had yet to share with Gilbert the danger Lord Burke posed to the home secretary and Lady Grace.

"*Ma chérie*, you are aware of how dangerous it is to tempt fate." Valois's tone was serious and ominous. "Come, or we will be late."

Lord Hadfield's eyebrows disappeared behind his mask, but his frown of confusion was clear for all to see. "Ready?"

Mary placed a hand on Gilbert's winged his arm and went on her tiptoes to whisper, "I must speak with you. Privately."

Gilbert asked, "What is the matter?"

Mary glanced at Lord Hadfield, who was staring.

She leaned a closer to Gilbert. "The comtesse shared with me that Lord Burke is planning a scheme that will place Lady Grace and Lord Archbroke in danger. I sent missives under the disguise of correspondence to Lady Theo, to warn them. But I don't understand why Lord Burke would want to harm Lady Grace."

Lord Hadfield came to stand in front of them. "I believe Lady Grace might have had a hand in Lady Cecilia assisting us to disrupt Burke's plans for Harrington and the others." He tapped his forefinger upon his closed lips. "When did you dispatch these letters?"

"The night before last." Mary searched Gilbert's features for reassurance.

Gilbert patted her hand that rested on his arm. "That was very clever of you to address them to Archbroke's wife."

Lord Hadfield and Valois said in unison, "We leave at first light." Without further discussion, the men led their party through the maze of hallways.

Slowing his gait as they approached the door to the

ballroom, Gilbert whispered, "Be very cautious this eve. As soon as Hadfield and I have obtained the information we seek, I'll find you."

"I'll be careful."

Mary's stomach knotted. She would carry out her assignment, but she had yet to devise a plan that did not carry a mountain of risk.

CHAPTER TWENTY-ONE

*A*s they entered the ballroom, Gilbert could feel the tension radiating off Mary. Her normally regal posture was replaced with a rigid stance, and the slight tilt of her nose in defiance was a sure sign she was not as confident as she appeared. He didn't want to leave her side. In light of the threat Mary had shared, they desperately needed the details of Comte Boucher's plans.

Gilbert squeezed Mary's hand one last time. "Let us escort you over to our host."

Both comte and comtesse were surrounded by elegantly garbed guests. Mary's eyes went wide as she took in their hostess's gown and mask. While Comtesse Boucher's dress was not an exact replica of Mary's, it was fashioned out of a similar dark blue material, and her ruby-red mask was adorned with sparkling diamonds compared to Mary's, which had pearls. The woman was even wearing a wig created from hair comparable to Mary's mahogany tresses.

Mary's nails bit into Gilbert's arm. "That wench has gone too far."

"Lass, do not let her make you lose focus."

"It is your focus that I'm worried about."

Gilbert leaned in closer and whispered, "Valois has promised to take care of the comtesse for us this eve."

Mary tilted her head and blinked. "You have engaged the help of my cousin? I thought you didn't trust the man."

He didn't trust Valois entirely, but without other reliable agents available, Gilbert was resolved to the fact that he had no other choice. "I've come to better understand your cousin."

They took another step closer to their hosts.

Hadfield fell into place next to Mary. "Waterford, we will need to move quickly. Valois heard it rumored Boucher has instructed his son to depart after this evening's festivities. We need to obtain the lists and set out tomorrow."

Mary nodded and said, "I agree the sooner we leave, the better."

"I'm in favor of not dallying here any longer than necessary. What about Valois? Is he returning too?"

"Yes. Valois suggested we all return to his estate since it is on the way."

Mary shuddered.

"Lass, are you cold?"

"No. I'm well. Do not worry about me."

But he did worry. He too experienced an intense tingling along his spine at the mention of returning to Valois's estate. A clear sign that trouble awaited them.

GILBERT AND HADFIELD marched toward the doors. The skin on the back of Gilbert's neck prickled. He swiveled once more and rose on his tiptoes to catch a glimpse of

Mary, who happily chatted away with a small group of women that had formed next to the comte and his wife.

"Waterford, please lead the way and stop worrying over Mary. You said you trusted the woman. Now is the time to prove it."

"I have an awful feeling about this evening and our plans to return with Valois."

"Without the assistance of Valois, we will not be able to beat Boucher's son back to England. We need his help."

"I understand it is our only choice, but it still doesn't dispel the knot growing in my stomach."

He marched in front of Hadfield, and they silently made their way to the private wing that housed the Boucher family chambers. They would search those first and then proceed to search their host's private study and library and every other room on the estate if need be.

As they reached the comte's chamber, Waterford checked the door handle. Locked. He had expected as much but was hard-pressed not to complain at the delay. Reaching into his breast pocket, he withdrew his tools and turned to find Hadfield already down on one knee and working the lock.

Click.

Hadfield entered the room, leaving Gilbert alone in the hallway to stand guard.

The sound of women giggling alerted Gilbert to a group approaching. He tapped on the door with his knuckle three times. He reached for the handle behind him, but all his hand came into contact with was air. Rotating at the waist, he came face-to-face with Hadfield.

Gilbert whispered, "Did you find what we need?"

"It isn't here. But I will say the comte has some rather peculiar hobbies and instruments stored in his room."

Gilbert recognized a male voice to belong to André,

Boucher's son. "Ladies, let's experiment with some of the new toys *mon père* has recently acquired."

The women replied in unison. "Yes, master."

They needed to move quickly.

Gilbert whispered, "The room across the hall."

Hadfield nodded and closed the door to the comte's chamber. He made quick work again of resetting the lock.

Backing into the room as André came into sight, Gilbert carefully closed the door but left it slightly ajar, spying on the young man as he made his way to his papa's chambers.

In a harsh whisper, he asked, "Are you certain it wasn't inside his chamber?"

"Waterford, are you questioning my abilities now? It is a little too late for that. Can we make our way to the comte's study or not?"

Gilbert had hoped the information had been hidden in his host's chamber; otherwise, it might very well be a long night searching each room. He shook his head. The young pup had left his papa's door ajar. They'd have to wait until the trio was well occupied before leaving.

"Whose room do you think we are in?"

Gilbert turned to take in his surroundings. The room was sparse compared to the lavishly decorated ones he and Hadfield had been assigned to. There was no bed. A simple pallet lay on the floor in the corner.

No pillows.

No wardrobe.

No adjoining changing chamber.

Whose room indeed.

A small desk and chair placed under the window were the only pieces of furniture. Hadfield made his way over to the desk with a stealth that Gilbert likened to a ghost floating across the room. Silent, effortless, and quick.

Hadfield ran his hand along the edge of the desk and then the underside. Crouching, he then inspected the underside of the chair. The sound of rustling paper caught Gilbert's attention.

"What did you find?"

Hadfield ignored him and carefully turned the chair over to inspect the seat. After prying a folded parchment held by a few drops of wax from the chair, Hadfield lifted it to his nose and sniffed.

What was the man doing?

Hadfield ran a finger along the crisp fold with reverence. Turning his back to Gilbert, he stepped closer to the uncovered window where only a sliver of light peeked through the cloudy night sky.

In a harsh whisper, Gilbert asked, "What does it say?"

The obtuse man ignored him, swiveled, pocketed the paper, and walked over to the overturned chair to return it to its original position. With glazed eyes, Hadfield said, "Let's be off."

The man's inexperience wore on Gilbert's patience. "We should check under the pallet before leaving." He would have to return to the comte's chambers to ensure Hadfield had not missed any clues. Gilbert growled. The additional task would delay him further from seeking out Mary.

Frowning at Hadfield, who remained unmoving, Gilbert walked over to the straw mattress and turned it over.

Nothing.

Wanting to be done with their search, Gilbert asked, "Did the note contain the information we seek or not?"

Hadfield shook his head. "It did not."

Gilbert scanned the room to ensure they left it as it was

when they entered. "Which should we attempt to search next, the study or the library?"

"Neither. I want to inspect Valois's chambers."

Gilbert frowned. "Are you certain?"

Hadfield opened the door and slid out to the hallway.

Gilbert clenched his fists. If the man continued to refuse to answer any of his questions, Gilbert would simply beat the information out of him. To hell with Archbroke's orders to protect Hadfield.

Slipping into the empty hallway, Gilbert jogged to catch up. He almost ran into Hadfield as the man slowed and placed a hand along the wainscoting of the wall.

It was apparent that Hadfield had paid a great deal of attention to the goings-on of the household while he had been preoccupied with a lady who was now entertaining another man. The thought of Mary alone with Boucher had Gilbert clenching his jaw.

"Come along, Waterford. We don't have all evening." Hadfield waved him into what looked to be an old servants' entrance. "Peculiar that the comte didn't board up the old passageways."

"Unless he still has a use for them." Gilbert squeezed past Hadfield to lead and walked directly into a spiderweb. "Although it appears it hasn't been used recently."

"Or used by someone a lot shorter than you."

The comte and his son were of similar height. "Who are you referring to?"

"No one in particular. Simply an observation."

Gilbert had underestimated the man before him. He wouldn't do that again.

CHAPTER TWENTY-TWO

*S*eated at the card table, Mary rolled her head forward to stretch her neck. She had been playing faro with the comte for hours. If she never engaged in another game of faro in her life, she would be a happy woman. Mary pushed the mounting stack of coins in front of her slightly to the side to rake in another round of winnings. The darkening of Comte Boucher's features did not bode well. While her host's frustration at her besting him at cards increased, her bravado was beginning to wane.

She was at a loss. She had calculated the odds, and despite placing her wager on what she believed to be the highest risk of losing, the outcome still came out in her favor. As the comte's stack had dwindled, one by one, the other players had made excuses and left the table. Only the two of them remained.

Comte Boucher glanced at the discarded pile, and then he shoved the remainder of his stack upon the three of diamonds and commanded, "Deal."

Steadying her hand, Mary counted out coins to match the comte's wager. His calculations had been meticulous all night, but luck had not been on his side. She placed her own coins next to his.

Her heart pounded. Mary prayed that the dealer would turn any card over but a three to bolster the comte's stack. If the three appeared, the comte would be bankrupt, and then what would she do to retain his attention? Gilbert had instructed her to not let Comte Boucher out of her sight until he came and found her. There was no sign of Gilbert or Hadfield magically appearing. She sat silently, wishing she had the assistance of Lady Frances or any of the others to gauge how long she must keep up fawning over her overbearing host.

Mary squeezed her eyes shut as the dealer turned over a three of hearts. They had both lost. She slumped forward and closed her eyes in disbelief, then opened one eye only to find the comte staring. Not at her face but rather at her décolletage, which had slipped lower as she pressed up against the table.

Turning to face the comte, Mary gave him a weak smile and said, "You have been such a gracious host. I must thank you for a lovely evening."

The man's gaze remained upon her chest as he replied, "*Au contraire*, the pleasure is for me. Let us move to another room."

Mary's hand stalled upon the table at Comte Boucher's words. The man was not as fluent in English as his wife. Perhaps she had misinterpreted his meaning. Surely he wasn't implying they should retire to *his* rooms.

With a nervous laugh, Mary asked, "Do you have a billiards room?"

"You play?"

Releasing a sigh of relief, she grinned and said, "I must warn you, Comte, I grew up with three brothers who never played simply for fun."

The comte's eyes blazed with interest. "And the stakes?"

Looking down at her pile of coin, Mary said, "Double or nothing."

With a loud bark of laughter, the comte nodded. "*Oui*, double or nothing."

He pushed back his chair and rose and gallantly held out a hand to assist her. Mary stared at the comte's sweaty palm and debated if she genuinely wished to be touched by the man. She searched the room once more for a glimpse of Gilbert.

Blast.

Lightly placing her hand upon the comte's, she rose quickly. Blood rushed to her legs, and she faltered. She squeezed the man's hand, but he pulled her closer. An impish grin appeared upon the comte's face as he looked down at her. His eyes were glued to her bosom, specifically the spot his hand had brushed up against. Mary's nose twitched and burned with the overpowering scent of cologne, which masked the putrid smell of stale sweat.

Regaining her footing, she stepped away from the gaming tables and allowed the comte to lead her through the crowded cardroom. Entering the cooler corridor, Mary spotted a couple in a rather intimate embrace. She inhaled sharply as she spied the dark blue gown similar to her own, and fake long brown tresses wrapped about the man fingers.

The comtesse had a man pressed up against the wall, and her hands roamed freely over his form. There was a familiarity about the man, but in the dark, Mary couldn't be sure who he was. When the comtesse pulled back from her victim's lips, his head fell to rest on her shoulder, and she turned, catching Mary's gaze. The witch winked.

Sliding a quick look at the comte beside her, Mary saw that the man's eyes were affixed to her chest, and when she looked down the hall once more, the couple had mysteriously disappeared. While the man hadn't pushed the comtesse away, he didn't appear to be fully engaged in the assignation.

Mary's gut clenched. She didn't want to believe it was Gilbert. But the man was known to do whatever necessary to carry out his duties. If that meant distracting the comtesse to allow Hadfield more time to conduct his search, without a doubt, Gilbert would carry out his assignment.

The swoosh of air as the footman opened the double doors in front of them brought the repugnant stench back to Mary's nose. Wrapping her arm about her stomach, she followed Comte Boucher as he strode into the extraordinary large room.

The footman raced about the room lighting more candles, illuminating a billiards table. Mary squinted. The solid wood legs were intricately engraved with layers of garden scenes. Some even had couples in them. She glided a hand over the table. The exquisitely fine wool was similar in texture to that of the plaids found in Scotland. An image of Gilbert dressed in a lawn shirt and kilt transformed into the gentleman she had spied moments before in the hall. Mary gave her head a shake. She needed to focus upon her assignment—Comte Boucher.

She clasped her hands behind her as she turned to admire the walls filled from floor to ceiling with paintings ranging in size and subject matter. The frames were varied, varying from simple wood to ornately designed metal casings. A narrow picture of a young maiden kneeling in a clearing caught Mary's eye. She stopped to examine it closely and took a quick step back. The fresh-faced lady in the painting was Lady Frances! It was a sign. But what did it mean? Was Mary to use caution, or was it an indication that the comte was a friend, not foe?

Shuffling forward, Mary blankly stared at the paintings until her gaze fell upon a large portrait in the center. It depicted the comtesse naked with a white sheet draped over one shoulder.

Comte Boucher chuckled behind her. "At the time, I believed my wife— *une belle âme*."

Mary swirled to face the comte. "A beautiful soul?"

"*Oui.*"

"Your wife has been a very gracious hostess."

The comte sniggered and walked to stand before the painting with his hands on his hips. "*Non.* She is a devil. But mine." He continued to speak to the canvas. "We live in accord."

The faraway look in the comte's eyes, the downturn of his lips, were all too familiar. The sadness that dwarfed Mary's mama every time her papa was unfaithful descended upon the man who only hours ago had seemed unfeeling.

She asked, "Are you happy?"

Chuckling, the comte answered, "Blah. Happiness. I have André. This is all I ask."

"You are not bothered by her—"

"*Liaisons?*" He turned to face her. "*Non.*" The comte retrieved two cues from the corner and brought one over to her. "*Prêt?*"

Mary looked at the stick. Her gaze slid back to the

comte, who gave her a watery smile. Something had changed. She didn't need Lady Frances to tell her. She sensed the man's guard had lowered. Now was her chance to prove to herself she was more than capable of aiding in the mission. Especially since it appeared Gilbert might be detained for a while.

Mary replied, *"Oui. Allez."*

"Mademoiselle Mary." The comte laughed heartily. He was no longer leering at her. Now his looks were more like those of her father. "You are *naïve*—How to say in *Anglais*—"

She wasn't that innocent, not after the night she shared with Gilbert.

Smoothing out the slight tug at the corner of her lips, Mary pretended not to understand him. "I'm sorry. My French is as rusty as your English. Shall we play?"

The comte gathered a collection of balls in a hoop.

"In England, we play with two white balls and one red. How do you play?"

He rolled the cue ball to a dot that was midway between the sides of the table. "One point for each ball hit."

"And how do you determine the winner?"

"Who gets fifty points."

Mary counted the balls inside the rack. Fifteen. The game seemed simple enough. When the comte removed the hoop and hit the white ball, scattering the balls about the table, Mary released a loud sigh. Again, the comte smiled at her and waved her to the table.

This would not be as easy as she initially thought. While she could trounce her brothers, this again was altogether a new game for her. Instead of doubt and sweaty palms, she was overcome with excitement at figuring out the complex angles and probabilities that lay on the table before her.

The comte leaned against the table. *"Allez."*

"Do we alternate turns?" Staring at the balls sprinkled about, Mary calculated the chance of her hitting more than one in a single strike.

"Non, you play until you miss."

Ah, that changed her strategy. She could hit one and try to position the white to her advantage. Leaning over the table, she aligned her shot. She pulled back the cue, hit the ball square on.

Click.

Satisfied at the positioning of the white ball, she moved to reposition and take another shot.

"Advice, Mademoiselle Mary. Men do not prefer femmes that can best them at games."

The cue slid against her chin as she lined up her shot. "Then I am content to remain a spinster."

She pulled back, poised to bank the ball, but hesitated as Comte Boucher asked, "Spin-t-star? Is what?"

Instead of taking her turn, she stood and stared at her opponent. "A woman who remains unwed."

The man's cue hit the edge of the table hard as the comte bent at the waist and burst into laughter.

"What is so funny?"

Between gasps for air, the comte said, *"Invraisemblable!"*

"Why is that impossible?"

"Non." He shook his head. Brow furrowed, he said, "Unlikely."

"Comte Boucher, you flatter me. As you pointed out moments ago, men do not find my abilities all that attractive."

His gaze roamed over her entire body. "You are— *magnifique."*

Mary bent and steadied her hand as she took her shot. "Not as beautiful as your wife."

The cue ball sailed past its intended target and sunk into the corner pocket. Blast. Comtesse was ruining her evening in every way possible.

"*Oui.*"

The comte's agreement stung. It shouldn't. Mary was fully aware she didn't compare to the comtesse. Mary gripped the cue until her knuckles were white. Images of Gilbert in the arms of the gorgeous woman floated before her. Her stomach clenched. The room tilted as she leaned on the wooden stick in her grasp. Her nails bit into the flesh of her palm. The visions weren't real. Evening out her short shallow breaths, she slowly relaxed her fingers, allowing the blood to rush back into the tips.

Click.

Click.

The comte scored two points.

He said, "On the surface." Hunched over the table, he waited for Mary to meet his gaze. "But you. You, *mademoiselle*, are radiant."

Heat rose on her cheeks at the compliment. "I'm sorry we are leaving tomorrow. I think I would have enjoyed spending more time in your company."

Click.

Another point for the man. "After tonight's festivities, everyone must go."

Mary rounded the table to assess his next shot. "Are you ready to be rid of all your guests so soon?"

"*Oui.* I have much business to attend to."

"Your wife mentioned you were responsible for managing a great number of trade lines throughout the Continent."

175

"*Non*. Matters—" His lips thinned. "Affairs I've neglected. Things must change."

The ball whizzed by and missed by a hair.

Pretending to not have heard him, Mary moved into position to take her turn. "You are lucky you have André to assist you."

Click.

Click.

The two points put her back in the lead.

Comte Boucher scowled at the balls that remained scattered. "André is still young. But he will learn quickly. I'm sending him to visit your homeland, England."

"How wonderful. I can introduce André to my father, the Duke of Seaburn."

Click.

At this rate, it would take many hours for her to accumulate the necessary points to win.

"Mademoiselle Mary, do you know Lord Wharton?"

Mary stood and refocused her attention on the man speaking to her. Why was he inquiring about Lord Burke's son?

"I believe Lord Wharton might be acquainted with my older brother Thomas, Lord Roxbury." She had the comte's full attention.

"Rumor, he is— *le gaspilleur*, true?"

Mary repeated, "*Le gaspilleur*?" She wasn't familiar with the French term. Where was Lady Frances when she needed her?

The comte was waiting for an answer. His lips formed a deep frown. "Wharton— *pas bien*."

"*Pas bien*. Not good." Mary's shoulders stiffened. "Are you asking about Lord Wharton's character?"

The man's eyes rounded. "*Oui.*"

176

"I've not met Lord Wharton. However, I'd be happy to make inquires for you."

The comte nodded and waved at the table. Apparently done with the conversation, he ordered, *"Allez."*

Realizing that it would take the rest of the game for her to ascertain the man's motives, she would win the game by accumulating one point at a time.

CHAPTER TWENTY-THREE

*B*linking, Gilbert let his eyes adjust to the darkness.

Since the moment he laid eyes on Mary in the exquisite gown, the image of her had been burned into his mind and appeared every time he closed his eyes no matter how brief. The woman was constantly on his mind.

He inhaled a deep breath. Unable to comfortably fit in the narrow passageway, he sidestepped through the passage until there was a sliver of light at his feet. He flattened his hand against the wall, searching for a latch or some mechanism to enter.

Hadfield whispered, "Lower."

Bent at the knees, Gilbert resumed his search until the pads of his fingers came across the seam in the wall. Inching his hand over, he finally found the latch.

Hadfield was on his tiptoes, peeking through a hole. "This is the room."

Secret passageways. Peepholes. The estate was riddled with evidence that the comte was involved in some rather strange dealings. It was good that they were to leave in the morning. Gilbert didn't want to reside on the estate any longer than necessary.

He slid through the door. Sounds of a woman's moans and the rustling of clothing came from the adjoining chamber. He put out a hand to stop Hadfield from following him.

Hadfield pushed his arm out of the way and barged through the door. "Get out of my way."

"We cannot go in. There is someone in the room next to us."

"Sounds like they are too busy to investigate any noise we make." Hadfield made his way to the candle burning near the entrance. As he peered into the room, his whole body stiffened. "I was mistaken, this is not the correct room." Hadfield replaced the candle and marched over and pushed Gilbert back toward the door they just entered from.

"Wait. You said you wished to search Valois's chambers. Why?"

"Now is not the time for discussion. Let's just go."

Gilbert planted his feet and refused to budge. "What did you see?"

"Nothing— I was wrong about our location." Hadfield used his shoulder to try maneuver toward the passageway.

Hadfield's left eyebrow twitched. The man was lying.

"Wrong or not, we should search the room. I still don't trust the man." Gilbert glanced about the room. "I'll keep a lookout."

"Very well, move out of my way so I can begin."

Gilbert turned to his side to let Hadfield pass. Quiet as a mouse, Hadfield began to meticulously search every nook and crevasse of the room. Perhaps the man wasn't as inept as he had led Gilbert to believe. Which would mean Gilbert wouldn't have to venture back to Comte Boucher's rooms. The sooner they were done, the sooner he could seek out Mary.

A deep masculine groan came from the other room followed by soft moans of a woman.

Gilbert tiptoed over to the doorway.

The sparkle of jewels in the candlelit room brought his attention to the pool of dark blue velvet that lay upon the floor next to the bed—Mary's dress.

His gaze rose to fall upon luxurious brown mahogany tresses flowing down a woman's creamy back. Locks that swayed back and forth against her skin as she rocked back and forth, riding the man beneath her.

Gilbert's vision blurred.

The deep voice of Valois reached Gilbert's ears. *"Plus lent, ma chérie—."*

Slower! *Ma chérie!* Valois had used the endearment with Mary many times before.

Gilbert inhaled as his mind raced. Stars appeared behind his eyes that were clenched tight.

Images from his dreams—breasts pert at attention, skin flushed in places lips had ravished the skin, the sway of soft brown curls appeared before him. Gasping for air, Gilbert reached out to lean against the doorframe.

Another pleasured moan from the woman had his fingers digging into the wood casing.

A rush of blinding jealousy and anger roared through his veins.

Gilbert jumped as Hadfield's hand landed upon his shoulder. His eyes flew open. Hadfield's lips were moving, but his brain wasn't registering what the man was saying. Inhaling a deep breath, he attempted to focus. His preoccupation with Mary was obscuring his logic.

They were in Valois's chambers, and woman riding him had to be Comtesse Boucher—they had assigned

Valois to keep an eye on the she-devil. Then why was his blood boiling with jealousy?

Hadfield gave him a good hard shake. "Did you hear me? I have the information we need. Everything. The list of names and Boucher's plans for Lord Burke's demise. Time to go."

Gilbert peeked into the room once more.

Hadfield tugged Gilbert back away from the doorway. "What the devil is wrong with you? We are trying to avoid detection."

He met Hadfield's deathly serious glare but quickly lowered his eyes. Gilbert's hands shook at his sides and his chin dropped to his chest. How could he have entertained the outrageous thoughts of Mary being in the other room with Valois?

"You fool!" Hadfield pointed to the other room. "Tell me you didn't think for a moment that the woman in there was Lady Mary."

Gilbert was no liar and was terrible at hiding his thoughts. These constant hallucinations of Mary were muddling his brain.

"I should box your ears for even thinking the woman you love would do such a thing."

Hadfield was right. He deserved a beating. Mary wanted a man who had complete and utter faith in her, and he had failed.

"We need to find Lady Mary and ensure she is safe." Hadfield released a sigh. "She has been in the comte's company long enough. Do you want to search for Lady Mary, or shall I?"

He wanted to be the one to go and find Mary, but her keen senses would detect his guilty feelings immediately. "I'll take care of the papers and make arrangements for our departure at first light."

CHAPTER TWENTY-FOUR

*S*lowly sliding her hand under her pillow, Mary reached for her dagger. She wasn't sure what had prompted her to sleep with it tonight, but she felt it necessary. She was glad now that she had. A shadow slipped across the room where no shadow should be. She wrapped her fingers around the cold steel.

The mattress sank beneath the intruder's weight. It was no shadow but a man. Her heart wailed against her ribs, but she swung the blade toward him in a confident arc.

The man caught her, twisting her wrist painfully. She dropped her weapon with a curse, searching for another escape, another means of attack.

"Lady Mary, it is I. Hadfield."

"Lord Hadfield?" Mary rubbed her wrist. "What are you doing here?"

"I've been looking everywhere for you. You were to remain with Comte Boucher until we found you."

Still foggy from sleep, Mary blinked and then stared at the man before her.

"Waterford is seeing to the arrangements for our travel tomorrow. We are to leave at first light."

More likely, Gilbert was still preoccupied with the comtesse. Pushing aside the absurd disappointment that it was Hadfield who was in her rooms instead of Gilbert, Mary said, "I entertained the comte as long as I could. I played countless rounds of cards until I emptied the man's pockets. After I trounced him at billiards, he declared he was off to seek other entertainment—the kind I was not willing to provide."

"I'm sorry for not arriving sooner, but we—"

"No need to apologize. Did you obtain the details you were searching for?"

Lord Hadfield nodded, but his gaze remained lowered as he said, "We did."

"I know you mentioned you were dubious about the comte's motivations, but after my discussions with him tonight, I believe he is an ally, not a foe."

He looked at her sharply. "What led you to this belief?"

Lord Hadfield's intense stare settled deep into her bones and disconcerted her. What it didn't do was set her heart aflutter.

Shaking her head, she said, "Comte Boucher wants André to locate Lord Burke's son. He wants to determine if the rumors about Lord Wharton are true. His informants alluded that Wharton is not at all what the gossips say and is in hiding, waiting, plotting against his own papa."

"The evidence I found tonight would support your claim that Boucher is privy to such sources and that he is indeed an ally rather than the enemy."

"Would you have believed me if you hadn't found proof of Boucher's ties?"

"Of course. Why wouldn't I?"

She stared at Hadfield.

Nothing.

No tingles, no rapid pulse, no anticipation. What was wrong with her? Hadfield was a jewel among gentlemen— titled, with healthy coffers. But she remained cool and steady around him. "Waterford would have asked me questions or required me to explain myself further."

"I am not Waterford. But I, like him, will protect you and your honor."

"Lord Hadfield, I do appreciate the offer. However, I've learned over the past week that I am capable of many things and possess a multitude of talents I never knew prior."

"You are an amazing woman. It would be an honor if—"

She raised a hand, preventing him from continuing. "Lord Hadfield, you are a wise man, and it is very generous of you—" Mary stared into his eyes. Remorse. She didn't need Lady Frances's assistance in this instance to deduce that the man's heart belonged to another. Clearing her throat, which was constricted with empathy for the man before her, Mary continued to say, "As I informed Gilbert, I will only marry a man whose belief in me is unwavering."

"Unwavering, you say." Lord Hadfield's lips pressed together in a slight grimace. "Did you share this requirement with Waterford?"

She had lain in bed for hours waiting for Gilbert to find her so she could ask him directly if it had been him in the hall. But after her emotions ceased to volley about, she had rationally contemplated what she had spied in the hall and had concluded that Gilbert would never betray her.

Mary considered Lord Hadfield's posture and tone and was overcome with doubt. "Yes. Gilbert knows it is my wish to marry a man who is willing to place his trust in me. Why do you ask?"

Lord Hadfield inhaled deeply and released his breath ever so slowly, postponing his answer. "While we were searching for the documents, we came across Valois. He was being— entertained by a woman. From Waterford's vantage point, the lady appeared to be—" Hadfield's brow creased as he took another deep breath before continuing. "Well, one could have assumed it was you in the room. I know it was not you but the comtesse. Valois agreed, like you, to entertain our host until we obtained what we needed."

Relief flowed through her that it was her cousin whom the comtesse had managed to corner and not Gilbert. She had rationalized earlier that she must have been mistaken.

"The dress. The hair. One might have confused you with the comtesse at first glance." Lord Hadfield reached out to take her sore wrist and rubbed it with the pad of his thumb. It was a soothing gesture, and again she was disappointed it wasn't Gilbert.

"Were you confused?"

The man stiffened as if she had slapped him. "Of course not!"

"But what you are trying to tell me is—" Mary paused. Swallowing hard and fists curling into balls, Mary pulled her hand away. "Gilbert thought it was I and not the comtesse who was entertaining my cousin, didn't he? Gilbert doesn't trust me, and never will."

Mary wrapped her arms in front of her stomach.

Hadn't she herself believed that Gilbert had let the witch have her way with him in the hallway?

It had been her cousin, not Gilbert carrying out the duty of entertaining the comtesse. She was a hypocrite. If she wanted Gilbert's ultimate trust, she would have to trust him equally. Her mama had placed her faith in her papa over and over only to be disappointed time and time again.

"I'm sorry." Lord Hadfield's palm lay open in invitation.

Mary shook her head. "There is no need to apologize."

Standing, Lord Hadfield tugged on his coat sleeves. "Oh, but there is. It was not my intention to upset you. I clearly failed. I—. I thought you should know in case Waterford behaves oddly tomorrow."

She lay back, pulling the covers up to her chin. "I expect Waterford will do what he does best. Focus on executing the assignment and ignore me. He has for years."

Hands clasped in front of him, Lord Hadfield smiled and revealed a charming dimple. "You are an extremely clever woman, and I'm certain I'm not telling you anything you are not already aware of. But once we arrive at Valois's estate, you *will* have to make a choice as to which of us will have the honor to marry you."

All she could manage was a weak smile.

Hadfield turned to leave.

The devil got the better of her as she spoke to his back. "Convention would dictate that to be the rational course of action. However, I've never been one to adhere to society's rules, and I'm not about to begin now."

Two quick strides and he was back on the bed sitting next to her. "Lady Mary, I must insist. If not Waterford, please consider my offer. I am not a bad sort once you get to know me better."

Sadness filled his eyes, contrary to his words.

"You are the best sort of gentleman, and I'm truly honored by your offer. But I have a feeling you have already lost your heart to another, but are too afraid to approach her."

Lord Hadfield tilted his head to the side and said, "Waterford warned me of your intuition. But I do not fear it like he does. It is what makes you unique, a quality to be treasured."

She sat up, wrapped her arms around him, and gave him a sisterly hug. There were no shooting stars. No tingling in the most intimate of places—no zing. Her pulse remained steady. She pulled back and shoved him off the bed. "Thank you. I shall think upon it."

It was a lie, but she needed him to leave, for the tears were welling behind her eyes and threatening to appear. If she did not get rid of him, he would see exactly how much Gilbert's lack of faith in her affected her.

Just as he had entered her room without a sound, he left the same way. Mary's gaze shifted to the adjoining chamber. Greene's shoulders were slumped, and she shook her head as she turned away.

Alone.

Mary buried her face in the pillow and let the feathers absorb her sobs.

CHAPTER TWENTY-FIVE

*B*lurry-eyed, Gilbert padded over to the window. The storm clouds hovering overhead reflected his dark mood. He hoped they would be able to ride out of range before it began to rain, for he dreaded the idea of being cooped up in the coach with Mary and Valois. He couldn't banish the image of Mary riding him. His twisted mind had somehow replaced Valois with his own likeness, and thus he had remained awake throughout the night.

Raking a hand through his hair, he muttered, "The woman has me going mad." He stuffed a leg through his breeches. "Valois. I'm not jealous of the frog."

For years the French had been his enemy. They shot at him. They tried to kill him. But he could rationalize that Valois was not the enemy. In fact, the man had aided the British forces by hiding captives and providing safe harbor on long treks through France.

Tarnation. It pricked his ego that the comtesse, who had been chasing after him since the day he set foot on the estate, had turned her attention to Valois, the man who

Mary seemed to prefer over his own company—which made his jealousy worse.

Jamming his shirttails into his breeches, he adjusted his falls. The mere thought of Mary had his body at the ready. The scratch at his door came as he was fastening the last button of his breeches. "Enter."

Hadfield waltzed into the room, looking refreshed and ready for the multiday journey. As per his habit, he headed for the window. "André will be joining our group."

"What?"

"I spoke with the comte this morning, and the arrangements have been made. Lady Mary and Valois will ride together as before, and the three of us can take turns resting in the extra coach."

"Mary will ride with me and not Valois."

"That is not the plan." Hadfield's tone held an edge to it Gilbert had not heard before. "Last night, I found Mary in her chambers. Safe and asleep."

"Her bedchamber! You sneaked into her room. Please tell me you left right away as soon as you saw she was slumbering."

"No. Mary and I had a very informative chat. She was able to provide me with a wealth of intelligence that she had pried from the comte before retiring to her own rooms —*alone*."

"Tell me what information Mary was able to obtain?"

Hadfield briefly shifted his gaze from the window to Gilbert and then back to the window. "Always about the mission. Very well. She confirmed my suspicions that Boucher is, in fact, a friend to our cause, not an enemy, and has access to far-reaching resources. As the paperwork we retrieved last night suggests, Boucher and his son are on the hunt for Burke's own offspring, Lord Wharton."

Gilbert blurted, "Wharton! The man's an imbecile."

"Boucher has informants that have him believing that Wharton is actually conspiring against his own papa."

"And we are simply going to trust Boucher and his informers."

Hadfield rested a hand on the window casing. "Yes."

"My assignment was to ensure your safety, not to question your sanity."

Pushing away from the window, Hadfield replied, "Perfect. Let's be off. I'm eager to reach Valois's estate and have my fate determined. Living in limbo like this is grating on my nerves."

"What are you rambling on about now?"

Employing a tone one would use with a child, Hadfield said, "I want to know what Lady Mary's final decision is, which of us will she agree to marry."

"She gave *me* permission to court her, not *you*."

"Oh, I don't believe you are even a contender anymore after you failed her last night. I was referring to Valois or me."

Gilbert felt like the imbecile he had called Wharton. Hadfield was making no sense to his tired mind. "How did I fail Mary?"

Hadfield raised an eyebrow, turned, and left him to mull over the answer.

FOR THREE DAYS, Gilbert had tried to capture Mary's attention.

He had been an utter dolt for even thinking for a second the woman on her knees had been Mary. The buffoon that he was believed that all he had to do was simply ask for her hand and she'd be overjoyed and agree immediately. After years of rebelling against what he viewed as an arranged marriage of sorts, Gilbert was now faced with the fact that he might never have the chance to marry the woman who was so much more than the girl he feared with the ability to see and speak to the dead.

It had been hours riding alongside the closed curtain of Valois's coach in hopes of catching a glimpse of the woman who had completely shut him out. She hadn't even greeted him the morning of their departure. Instead, she'd waltzed right by on the arm of Hadfield, who had transferred her into the coach that she shared with Valois. For miles, the man had droned on and on about how Mary should remain in France and all the advantages he believed went along with becoming a duchess. Either Mary had dozed off, or her responses had been nonverbal, for though Gilbert had hoped to hear her decline, there wasn't a note of her musical voice.

As they rounded a bend and the gates of the ducal palace came into view. Gilbert recalled the childhood image of his abandoned estate in the highlands. It wasn't as large or as imposing as the monstrosity that lay before him, but it had the most spectacular views. Which would Mary prefer?

Phillip's voice pierced through his thoughts. *Location is not the issue, you imbecile. It is you whom she should choose. Prove to her you are worthy of forgiveness.*

Her brother's voice had been a nuisance over the entire journey. Constant reminders of why Mary was perfect for him and why he was an idiot for making such a hash of matters.

The window curtain was pulled back, and Mary's tired, withdrawn features were in full view. She peered down the drive, but as soon as she spotted him, she pulled the material back up as a shield.

Moments later, he heard her address Valois. "It appears you will have my family to contend with also."

"I invited them."

"You did? I wonder whom Papa brought with him."

"Everyone. For the ceremony."

"What ceremony?"

"Your wedding, *ma chérie*. But your papa will want to know which man will be lucky to have you, *non*?"

Who had Mary decided to marry? Trying to catch Mary's response, Gilbert leaned closer. His horse shifted away from the moving vehicle, and he nearly fell out of his seat. To his dismay, he hadn't managed to hear Mary's response.

His heart raced as he caught sight of the entire Masterson clan assembled on Valois's stairs. What was he to say to Mary's papa? For years he had readily made promises to see to Mary's care, the same promises he made to Phillip on the battlefield.

Gilbert dismounted and strode over to the coach, but Hadfield had somehow managed to reach Mary first. Gilbert's hand curled into a fist. Mary nearly slipped disembarking from the coach, and it was Hadfield who caught her and was the recipient of her alluring smile. It should have been him who was there for her. Not Hadfield.

CHAPTER TWENTY-SIX

*D*ucking her head, Mary withdrew from Lord Hadfield's arms. She wasn't ready to face Gilbert. Running up the wide stone stairs, she flung herself into her aunt's arms. Without hesitation, Aunt Agnes wrapped her arms about Mary. "Shhh— sweetling."

Her aunt's warmth was reassuring, and Mary squeezed the older woman closer.

"Let go of your aunt Agnes this minute," her papa ordered. The duke hated public displays of affection, claiming them to be unbecoming and uncouth.

Her aunt responded, "Oh. Shoosh, Rupert. The child is upset. Leave her be."

Shielding Mary from curious stares, Aunt Agnes ushered into the house. "Dinnae worry about your papa. Leave him to me."

Mary nodded, relieved to have an ally in dealing with her meddling family. Her head ached. She had to decide and soon. Blindly following her aunt through the halls, Mary wasn't aware that she was in the guest chamber she had been assigned to until after she was stripped of her clothing and Greene was pulling a night shift over her head.

Crawling into the plush bed, she settled between the soft sheets and placed her weary head upon the soft feather-stuffed pillow. Mary sighed and then let the tears fall.

What was she to do?

She couldn't stay in France.

Lord Hadfield's heart belonged to another.

She didn't want to marry a man who had little faith in her and was capable of believing the worst of her.

Aunt Agnes rubbed her back. "The git is sorry, but you need to make him grovel before accepting his hand."

"Gilbert?"

"Aye."

"I won't marry a man who doesn't want me."

"Oh, my child, he wants you."

"I don't mean to bed. I want a man who will value all my abilities."

"Have you not learned that in order for others to see you for what you are worth, you first must believe in yourself?"

"I have learned much while being on the Continent and all without the help of Lady Frances."

"What do you mean without her assistance?"

"I no longer have the ability to see or hear them. They have all disappeared."

"What do you mean? She is sitting right next to—" Her aunt tucked her hair behind her ear. "Child, look at me."

Mary rolled and faced her aunt. "I miss them."

"They will never abandon you. It is you who has to learn to value your gift and believe in your capabilities."

"But I do."

"If that were the truth, you would hear the blistering words our dear Lady Frances is now sharing with me."

"What is she saying? Why can I not hear her lecture?"

Her aunt raised a hand to her cheek and wiped a tear away with her thumb. "I have explained. It is up to you. Figure the rest out. I suspect once you are in accord with your fate all will return to normal."

"I will not accept that I'm meant to marry Gilbert. It can't be so. Why would the universe want to burden me with such a man?"

"You have always had a stubborn streak to you, but now is really not the time for such behavior. Rest, and we will deal with matters in the morning."

Mary closed her eyes and slipped farther under the soft linens and waited for her aunt to leave. She wasn't willing to wait until morn to deal with her future or allow others to determine it for her. She would take care of matters tonight.

IF THEY WERE all assigned the same rooms as before, Lord Hadfield's room would be to the right of her cousin's chambers and Gilbert's to the left. Mary stood in the middle of the hallway and looked at each door.

There was only one sensible choice.

Her heart raced as she took a step toward Lord Hadfield's chamber. The door began to open, and she swiveled and dashed into Gilbert's instead.

Leaning her forehead against the door, she let out a sigh.

"Mary?" Gilbert's voice was gravelly from sleep. "Is that you, lass?"

Maybe if she stayed still and didn't utter a sound, he'd

close his eyes and go back to sleep. She was about to straighten and flee from the room when his large hands grabbed her by the upper arms and spun her around.

Face-to-face, he asked, "Lass, what are you doing here?"

What was she to say—*I meant to enter Lord Hadfield's chamber, but at the last moment, I got scared and hid in yours*?

She was no ninny. That would surely anger the man, whose touch was threating her resolve.

"I came to tell you I've made my decision to marry Lord—"

Gilbert's eyes widened, and then he barked, "Over my dead body."

"Gilbert. There's no reason to be dramatic. It is the most sensible choice, and I wanted to be the one to inform you of my decision."

"How does marrying Hadfield make any sense?"

"He respects me and—"

"But he will never love you as I do!"

"Love? What does love have to do with anything?"

Gilbert's stiffened at her declaration.

"In any case, you don't love me. If you did, you wouldn't have thought me capable of—"

He grabbed her hands and held them tight. "It's because I *am* in love with you that I lost my mind." He rubbed his thumb over the back of her hand, and she lifted her gaze to meet his. "Lass, I've loved you even before I laid eyes upon you. Phillip shared your letters at school, and I'd fallen in love with your wit, the selflessness of your words, and the affectionate tone in which you wrote. I was a lout the first time I met you. I didn't want to be forced into a marriage like my parents, so I ignored the intense attraction I felt for you."

Gilbert wasn't a liar. Did she dare believe that they

could have shared a bond even before meeting? She herself had admitted to having feelings for the version of Gilbert Phillip had spoken of. The man that had appeared on rare occasions over the years. The man that made her feel safe and warm merely a week ago.

Gilbert squeezed her hand. "You're cold. Come warm up under the covers."

Mary pulled her hands from his grasp. "No. I'm going to return to my own chambers, and I'll be informing my papa of my decision in the morn."

"I had hoped my admission of mistakes and declaration of my feelings for you would have changed your mind." Gilbert cupped her face with both hands and bent until they were eye to eye once more. "Mary, I signed the marriage papers over a year ago."

"How can that be? A year ago you departed the Devonton house party early and headed straight for the Continent."

"Your mama brought the papers with her to Devonton's, and I signed them before I left. It was then that I agreed to a ceremony upon my return. Until then, you were to remain in Scotland with your aunt."

Anger rolled through her body. No one had even bothered to ask what her preference was. Gilbert hadn't even bothered to ask for her hand. It was she who was to be forced into a marriage she didn't want.

What she wanted was to box his ears. Or simply punch him. The arrogant fool! She firmly clasped her hands in front of her and shifted away from him, if not lessening the urge to inflict bodily harm to her betrothed, then at least making it more difficult to do so.

"I'll escort you back to your rooms." Gilbert turned and walked over to retrieve his banyan from the foot of the bed. Instead of donning it, he wrapped it about her shoulders and then grabbed his breeches and shirt, which lay nearby. "Mary, I do love you and believe our union will be a happy one if you can ever find it your heart to forgive me."

Time.

She needed time to think. Gilbert walked her back to her chamber and tucked her in bed like a small child. Once he was gone, Greene's head peeked out from the adjoining room.

"Greene, were you aware that I was betrothed to Lord Waterford this past year?"

Her maid dropped her gaze to the floor and wrung her hands in front of her. "Yes, my lady. I was informed."

"Why didn't you tell me?"

"I was hoping he'd not make it back from the Continent this time. Your family waited all those years to see if he would return from the war, and then when he returned, your papa told him his time was up. His Grace threatened to marry you off to another if he didn't sign the papers."

In her formative years she had accepted that there were events and disappointments that one could not avoid. Aunt Agnes and Lady Frances foretold Gilbert was the man she was destined to marry. She understood that some things, no matter what choices you make, are unavoidable, but for her parents and others to have acted as they did— blast them all!

Suppressing a surge of indignation, Mary calmly said, "Thank you for sharing this with me. Sorry to have awoken you. Please go back to bed."

Mary laid her head back upon the pillow and stared at the canopy above, mulling over the fact no one had cared or bothered to consult her about her wants, needs, or wishes.

CHAPTER TWENTY-SEVEN

*S*tomping back to his room, Gilbert flung himself atop his bed. Mary hadn't uttered a single retort to his confessions. Sliding his hands behind his head, he closed his eyes.

Hadfield. When she believed she had a choice, Mary had chosen Hadfield and not him. How was he to convince her a life with him would be ultimately better than marrying the man across the hall?

Phillip's voice whispered once more. *Remember what I shared with you.*

The letters!

Scrambling off the bed, he pulled out his satchel hidden beneath the bed. He reached in to retrieve the stack of letters Mary had sent to Phillip during the war. He hadn't read them, despite his promise to Phillip he would. The man really had a long list of wishes upon his death.

Gilbert untied the blue ribbon that held the tattered letters together. Phillip had placed them in chronological order with the very first letter he received on the top. His fingers trembled as he unfolded the parchment to read:

Dear Philly,

I'm stuck inside again today. Mama refuses to allow me to ride in the rain.
But I long for the bite of the wind against my cheeks and the balm of the fresh, clean water seeping into my pores.

Enough of my woes. To answer your question, do I agree with the theorems of Joseph Fourier? His ideas on time and heat are of particular interest. However, with the limited resources available to me, now that you have abandoned me, it will take me a few weeks to organize my thoughts, but do not fear. I will endeavor to provide you with a thorough analysis.

Your devoted sister,
Mary

Mary had always exhibited a keen mind, but her interest in the complex theorems relating to the transfer of heat and energy between physical systems was surprising. He certainly couldn't deny the heat that he generated whenever she entered a room.

Gilbert read through the letter again. What a dunce he had been! Mary's intense curiosity had been facilitated by her brother. Phillip had been her confidant and conspirator, assisting in obtaining data for her research and gaining introductions for her to go on explorations.

Without Phillip, she needed a husband that could provide her access to information and adventure. He could provide exactly what Mary wanted. His duties ensured he was constantly on the hunt for new intelligence and led him on more than one escapade.

A bead of sweat ran down his spine. By involving her

in his missions, he would be placing Mary in danger. Was marrying Mary while in the midst of an assignment a wise decision? Gilbert glanced at the paper in his hand. No more excuses. Mary was going to be Countess Waterford by day's end.

Footsteps sounded in the hall. He hastily replaced the letters in the satchel and kicked it under the bed. Hadfield swept in, not even bothering to close the door. The man pulled back the curtains. Muted streaks of sunlight filtered through—what time was it?

After scanning the room, Hadfield's gaze settled upon him. "Lady Mary is missing. We need to find her before her papa does." He released the curtain and bent to look under the bed. "His Grace is in no mood for games and wants a ceremony to be held later this afternoon."

Without sleep, Gilbert's brain was not fully functioning. "Afternoon? A ceremony today? Wait, Mary is missing?"

Striding to the adjoining chamber, Hadfield placed a hand on each side of the door casing and stuck his head in. When he emerged, he said, "Yes. Her maid awoke to find Mary's bed empty this morn."

Hadfield was here to search his room.

"She's not in here." No. After telling her the truth, he had seen to it that Mary was safely tucked away in her own bed. "I'm sure she is somewhere about the estate." Gilbert bent to retrieve and put on his boots.

"No one has seen Mary, and Valois has already questioned all the staff. None have laid eyes on her since last eve. When did you see her last?"

Gilbert did not care for Hadfield's question or tone. "Why do you want to know?"

"She has been withdrawn ever since we left Comte Boucher's estate. Making a decision has weighed on her heavily."

Donning his coat, Gilbert said, "There is no question as to who she is to marry."

Hadfield stood directly in front of him. "That is a rather bold statement. Do you care to explain?"

"Her papa and I already signed the settlements. Mary is betrothed to me."

"Why did you fail to mention any of this before?"

If Mary was genuinely missing, now was not the time to discuss how foolish his actions had been.

Gilbert asked, "Has Valois searched the grounds?"

"It's raining. Surely she wouldn't have ventured outdoors."

His blood pumped faster. Rain. Hadn't he learned just last night Mary loved to venture out in the rain—to feel the moisture soak into her pores. He felt in his bones she was out roaming the estate grounds. "Very well, you continue to search indoors, and I'll conduct the search outside."

He needed to find her. The possibility of Mary lying injured in a ditch or lost in the dark and cold sent a chill down his spine. He shook off the morbid thoughts. Mary was a skilled horsewoman. Tarnation! Accomplished or no, the dark made every unseen obstacle deathly.

Gilbert rushed to reach the door.

From behind, Hadfield said, "André and I are leaving tomorrow at first light. We must return to London."

Gilbert turned to meet the man's hard stare.

Hadfield continued, "Your assignment ends here."

No way Gilbert wasn't going to complete the mission. Mary wanted adventure, and she had proved more than capable during their visit to Comte Boucher's estate. Once they were married, he wouldn't be distracted by the woman who had his mind and stomach tied in knots.

Gilbert marched up to Hadfield. Nose to nose, he said, "I only take direction from one man, and that is Archbroke. My orders were to see you safely returned to English soil when you were ready, and that is precisely what I plan to do."

"What is the matter with all the agents of the Home Office? You are all dunderheads to place duty before all else. Mary is to be your wife. She is to be your number one priority. If you insist on continuing, she will no doubt want to accompany us. Are you willing to place her in danger?"

"Mary will not be a burden. If anything, she will be a valuable asset to our team."

The smirk Hadfield gave him reminded Gilbert never to underestimate the man. "We'll find her first."

Hadfield was right. He needed to locate Mary, convince her to marry him, and then deal with details of his assignment.

GILBERT WALKED in the blinding rain. What had started as a relatively light shower had become a torrential downpour.

Cupping his hands about his mouth, Gilbert yelled, "Lass, where are you!"

He glanced at his pocket watch once more. He had been out wandering the estate for hours, finding no hint of which direction Mary might have headed. Oddly proud of her stealthy skills, he was simultaneously concerned he might never figure out how to find her. He had been so sure Mary would have been hidden in the gamer's cottage, but when he found it empty, his heart sank with disappointment. Continuing to trudge through the woods, Gilbert stopped to tug his coat tighter about him.

"What is taking the obstinate man so long?" Mary's mutterings reached his ears, but her voice came from above. Raising his gaze higher, he spotted a small wooden structure mounted high up in the branches.

How had the woman found such an obscure hideaway?

Making his way to the decades-old tree, he began to climb the wood slats nailed to the trunk. Gilbert froze as Mary continued to rant.

"How could he believe I'd simply agree to marry him?"

After a minute of silence, he was about to take another step when she continued.

"I certainly will not."

Again silence. Who was she talking to? Considering the length of the pauses between her outbursts, he guessed the voices had returned.

"Gilbert, I know you are out there. Are you coming up, or shall I come down?"

Yes, even her sharp-witted tone had returned.

"I'll come to you." With each rung, he mentally reiterated each reason why she should marry him—preparing for the battle he was about to enter. With his eyes peering over the platform, he caught sight of her riding boots. Odd. He hadn't seen a mount tied up nearby. As he took another step up, his eyes traveled up along her long legs clad in breeches, revealing every curve of her delicious body. "Lass, you have everyone worried and looking for you."

"Oh, so *now* everyone is concerned about my whereabouts."

Climbing up to the platform, he had to bend at the knees to prevent hitting his head on the wooden ceiling. "Lass, please let me explain."

Without hesitation, she walked up to stand before him. Her honey-brown eyes were ablaze. "You said more than enough last night. Today, it is my turn to speak and for you to listen."

Gilbert was a seasoned soldier accustomed to taking orders, and he'd willingly take them from the woman in front of him as long as she agreed to become Countess Waterford.

He bowed his head in assent.

"Aside from running away and assuming a new identity, I see I have no other choice but to marry you. While I considered the advantages of becoming someone new, I adore my nephews and niece too much to cut off those familial strings." Mary took two steps away, but due to the cramped conditions, she turned again and, after a moment, ordered, "Sit."

He looked at the tiny chair, uncertain that it would hold his weight. It was worth the humiliation of landing on his rear if it meant Mary continued her impassioned speech.

With the extra room, Mary managed to take four steps. She began to pace wall to wall. Four steps away, four steps back.

"Where was I?" Her forefinger tapped against pursed lips. Lips he desperately wanted to kiss. "Do you intend to ship me back to Scotland?"

Mary's question snapped the wayward thought from his mind.

Should she venture to Scotland? Yes, if only for her safety. No, he wanted Mary with him, always. He hadn't made any plans. His attention for the entire day had been focused on finding her. With eyes trained on the floor, Gilbert said, "I intend to return to London with Hadfield in the morn. If you wish, you can journey back at a more leisurely pace with your family. I'll come to fetch you when my assignment is complete."

Mary snorted. "Once this one is complete, Archbroke will simply assign you to another. And thus you shall remain 'on assignment' until you no longer can complete them, allowing you to avoid me for many more years to come."

His face flushed. Based on his past behavior, he could not fault her reasoning. "Then I shall inform Archbroke that I wish to retire, and this shall be my last mission."

Mid-step, Mary whirled to face him, eyes filled with worry. "Why would you do that?"

"Because it's time I tended to my other duties as a lord."

"To produce an heir." Mary's hands shook. She quickly clasped them behind her back.

Gilbert nodded. "Among other things, yes."

"And what if I told you that I'm not willing to bear you a child? Would you assist me in convincing my papa that the match is not a suitable one."

Gilbert considered Mary's statement for a moment. She had spoken the words as if she had shared a deep dark secret. Were the obligations of his title and her desire not to reproduce what prevented her from accepting his offer? No, that couldn't be the reason for her refusal. Hadfield was also titled.

"No. I will not assist you in persuading your papa to allow you to marry another. If we do not produce the next Earl of Waterford, the title will pass to my cousin. He's a good fellow."

Mary stared at him with wide eyes as if he had gone mad. "What?"

"If you have no desire to have children, there are ways to prevent a child from being conceived. I have no objection to your wish." He spoke the truth. All he needed was Mary.

Mary stared at him. "I'm very serious, Gilbert. While I love Thomas's offspring, I'm quite happy when they return to their parents' care and I'm able to continue with my hobbies. It sounds selfish, but I do not believe I'm the maternal sort."

What was he to say? Not having younger siblings or any siblings to produce nieces and nephews, Gilbert hadn't been exposed to little ones. He searched his heart. Mary was more than enough for him. If she preferred not to have any children, then he would gladly spend the rest of his days with her and her alone.

How to convince her of his agreement?

Her hands still tucked behind her, Gilbert waited until he managed to capture her gaze. "You will gain no argument from me on the subject. Did you think that I would not want to wed you or that I'd love you less if you preferred not to have my child?"

Mary's eyes bore into him.

He ached to reach out and hold her. "Sorry to disappoint you, lass, but we *are* going to marry as soon as we return to the house, *and* you will be subject to my company for the rest of your life."

Turning away from him, Mary said, "If that is the way it is to be, I'd prefer to remain here in France until you are done with your duties."

"No." The image of the Valois taking advantage of a lonely Mary flashed before him. He would not be cuckolded.

Mary muttered. "See! He still doesn't believe in me." Hands on her hips, she turned to face him. "Don't try to deny it. It is clearly written upon your features."

For a moment, he had been confused as to whom she had addressed. He would have to accept that she saw and spoke to others whom he was unaware of, but first to convince her to willingly return with him and accept his hand. He partially stood. "Mary, it is your turn to sit and listen."

She huffed but shuffled past him to plonk down in the small chair he had just vacated.

Gilbert knelt and reached for her wrist, needing to determine if her pulse was racing as fast as his. "Tell me what your ideal future would entail, with the caveat that I am included in that scenario."

"Why waste our time? We should discuss the reality of the situation, not some fairy-tale ending."

Yes, Mary's pulse was racing. He lifted her wrist to place his lips upon the delicate skin on the inside. "Indulge me."

"Very well. I would prefer our union to be a partnership of sorts. I'd like to travel with you when you are on assignment and work for your confidence. I believe I could be of assistance." Mary looked down at where they were joined. "I do not wish to be banished to some remote part of Scotland."

He couldn't prevent the grin from appearing on his face. "Lass, if I promise to do everything in my power to grant you the life you just described, will you do me the honor of becoming Countess Waterford?"

Her forehead wrinkled, and then to his relief, Mary smiled.

The idea of having her by his side every day was appealing, not appalling. He could wait for her to return his affections. He had the rest of his life to beg for forgiveness and prove to her he was worthy of her love.

Mary remained nervous—the quickening beat of her pulse against his fingers told him so.

"Do you swear?" The steel in her voice belied her anxiety.

Gilbert released her hands and raised his right hand to cover his heart. "I do."

How long was she going to make him wait?

Even as the seconds ticked by, he was flooded with remorse for all the years he had made her wait.

The corner of Mary's lip turned up into the most alluring smile. "Very well. I agree."

Gilbert exhaled the breath he was holding. "Finally."

She cupped his cheek and bent down to press her sweet lips to his. How he hungered for her touch. Capturing her by the waist, he stood to haul her into his arms but hit his head hard as he straightened. "Oof."

Mary's giggle had him smiling too as he rubbed the top of his head. "We should head back. There is still much to organize."

"By the time we reach the estate, Valois will have already had everything arranged." She looked down at her attire. "Will you require me to change before we say our vows?"

He thought she looked rather delectable—white lawn shirt peeking from beneath her unbuttoned greatcoat, breeches, and Hessians. "No. I'd rather you say them before you have a chance to change your mind."

"You are willing to marry me as I am?"

Grinning like a fool, he said, "Exactly as you are."

After a chaste kiss, he released her and began to lower himself down the entrance, balancing on his toes upon the makeshift stairs. Glancing up, he was pleased to see Mary carefully lowering her foot down the tree trunk to find purchase on each rung. It also gave him a perfect view of her derrière. He hoped they would have time this eve to consummate their marriage.

On the ground, with his feet firmly planted, he reached up and grabbed Mary by the waist to haul her against him.

She slid down his chest, sending sparks of energy flowing though his entire body. Mary was to be his wife. Spinning her, he claimed her lips with a hunger he doubted would ever abate. In return, Gilbert was rewarded with one of Mary's passionate moans.

She wound her hands about his neck and kissed him soundly before pulling back. "Thomas is approaching."

"Hopefully, Roxbury brought an extra mount with him."

"He did." She looked back at him once more. "You no longer consider me a witch or mad?"

"I will become accustomed to you knowing things before me soon enough. It may well be an extreme advantage while we are on assignment."

The smile he received for his response had him bursting with pride as if he had given her the sun, moon, and the stars.

CHAPTER TWENTY-EIGHT

*B*last Thomas and his timing.

Oh, how she had missed Gilbert's kisses. Mary reluctantly withdrew from Gilbert's embrace.

Phillip, years ago, had advised Mary that Gilbert would not object to her wish not to conceive. When she had pressed for an explanation, all Phillip had said was that it was his firm belief that Gilbert held no strong attachment to the idea of having children of his own. Without sound reasoning or logic, she had not believed Phillip.

Gilbert was no liar. Hearing him state that a childless union was of no matter to him shattered all her remaining doubts, and her heart burst with joy over his agreement to allow her to accompany him on missions. A smile remained on her face. His admission that he would find her useful was better than his admission of love. Finally, the feeling of being wanted had her heady and looking forward to the wedding ceremony.

Thomas rarely donned the Seaburn ducal scowl, but it was out in full force today. "Waterford, you're not married yet. Take your hands off my sister."

"Not a chance. Now that I have Mary's consent, I'll not let her go for anything." Gilbert laced his fingers through hers, and she followed alongside him as he marched over to the mount Thomas had brought with him.

Gilbert released Mary's hand momentarily to give her a boost up onto the horse. Once she was seated, he mounted up behind her and pulled her against his chest. Warmth seeped into her bones. She leaned back and gloried in the safety of his care.

Her brother stared at her square in the eye and said, "Mary, don't get too cozy. As soon as we are within sight of the estate, you'll ride with me." Thomas looked at Gilbert. "Not negotiable."

As they approached the edge of the trees, Gilbert whispered, "We will have to leave early in the morn to ensure Hadfield's safe return. I would prefer to—"

Thomas stopped a few yards in front of them.

Mary asked, "What is it? I won't let you change your mind or allow you to renege on your promise."

"I've never broken a promise, and I don't intend to start now. What I was trying to say is that we can postpone the consummation if— if that is what you would prefer."

Heat flooded her cheeks. "I honestly hadn't considered the matter. Can I— decide later?"

Gilbert looked up at the sky. "There is not much more time for you to decide, but we will need to be ready to leave at first light."

"Does it take all night?"

"Ahh— well."

Thomas interrupted, "Come along, Mary."

Gilbert barked, "Just a minute."

Thomas coughed and mumbled, "That's about as long as it will take."

Confused by the conversation, Mary slid to the ground. "I'll give you my answer when I see you next."

Gilbert scratched the back of his neck—a telltale sign he was nervous about the outcome. Why was he so nervous? What did she not know?

Gilbert came to help her mount. Seated behind Thomas, she wound her arms about his waist just as she had when she was a little girl. Not that it was necessary, but Thomas was still her eldest brother, and she rarely had opportunities to show him how much she cared for him. It reminded Mary of how much she missed Phillip's hugs.

She rested her cheek against Thomas's back and released a contented sigh.

He peered over his shoulder.

Mary leaned back and said, "Your smile has me worried."

"And you should be. I can't imagine Mama doing well having a go at explaining the marriage bed. Papa made a total hash of it."

She wouldn't seek out their mama for information. Ellen, Thomas's wife, was kind and intelligent. Yes, she would be able to explain what occurs rationally.

Peering around Thomas, she groaned at the sight of servants rushing about like ants and her family milling nearby ready to pounce as soon as they were within range. The only person who appeared calm was Aunt Agnes, who stood at the foot of the stairs, hands firmly clasped in front.

Thomas chuckled.

Mary asked, "Why are you laughing?"

"Because I finally won a wager against the old woman. When we set sail across the channel, Aunt Agnes was of the opinion that Waterford had made an irreparable mistake and it would be a waste to bring the vicar along. But Papa insisted, and for once, I sided with the old man."

Was Aunt Agnes losing her ability? Mary recalled the drawings her aunt had passed along to her before her departure. Not one had become a reality. How odd. Her aunt's predictions had always materialized in the past. Curious, Mary asked, "What was the winner to receive?"

"If she won, I was to repair the crumbling estate she lives in."

"And if you won?"

"She was to return to London and reside with Ellen and me."

Mary slapped her brother on the arm. "You can afford to pay for nannies and such to take care of the children. Why would you—"

"Aunt Agnes won't be with us for much longer, and she should be with family, not alone in some abandoned castle."

Male logic continued to baffle her. "But Thomas, that is her home. You can't expect her to want to leave the resting place of her husband."

"Mary and I will reside with Lady Agnes until the repairs on my estate can be completed." Gilbert interjected. Her betrothed's words warmed her heart.

Thomas eyed Gilbert. "Why would you do that?"

"It is close enough for me to oversee the work on my own dilapidated castle, and it will allow Lady Agnes to remain in her home." Gilbert's gaze landed on Mary. He was fulfilling his promise to do everything in his power to make her happy.

Coming to a stop before the woman whose face was now streaked with tears, Mary jumped down and embraced Aunt Agnes, who was more mother than an aunt. "Don't cry, Aunt Agnes. All will be well. Waterford will see to it."

Her aunt gave her a squeeze and pulled away. Gilbert

approached and was wrapped up in a big hug from her aunt, who said, "I'll forgive you for your tardiness if it means I get to remain in my home."

Gilbert replied, "I was expecting you to make me beg."

Nodding in Mary's direction, Aunt Agnes said, "I'm still unsure how you convinced her to forgive you—"

"I don't believe I've gained her forgiveness, merely her consent to marry. I expect it will take me the rest of my life to make it up to her."

Her aunt patted Gilbert's chest. "As it should be then."

Grinning like the cat who ate a mouse, Aunt Agnes turned and linked arms with Mary, escorting her into the house. "Now—" Her aunt glanced down at her attire. "We need to get you ready quickly. Your papa has lost all patience, and your dear mama won't be able to delay him much longer."

Mary said, "I'm ready now."

"Oh no, my dear, I've allowed you much freedom in the past, but you will conform to convention and wear a dress to your wedding."

Mary jumped as Gilbert began to say, "Lady Agnes, if Mary—"

"Not another word from you, dear boy." Aunt Agnes turned at the waist and ordered, "Roxbury, make sure he is presentable."

"Yes, Aunt."

From the corner of her eye, Mary spied Thomas throwing an arm about Gilbert's shoulders. "It's been a long time coming, but let's have a drink, brother."

MARY STOOD in the middle of her chamber waiting for Greene to arrive with a gown. She tracked her aunt's flurried movements. "Do you know where I might find Ellen?"

Aunt Agnes absently waved her hands toward the door. "I sent her to see to the flower arrangements."

Mary wiped her palms down her skirts. Should she discuss the bedding with her aunt?

Wide-eyed, her aunt stopped and turned to face Mary. "Not another word from you. I shall ask Greene to go and locate Ellen for you."

"Is it that terrible that no one will be forthcoming?"

Lady Frances's voice rang clear. *Agnes, be done with it. Tell her!*

Wringing her hands, her aunt said, "Child, the first time can be rather underwhelming."

Mary asked, "And after the first time?"

"I'm sure Waterford will do well enough. Now, where is that maid of yours?"

Greene came rushing in with a gown that Mary was sure Madame Auclair had created.

"Aunt Agnes, tell me. Is there anything I can do to make the experience better?"

Greene snorted at Mary's question. Her aunt frowned and smacked her maid on the arm. "Relax and follow your instincts."

That didn't seem difficult. If it was anything like the night she spent with Gilbert, then she had nothing to fear. But now that she reflected upon it, they had spent most of the night awake. It would do them no good to be weary for the journey back to England. They needed clarity of mind. Now that she gave it more thought, Mary better understood Gilbert's dilemma. However, if they did not consummate the marriage tonight, it could be deemed illegitimate. But if they did engage, they could be placing themselves and the others in danger for the journey.

Greene pulled Mary's corset strings tight. "Do as your aunt suggested, and all will be well. Do not worry."

"If I have not a thing to be concerned about, then why is everyone being so obtuse about the subject?

"We don't have time to discuss." Greene looked about, then said, "I'll not be traveling with you on the morrow. Lord Waterford instructed that I pack a valise for you, and that is all you will take. It will be but the four of you. His Lordship wants to keep the traveling party to a minimum, and that places you at risk. Are you certain you want to journey back with them? It would be safer to journey home with your family."

This time it was Phillip's voice that rang clear. *Mary, you must accompany the men.*

"I must accompany Gilbert."

Greene muttered, "Why you are so devoted to the man I'll never understand." Her maid turned her to face the looking glass and smiled. "You look beautiful, my lady."

Mary took in her image. The woman looking back at her would be the Countess of Waterford. Strangely enough, she was at peace with the idea and wanted the ceremony to be done so she could begin her life as the wife of an agent to the Home Office. A life surely filled with adventure. Ready, she walked with her aunt down to the study, where her family awaited.

CHAPTER TWENTY-NINE

*H*ow long was Mary going to make him wait? The idea that Gilbert might not be consummating the marriage had his skin itching, and he had rubbed the back of his neck raw.

Roxbury nudged him in the ribs. "Good Lord, man, stop fidgeting. I'm sure Ellen allayed any of Mary's fears."

"Ellen has been by your side most of the night, and I have no faith that Lady Agnes—" His words caught in his throat as Mary entered the study.

She looked magnificent. Her white gown of semi-transparent mull was adorned with embroidered white satin stitching in the design of what seemed to be a variation of his mama's family crest. He wasn't certain as Mary swooshed past with her head held high as she walked directly to her papa, who simply nodded, while her tearstain-faced mama simply embraced her.

His Grace barked, "Let the ceremony begin."

The vicar, whom Mary's papa had brought along with him, and Valois's priest both stepped up to conduct the proceedings.

Gilbert swallowed a groan. *This was supposed to be a quick event.*

Neither priest nor vicar was willing to relinquish their duties, and so the ceremony was conducted in both French and English.

Rolling his eyes to the ceiling, Gilbert resigned himself to endure the extended service. It would be a test of what little patience he had left.

Standing next to Mary, he glanced down once more at her dress. This time the outline of the rosemary leaves with little flowers embroidered around his clan's crest of an angel with harped wings was clear. The symbol of those who serve and assist the three families delegated as Protectors of the Royal Family—unflatteringly known as PORFs. Where had Mary obtained the gown from, and was she aware of the significance of the design? He would have to explain to her that from this day forward, she was bound to aid and serve the PORFs—those that held the Burke, Archbroke, and Hadfield titles. Consumed by thoughts of how to explain the complex network Mary was marrying into, Gilbert had missed most of the proceedings.

His focus returned as the vicar asked, "Gilbert Elliot Talbot, Earl of Waterford, wilt thou have this woman to thy wedded wife? Wilt thou love her, comfort her, honor, and keep her in sickness and in health; and, forsaking all other, keep thee only unto her, so long as ye both shall live?"

"I will."

"And do you, Mary Eloise Masterson take Gilbert Elliot Talbot, wilt thou have this man to thy wedded husband? Wilt thou obey him, and serve him, love, honor, and keep him in sickness and in health; and, forsaking all other, keep thee only unto him, so long as ye both shall live?"

Would Mary object? He had sworn to love and comfort her, while she was asked to obey and serve him.

Mary's eyes raked over the length of him and then landed squarely upon his lips. "I will."

Was she as eager as he was to consummate their union?

A couple more promises, then they were off to sign the registry—two in this case. As Mary bent to scrawl her name, he got a glimpse of her creamy flesh. He was dying to know what she had decided. He would obviously honor her wishes, but the anticipation was gnawing on his nerves.

Straightening, she caught him staring. With both eyebrows raised, Mary whispered, "Husband, will you escort me to your chambers?"

Unable to answer, he simply nodded.

Ignoring Mary's family and the officiants, he winged his arm and placed a hand over hers to whisk her away. Mary was his now, and he intended for her to remain by his side until he took his last breath.

As THEY MADE their way to his bedchambers, he was acutely aware he should say something, but his brain was only focused on one thing—bedding Mary.

He sneaked a sideways glance at his wife. Mary didn't look to be nervous. In fact, her resilience was one of the things he most admired about her. She was unflappable.

Over the years he'd seen the woman anticipate and preempt disaster after disaster. Did the voices always alert Mary as to what was to occur next? So many questions came to mind. Was she ever surprised by events? Could he surprise her? There was still much to learn about his wife. He felt certain she would never stop intriguing him.

Click. The door latch slid into place. Gilbert shook his

head, blinked, and squeezed his clenched hands behind his back.

They were alone in his chambers. This was no dream.

Mary stood before him.

His wife raised a hand to slide a hairpin from her elaborate coiffed hair.

Cheeks red, Mary asked, "Are you going to stand and watch?"

"If you don't mind."

Mary shrugged, but he caught an impish twinkle in her eyes. Gilbert rubbed the back of his neck. She removed another pin, brought it to her mouth and popped it between her lips.

The minx was going to kill him before the night was over.

Mary repeated the motion, pin after pin until her glossy mahogany tresses fell about her shoulders. He was about to step forward when she gave her head a little shake. Snaking her hands down to her side, she found the tapes of her skirt and slowly tugged. Her eyes never left him. Gilbert swallowed hard as the material fell to the floor.

Mary presented her back to him and gave him a saucy wink. "I can't seem to reach the ribbons."

His hands shook as he reached for her.

"Husband, quit your stalling, we don't have much time."

He grabbed her by the waist and carried her over to the bed. Mary let out a loud squeal as Gilbert tossed her onto the soft mattress below.

Tarnation. His fingers fumbled with the buttons on his waistcoat.

Mary giggled. "It is rather entertaining to watch another undress."

Stripping as fast as he could, Gilbert chuckled as he wrestled with the last button of his falls. He kicked off his breeches and stood naked with his member at full attention. "I agree."

Mary's smile lightened his mood as he crawled up onto the bed and slid alongside her. Her eyes sparkled with anticipation. Absolutely no fear, thank goodness.

Gilbert placed a hand over her cheek. "You're amazing." He ran his thumb over her bottom lip. "Thank you for waiting for me."

Mary's tongue peeked out. Every fiber of his being screamed to take and plunder the gorgeous woman who was now wrapping her arms about his neck and pulling his head down for a kiss. For years he had envisioned this moment in his dreams. He wanted to savor every real moment. She deserved to be cherished.

Mary's lips feathered over his—her kisses soft with a hint of urgency. He let his lips languish over hers. *Go slow. Be gentle*. His body in opposition, ached to take and plunder the lush woman in his arms.

Pulling back from him, Mary cupped his face. "Aunt Agnes advised me to lie back and relax, but your kisses have me restless, and my body wants to move. I want to—"

Gilbert silenced her with a bruising kiss, rolling onto his back and pulling Mary partially on top of him. For if she continued with her emboldened speech, he might lose all self-control and take her right now.

Mary lowered her hand to run it down his side. Every inch of his body came alive, and he groaned as he realized this night, what remained of it, was going to test his restraint. Mary's leg fell between his as she shifted closer, pressing her glorious naked body against his. She molded her body to his until she found the perfect angle in which they fit together. He wanted to mirror Mary's actions, to run a hand over every delicious curve of her, but he sensed Mary would prefer he be the one to lie back and relax.

They had left the celebrations shortly after midnight, giving them but four hours until their departure. He could afford a little less sleep if it meant Mary's first time went well. He let his eyes close as Mary continued her exploration of him. Her lips grazed his cheek as they made their way near his ear. "Are you content to allow me to do with you as I please?"

Gilbert inhaled deeply and nodded.

"Excellent." The excitement in her voice sent shivers down his back.

Mary whispered, "I want to pleasure you with my mouth."

He opened his eyes. Mary loomed over him.

If he allowed her to do as she wished, would he be able to regain his strength to consummate the marriage?

Control. He simply had to exercise control and prevent himself from spilling in her oh-so-sweet mouth.

Gulping Gilbert said, "Wife, if you do that, I warn you there is a good chance we might not be legally married by morn."

Frown lines formed on Mary's beautiful forehead.

"There is not much time left this eve, and if you succeed in—" The glow upon Mary's features faded as he continued to speak. To hell with the consequences. "Never mind, lass. Carry on, dinnae worry. Do with me as you please."

The smile she granted him was worth the risk of not making their union legitimate. No one but them would be the wiser. Mary was his, and he'd not let her go again.

She placed kisses along his neck and nibbled on his collarbone. He sucked in a deep breath. She ran a finger followed by her tongue down the center of his chest. Ah, what a clever lass to have learned the art of bed sport so adeptly. Gilbert groaned as her lips trailed past his navel, all the way down to his full arousal.

Glancing briefly up at him, Mary placed her mouth upon the tip of him. He wound his fingers in her soft tresses as she lowered her lips around him slowly, inch by inch, until there was no possible way she could take more. He shifted, not wanting to hurt her. She surprised him by winding her hand around the base and increasing the pressure of her lips. She began to slide her lips and tongue up and down his shaft, banishing any coherent thoughts he might have had.

He clenched his hand, tugging her hair. Mary moaned and her gaze locked on his face.

She released him. "Are you in pain? Were my brother's boasts of how—"

Gilbert reached for her, but she shifted back, inches out of reach. He ran a hand over his face. "Lass, I dinnae ken what yer brothers shared, but I was no' in pain."

Mary licked the length of him. "Would you like me to continue?" She eyed his erection like a candied nut—her favorite treat.

Gilbert replied with a hearty, "Aye."

Mary swirled her tongue over and down his shaft. Gilbert lifted his head to place both hands behind it. The sight of her sweet lips around his member sent a jolt of need through him. The tip of him hit what was undoubtedly the back of her throat, yet she didn't fully release him or choke; instead, she rolled her tongue about him. Every inch of his skin increased in sensitivity as her lips inched back up and then back down again.

Heaving for a breath, Gilbert croaked, "Lass—I'll not be able to withstand much more."

Mary slowly withdrew her lips but continued to pleasure him with her hand, gliding it up and down, as she asked, "Am I hurting you?"

"Ah—it's—not—that." Gilbert shook his head. He couldn't even manage a simple sentence. How was he to explain?

Mary smiled and returned her lips to his member. One of his hands slipped back into her silky hair. She flicked her tongue over him once before sliding her mouth about him. This time she increased the pace of her movements, and he couldn't tear his gaze from her lips wound tightly about him—she was magnificent. Hoping he wasn't gripping her hair too tightly, he felt his balls tighten, fully engulfed in her mouth. The surge of his release began at the base until he exploded into the back of her sweet throat. Mary pulled back with a pop as her lips left him. She continued to stare at his member.

Gilbert reached for her. "I—I'm sorry. I should have warned you."

Why was Mary still staring?

The woman's flushed cheeks heated his blood. He glanced at his cock, still straight as an arrow. He wanted her and mercifully so did his body.

She wiped her mouth with the back of her hand. Mary's smile was wide with satisfaction and awe. "We can both reach pleasure without risk of conceiving."

"Aye, but there are other ways to ensure you do not become enceinte."

Mary giggled. "Oh, and are you willing to educate mc tonight?"

Kneeling between his legs, the minx brushed the tip of her nipple along this erect member. *She will be the death of me if I continue to allow her full rein.* Rising to a sitting position, he ran his hands down her back as she licked and teased his balls with her tongue. He needed to be inside her.

Running a hand over her bottom, he slipped the tip of his finger into her crevasse. He let out a groan as the slickness between her folds covered his finger, allowing it to glide over her core. Mary was more than ready to take him, and he couldn't wait a moment longer. Trailing his hands up along her sides, he gripped her by the arms and raised her to meet his lips. Their mouths hungry for each other, he infused his kisses with raw need.

Mary edged closer, pressing her chest to his as she wound her arms about his neck. Leaning to one side, Gilbert positioned her leg to the outside of his leg and then repeated the action so that she straddled him. Now that he had her in position, he deepened the kiss, then pulled back to place a string of kisses down her neck. He wanted to taste more of her. Placing his hands upon her tiny waist, he raised her to her knees so her hardened nipples were in line with his mouth. Gilbert flicked the tip of his tongue over and over Mary's nipple until a moan escaped her. No longer interested in teasing her, he finally drew her breast into his mouth. His heart crashed against his chest as she screamed out his name.

He craved to make her scream his name every day for the rest of his living days. Reaching between them, he checked to see if she was still wet. Ready, he rubbed his tip over her slit until she lowered herself without his prompting or guidance. The woman was attuned to his needs and wants. She was small and extremely tight. He managed to wedge the tip of him inside when she froze. He immediately stopped loving on her breasts and glanced up to meet her gaze.

The uncertainty in her eyes had him lifting her up and back onto his lap. "Lass, did I hurt you?"

"No, it's—" Mary raised a hand. Her fingers curled to meet her thumb to form a circle. She tried to jam her fingers into the small opening. "We don't appear to fit together."

Gilbert gulped in a deep breath suppressing the bubble of laughter that threatened to escape. If he was going to make her his tonight, he needed to alleviate her fears. "Do you trust me?"

Mary leaned in and kissed him. "Yes, of course I do."

While he debated whether their current position was wise, Mary repositioned herself just above him. Her hand ran down his chest and reached between them, guiding him to her core. In full control, Mary didn't hesitate and steadily lowered herself. A frown appeared on her brow. Mary was extremely tight. Having never bedded a virgin before, the pressure against the tip of him was foreign. He ran his hands up her sides, over her pert breasts, and pulled her down for a kiss. Gilbert swallowed her yelp as she took all of him. Fixated on her mouth and not their joining, he continued to kiss her, infusing it with all the love he could muster. Mary was his, and he'd never leave her again.

CERTAIN IT HAD BEEN mere moments ago that he closed his eyes, Gilbert groaned as Hadfield's boots stomped into his room. Mary was abed with him. He shot up to cover her, but the bed was empty. Where was the woman?

"Your wife went to the kitchens to arrange food for us all."

Rubbing the sleep from his eyes, Gilbert asked, "What time is it?"

"An hour past our agreed-upon departure time. Mary convinced me to allow you to slumber awhile longer while *she* finalized arrangements and said her goodbyes."

"That was considerate of her."

His clothes hit him square in the chest.

"*You* don't deserve her."

"I know." He rubbed his jaw; he needed a shave, but there was no time for that. Dressing quickly and grabbing his greatcoat, he noticed Hadfield by the window, watching events below. "What has caught your interest?"

"Valois gave André an item."

"A letter?"

"No, something wrapped in cloth. What the devil is the man up to now?"

Gilbert peered down as André placed the item in his breast pocket. "We will have to question the lad once we are on our way." He turned to leave, but Hadfield's hand on his shoulder stopped him, and he glanced back out the window. Mary stood next to Valois and was now holding out her hand while she tapped her foot.

André retrieved the item as he shook his head. The lad's lips were moving until André's gaze met Mary's. Unable to hear the conversation was irritating, but once Mary had the item, she deftly tucked it into her décolletage, swiveled, and walked away.

"What do you think that was about?" When Hadfield didn't respond, Gilbert turned to find the room empty.

Hadfield had a good ten-step lead, but Gilbert was faster as they rushed downstairs and out through the doors. He barely won the footrace to reach their mounts and Mary first.

Gilbert looked up at his wife, who was looking regal seated upon her mare. "My thanks for the extra rest this morn."

"You are welcome, husband. I thought you deserved it." A blush rose on Mary's cheeks, and he wished he was whisking her away for a honeymoon instead of escorting Hadfield home.

Once he was seated upon his horse, he leaned over to give Mary a chaste kiss. "Shall we be off?"

"Finally," André muttered.

Mary shifted to address Hadfield. "If you don't mind, I'd like a word with you. Gilbert, please go on and take the lead."

Hadfield simply nodded and waited for Gilbert to pass. Curiosity gnawed at him, but she had asked him for his trust—to allow her to assist. He wasn't about to disappoint her on their very first day of marriage.

Resigned to the fact he might never be privy to all the woman's thoughts, he believed last night he had wriggled his way into her heart, even if it was only a smidgeon. Gilbert still had years' worth of neglect to make up for.

Setting a reasonably sedate pace in an attempt to eavesdrop on his wife's conversation, Gilbert was disappointed to find the woman spoke in hushed tones, eluding his petty attempts.

Giving up on gaining information from the two behind, he eyed André and asked, "What did you give my wife?"

André's entire body stiffened. "Merely a wedding present, my lord."

At the lad's obstinate features, Gilbert sighed. André was clearly not going to provide more information. He would have to wait to see for himself later when they stopped to rest. The idea of having Mary in his arms again had him shifting and urging his horse along. The sooner they arrived at the inn, the better.

CHAPTER THIRTY

*H*er husband might be an extremely skilled agent, but Mary had years of practice at being patient. Finally, Gilbert gave up his attempts to eavesdrop and moved along.

Raising a hand to her chest, she ran a finger over the outline of the coin. "I've been informed that I have an object in my possession that rightfully belongs to an individual who bears a particular mark. Would you happen to know who that might be?"

The devilishly handsome dimple appeared on Lord Hadfield cheek. "A mark, you say."

Unperturbed by the man's dimple, Mary said, "Yes. Not the type that one might find on a baby at birth, one that is intentionally placed upon a person's body with heat or ink."

"And what makes you suspect I would know this individual?"

The teasing tone of Lord Hadfield's question brought her ire up. He wasn't taking her seriously.

Narrowing her gaze, Mary said, "Theo stated you

would assist me if I asked. I'm asking if you can help me locate this person." The hair on the back of Mary's neck began to stand on end.

"Why did you not seek your husband's assistance?" His tone no longer teasing. Lord Hadfield's hazel eyes never left hers.

Flustered at the intensity of his stare, she said, "Really, I don't have time to explain. I was told it extremely important that I find a— well, a PORF."

"Why?"

Lord Hadfield hadn't blinked at her use of the term PORF. He must be well versed with the legends as they were.

The magnitude of what she was about to share weighed on her shoulders. "Because I have in my possession the treasure that Lord Burke was truly after. But I suspect you already know what the villain was after." A tingle ran down Mary's spine. Ignoring the sensation, she continued, "That is why you let Matthew take the crown jewels back to England while you did not return. You were still searching for—."

She paused at Lady Frances's frantic warning. *Alert Hadfield! You are being followed.*

Mary whispered, "There are others behind us."

"Yes, I heard them too. Act normally, as if we haven't detected them. Let's try to catch up to your husband."

Gilbert was a furlong away, not too far ahead. It was unlikely they would be able to outrun whoever was following them.

Phillip's voice urged, *Shift to the right.*

Pulling on the reins, Mary guided her mount closer to Hadfield on her right, causing his horse to startle.

Hadfield glared at her. "What the devil—"

An explosion sounded behind her. The air swooshed by her right ear.

From her right, Hadfield yelled, "Hell and Tarnation!"

Horses whinnied and the group scattered.

Mary took her eyes off the road to find Hadfield struggling with a bandit.

Why hadn't Phillip warned her? *Not enough time to change the outcome.*

The reins were yanked from her grasp. "Ow."

A meaty arm wrapped about her waist.

She struggled to remain seated, but the smelly brute hauled her down to the ground. Mary stumbled, falling to her knees. Scrambling to escape, her attacker grabbed her by the wrist and yanked her along with her mare toward a small clearing.

Mary cringed at the sight of three burly men with pistols. Gilbert and André were kneeling, their hands bound behind their backs. Blood trickled from the corner of Gilbert's mouth. Her chest constricted. She wanted to shout out to him.

Tugged away from the men, her attacker dragged her over toward the tree line.

Mary swiveled to glance at her husband.

Gilbert began to struggle. She shook her head but not in time—the shortest thug's fist connected with Gilbert's jaw. Losing his balance, Gilbert fell to his side.

Thwack! The tormentor's boot connected with Gilbert's ribs.

"Gilbert!" Mary's eyes teared at the sight of blood on the ground.

Filthy fingers dug into her arm. Her captor stared at her and said, "We were not expecting a lady to be traveling with this lot. We mean no harm."

Mary scowled at the offensive Englishman.

A lump settled in her throat. The bandit scanned her from head to toe. "Our master has sent us to retrieve an item; once we have it in our possession, you will all be free to go. Do you promise not to cause any problems?"

Fingers crossed behind her back, she answered, "Yes. My husband will be less an issue if you allow me to join him."

"Aye. But if I suspect you interfering, I will gag and bind you without hesitation."

Mary nodded, and her captor led her over to the group that now included Lord Hadfield.

Lady Frances confirmed what Mary suspected. *Be very careful. You have in your possession what they seek.*

Even tied up, Gilbert would not allow these men to harm her. The trick would be to ensure they had no cause to think to search her.

The brute left her next to Gilbert and said, "I'm seeking the gentleman who is marked." Their captor's gaze raked over Lord Hadfield and then André. Neither gentleman moved nor blinked.

"Lord Waterford, who shall I strip first?"

Mary gasped. "You know him?"

"He was a fellow officer who moved up through the ranks during the war. Mr. Thames, I believe."

"Well done, Waterford. What an excellent memory. Won't you assist me? We will release you and your lovely wife once we have what I've been sent to collect."

Gilbert answered, "Neither of them is marked. PORFs are but an old fairy tale."

Mary glanced at Gilbert. No one over the age of twelve openly discussed the term used to describe the Crown's protectors. Before this morn, Mary would have agreed with her husband's statement. She had heard the villagers and even Thomas tell tales of the Protectors of the Royal

Family as a child, but without real evidence of their existence, she had dispelled the stories as pure folk tales. Not until Phillip had instructed her to retrieve the item from André and seek Lord Hadfield's assistance in locating a PORF did she believe they were indeed real.

Mr. Thames stuck a finger in Lord Hadfield's chest. "What's this fellow's name then?"

"He is the new Earl of Hadfield. Sorry to disappoint, old man. Rumor has it that he inherited the title but not what you seek."

Mary wracked her memory for details regarding PORFs, but she didn't recall much.

Mr. Thames smirked. "Ah— but your information is out of date, Waterford. You were always a little slow to acknowledge what was right before you."

Gilbert asked, "What are you rambling on about now?"

"You are an extremely trusting fellow, Waterford. Do you still believe Devonton was the one responsible for the map that led you and your troops into direct enemy territory?" Mr. Thames chuckled. "I see you do. Let me tell you rumors and information from supposed reliable sources are not always accurate. Those maps that were provided to you were, in fact, not the work of the revered Lord Devonton." Mr. Thames walked over to André and placed his hand on the boy's shoulder. "It was the work of our dear French friend here and his papa, Comte Boucher."

Gilbert shook his head. "Comte Boucher provided sanctuary to our troops. He is an ally."

"You are a fool, Waterford. For years the comte has been working both sides. He remains loyal to no one but himself, providing aid to the party that bids the highest."

Gilbert's face was awash in anger and confusion. This

was the reason Gilbert had treated Lord Devonton with such distaste since his return.

Gilbert's eyes continued to follow Mister Thames as the man walked back to stand before him. Eye to eye with Mr. Thames, Gilbert asked, "And you have also adopted such a philosophy on how to lead one's life?"

"It has worked remarkably well for Comte Boucher. There was nothing for us when we returned home. Honest work is scarce, and after having sacrificed years, I wasn't even awarded enough for lodgings. So one must become resourceful." Mr. Thames took out a pointed blade and scraped it down Lord Hadfield's greatcoat, toying with the buttons.

Gilbert said, "I assure you, he's not the one you are searching for. You mustn't be paying your informants enough, for they have led you on a wild-goose chase for Hadfield."

"Hmmm—" Mr. Thames swiveled, glanced about the group. "I will grant you that our intelligence was fairly inaccurate. There had been no mention of a woman nor of Boucher's son."

"Thames. Do you really believe in the stories of PORFs? I'd not taken you for a fool."

"I've never believed in children's stories, but if it pays our way for the next six months, I'm willing to indulge my employer and search for the ridiculous brand that he believes Hadfield here is searching for." The tip of Mr. Thames blade disappeared, sinking into the material of Lord Hadfield's coat. "Or perhaps he has yet to locate it." Removing the blade, Mr. Thames moved to stand before Gilbert. "No, we were told Hadfield would not make arrangements to return to England unless he had the item in his possession."

Gilbert didn't even flinch as Mr. Thames waved the

blade about in front of his face. How could he be so calm? Every time the blade came near Gilbert's face Mary wanted to attack the odious man tormenting her husband.

Gilbert remained stoic, spine rigid and his neck elongated to give him as much height as possible. "I've been in Hadfield's presence for months. The treasure we found was returned with Harrington. That is whom you should be hunting down."

Lord Hadfield's features darkened as Gilbert spoke.

Mr. Thames looked at his men and then back at Gilbert. "You found Harrington alive?"

"Barely, but he was breathing. He has returned along with what you are searching for. Now, if you would be so kind as to untie us and let us be on our way, we will keep this little interlude private, shall we?"

Unconvinced, Mr. Thames returned to Lord Hadfield's side and began to pat him down and search his pockets. Finding nothing, he moved on to repeat the same search on André. The man growled as André's pockets were found empty. Mr. Thames looked at Mary then at Gilbert, whose features clearly stated he'd kill the man if he dared touch her.

Shaking his head, Mr. Thames asked, "Lady Waterford, what do you know of the children's tale?"

"All I recall is that the horrid term stands for Protectors of the Royal Family. It is as you said, a tale for young minds."

Mr. Thames stalked toward her. "Hmm— Do you not believe in the secret society led by three powerful families? Supposedly there are legions of families pledging their oaths to serve these PORFs."

All three men shifted, arms flexing, as they tugged on their restraints. Men of little faith.

With the sweetest smile she could muster, Mary said,

"Mr. Thames, did you not just enlighten my husband as to the foolishness of believing in rumors and gossip? I no more believe in PORFs than I do in spirits."

Gilbert's shoulders relaxed. He gave her an encouraging smile and then winked. Her heart soared. Gilbert believed in her.

Mr. Thames let out a hearty laugh. "You are correct, my lady." He turned to face Gilbert, "You are a lucky man to have married such a beauty but extremely fortunate she also has wit."

Mr. Thames made a circling motion to his men. "Let's be off. Lady Waterford can do the honors of releasing her traveling companions." He bowed and said, "My thanks for the horseflesh, they will fetch me enough coin to cover the expense of this wild-goose chase."

Mary faked despair. "You can't be serious. How are we to continue?"

"Ah, so the duke's daughter does have a petulant side after all."

To prove him correct, she crossed her arms and pouted. Mr. Thames gawked at her décolletage.

The man's eyes slowly rose to her protruding bottom lip. "Shame there isn't more time. You are a tempting morsel."

Gilbert growled. "Harm her, and you die."

"No fear. I'm not about to dally about any longer than necessary." He took the reins of his mount from one of his men and mounted. "Home, gents. We are to off to find Harrington and the loot."

CHAPTER THIRTY-ONE

Mary's hands shook as she loosened Gilbert's bindings. He had thought she was unaffected, but he was wrong. Mary was stoic, but she had a tender heart, and he had seen to it that she had spent the past year in isolation. It was his fault she had remained sheltered.

Gilbert wrapped her in a hug as soon as he was free.

Hadfield interrupted. "If you could untie us first, before mauling one another, I'd appreciate it."

Mary turned to assist Hadfield. "It is you, I—" She stopped midsentence.

Gilbert stiffened as he caught sight of Hadfield's narrowed gaze upon Mary's décolletage. Hadfield had been the one who she would have chosen to marry if he had not already signed the blasted marriage agreements. Jealousy again wiped all rational thought from his mind. He stomped over and grabbed Mary by the elbow to haul her out of Hadfield's grasp.

"Gilbert! What is the matter with you?"

"I'm aware you wished to marry Hadfield, but it is I who you pledged to honor for the rest of your days."

She pulled out of his arms and placed her hands upon her hips. "Gilbert Elliot Talbot. Let me be clear. I am in love with you, and only you. I thought you understood that last night. Are you always going to behave the jealous husband? Really, there is no reason."

"Yes, I fear when it comes to you, I become extremely and irrationally jealous. Lass, I'm deeply in love with you."

Mary wrapped her arms about his neck and pulled him down to her so that they were eye to eye. "Husband, there is no need to be jealous of another. I'll always be faithful to you. My heart has always belonged to you."

"As mine belongs to you."

Hadfield rolled his eyes and André muttered, "*Mon Dieu! Sauve-moi de tous ces couples!*"

Gilbert chuckled at the lad's plea—*My God, Save us from these couples*.

"I do have matters to discuss with Lord Hadfield. Would you please trust me and allow us a moment of privacy?"

He eyed Hadfield, who stood staring at Mary. "Lass, I trust you. It is Hadfield I do not trust, for he can't tear his eyes away from the tops of your creamy breasts."

She leaned up and kissed him soundly. "But not for the reason you ogle them. He wants what is currently hidden beneath my décolletage."

"What was it that André gave you?"

"I have no idea. Lady Frances instructed me to have André hand it over and to safely conceal it. There are times when you must simply follow blindly and hope for the best."

Mr. Thames's speech about him being a fool had unsettled him. He placed trust and faith in his superiors, and now it was time for him to do that with Mary.

"Lass, make it quick. I prefer to have you by my side rather than André." He patted her bottom as she strode to catch up to Hadfield.

André dropped back to walk alongside him. Head bowed, André said, "Mr. Thames spoke the truth. My papa has volleyed between sides, reasoning it was for our safety."

"And you believed him?"

"At first, but now I see that he was merely driven by greed." André kicked the dirt with the toe of his shoe.

A few paces later Gilbert asked, "What did you give my wife?"

"It is an old branding coin. Used generations ago to mark the members of three legendary families."

Branding coin? Gilbert had never heard of such a thing. "How did it come to be in your possession?"

André hastened his steps. "Valois."

"Yes, Yes, I know Valois was the one who gave it to you, but how exactly did such an item end up in your hands?" Gilbert lengthened his stride. Hypnotized by the subtle sway of his wife's hips, he absently said, "You're not going to tell me, are you?"

Their increased pace shortened the distance between them and Mary.

André cleared his throat. "Lady Mary is an extraordinary woman."

Gilbert nodded. Yes, his Mary was indeed amazing. At the mention of her, André's forlorn appearance disappeared. The young man almost appeared chipper.

André said, "She will know how to handle the matter of finding the marked one."

The words—*marked*, *branding coin*, *PORF*—all collided in

Gilbert's mind. "Is that who Valois instructed you to find and give it to?"

André nodded. "*Oui*. But your wife blackmailed me into giving it to her before we departed."

"Blackmail?"

André glanced about at their surroundings. "Lady Mary is privy to information I have no clue how she obtained, but I do not wish for it to be shared with anyone."

Interesting.

Gilbert was beginning to grasp the extent of Mary's gift. If Mary was kept informed by those that no longer existed on this earth, she had full access to a wealth of knowledge he had not been exposed to before. Perhaps he would become fond of Mary's Lady Frances after all.

Farther up the path, he could make out the silhouettes of a coach and outriders. But they were so far in the distance shouting for assistance would be useless.

He ran to catch up to Mary and Hadfield. "There are travelers up ahead. Mary, can you contact them?"

"How would I do that?"

"You know. Maybe your friend, Lady Frances, could assist."

She shook her head. "That is not how it works, my dear."

"In that case, Hadfield or I will have to try to catch up with them."

Hadfield didn't hesitate. "I'll go."

"Your lung condition. It's best if I go." He gave Mary a chaste kiss and started off at a jog but quickly increased his pace.

The farther he was from Mary, the more anxious he became until he caught up with the coach whose passengers were emerging from the tree line.

"Halo. Salut."

A young fellow looked at him and then turned to his companion. "Good Lord, Riley. I think I'm hallucinating. Is that Captain Waterford?"

His companion replied, "But it can't be. The cap'n swore he'd not set foot on French soil again. We really need to lay off the opium."

"Aye, you lads need to return home and not wallow in these French dens wasting away."

"Nothing for us to return to, Cap'n."

Isn't that what Thames had claimed?

"Well, I have a castle that needs repairing. If you lads would be so kind as to assist me in getting my wife and friends to port, I'll give you work once we are back on British soil."

Wide-eyed, the pair looked at each other than back to him.

"Maybe, Captain, we should escort you back home." They looked around him, but Mary and the others were not in sight.

"Don't leave."

Gilbert ordered one of the outriders to dismount. He grabbed the reins and vaulted into the saddle. Heading back the way he came, he realized he'd traveled a lot farther away from their group than he originally believed.

Rounding a bend, he finally spotted Mary. She sat upon a log, flanked by Hadfield and André.

He slowed his mount and dismounted with a jump. He knelt before his wife, reaching for her. "Are you hurt? Why are you all sitting?"

Mary brushed away his searching hands. "We are resting. We are not accustomed to marching for miles on end."

The war had conditioned him to travel long distances. Taking in Mary's features, she didn't appear in the least tired. Peering over at Hadfield, he was bent, head between his leg, gasping for air. The man's lung condition always worsened with physical activity.

Gilbert assisted Mary to stand. "I've found help. We need to make it about another mile, and there are some lads who will assist us in getting to port."

André stood and brushed the backside of his breeches. "How fortunate."

"I told you not to worry. I was right. Gilbert found help." Mary smiled at the lad, whose cheeks promptly turned red. She bent down to speak to Hadfield. "Are you ready to continue?"

Hadfield slowly rolled to his full height and asked, "You trust these men?"

The memory of the pair of soldiers fighting by his side, dried blood and dirt covering them, flashed before Gilbert. "With my life."

He gave Mary a boost up onto the horse. She reached for the reins and set a comfortable walking pace. None of the men were interested in engaging in conversation. Both André and Hadfield were in deep thought, while Gilbert's full attention was trained on Mary's beautiful silhouette. He contemplated how long would it be before they could be alone again—hours, days, both, too long in his opinion.

CHAPTER THIRTY-TWO

*G*ilbert bounded into the carriage and bundled Mary up into his arms. She was finally alone again with her husband.

"Lass, you look tired." Gilbert ran his knuckles down her jawline. "Did Hadfield's snoring keep you awake?"

Snuggling into his shoulder, Mary was shocked to find the man warmer than a summer's day. He'd been out in the cold, riding all night without sleep for close to twenty-four hours. She should be the one warming him up. Instead, he was rubbing the stiff muscles in her back, working the soreness out of them. They were still a fair way from port, but they were traveling at an unrelenting pace. By her calculations, they should reach Calais within the next day or so.

Mary answered, "No. I slept little due to my mind racing."

It had been Phillip and Lady Frances's heated discussions, all centered around the wrapped object that Mary had given to Lord Hadfield, which caused her to remain awake. Phillip had debated with Lady Frances over Valois's actions. Neither was aware of how exactly her cousin came into possession of the coin, but when his guides informed him it was imperative it be returned to a man who bore the mark, and that one was in residence, Valois had sent his maid to determine if it was Gilbert or Lord Hadfield who should receive the item. When Aimée failed to see Gilbert naked that first night, Valois made the curious decision to keep the coin, but when his guides informed him André had been instructed by his papa to seek out a man who bore the mark, Valois entrusted André with the coin. Phillip had argued he should have intervened instead of involving Mary and potentially putting her in danger. Lady Frances had argued it had all worked out and that she never doubted Mary would be able to handle any situation that arose.

From experience, Mary found it best to listen to all the arguments shared with her before making her own decision what action, if any, should be taken. For the very first time, she wanted to discuss her troubles with another—her husband.

Raising her chin, Mary said, "I gave Lord Hadfield the item Mr. Thatcher was sent to obtain. It's a branding coin."

"Did you see it?"

"No. Yes. Not exactly. When Lord Hadfield thought I was asleep, he carefully pulled back the cloth to reveal what looked to be a button. Curiously, Lord Hadfield closed his eyes and ran his thumb over it repeatedly, it was then that I sneaked a look at the round metal disk, with its distinctive design—the outline of a horse with a falcon perched on its back, circled by laurel leaves." Mary was sure she had seen parts of the design before, but never its totality. "PORFs are real, and Lord Hadfield is one. But who are the other two families?"

Mary rubbed the back of her husband's neck.

Gilbert frowned as he removed her hand from his neck and clasped it tightly. "Did you ask Lord Hadfield to prove his identity before you gave him the item?"

"I did." Mary attempted to pull her hand from his, but Gilbert held on tight. "Lord Hadfield explained that only those who share the mark are privy to a view of it. However, he surprised me by adding that there are others who are aware of the identities of those who bear the mark." She waited until Gilbert turned to face her directly. "You've known all along that Lord Hadfield is a PORF. Why did Archbroke choose you to protect him?"

Gilbert avoided her eyes. "I should have confessed this before we were married, but for as long as PORFs have existed, there has been a network of families that have pledged their allegiance to the Crown and to serve PORFs in any manner necessary. My mama's family was one, and I have carried on those responsibilities. You too will now be honor bound to serve and assist those who hold the Hadfield, Archbroke, and Burke titles."

"Archbroke *and* Burke are PORFs?" Mary mulled over all that Gilbert had shared. "Is it only the men who hold the titles that I am obligated to assist?"

"Technically it is any person who bears the mark of a PORF. That typically includes the wives and children, male or female, of those who hold the title. There have been a few traditions that the Neale family rejected, which resulted in Theo being the one to bear her family's duties for a period, but that was all rectified when Hadfield received the mark."

Frowning, Mary said, "So Theo was a PORF even before she married Archbroke. Well, it's no wonder their courtship was a whirlwind of misunderstandings. And because of your mama's family, I am now too part of a secret network." The burst of excitement and joy at being included had Mary smiling.

"Lass, the role comes with many responsibilities and dangers. Burke's actions have been in direct conflict with his role as a PORF, which means the others and the network have to—"

She placed a finger upon Gilbert's lips. Mary fully understood the dangers. Phillip's and Lady Frances's nattering all made sense now that Gilbert had explained her involvement.

"Not to worry. I believe I comprehend the dire situation." She leaned in and rested her head upon his shoulder.

Gilbert's hand came to rest upon her thigh. "I'm sorry that our wedding night was rushed. Rather than whisking you away for a romantic tour of the Continent, we are stuck traveling with a quad of men."

"This will be our future. Carrying out missions together. As long as you are happy for me to accompany you, I'm an eager travel partner." Mary raised her head. "I'm willing because I love you."

Gilbert's eyes flared to life. "Are you certain?"

"My heart has belonged to you for years. I've not wanted to listen to it."

"I am guilty of the exact same behavior. Will you forgive me for making you wait until I came to my senses?"

"We weren't ready all those years ago."

"You are right." Gilbert yawned. The poor man was exhausted. Mary shifted to give him more room but found herself lifted and placed upon his lap.

Eye to eye, she said, "I usually am." Mary threaded her fingers through his hair and guided his head down so that their lips met. Once she began kissing the man, she couldn't stop. She should stop. Gilbert was exhausted, but as his hands roamed up her side and landed upon a breast that sorely missed his attention.

Mary's tongue trailed down the side of his neck. From their wedding night, she had learned if she could garner a guttural growl from him and lingered long enough upon particularly sensitive spots, she could induce the man to remain erect for an extended period. She gently sucked and circled her tongue over his ear lobe, mimicking the actions she longed to be making upon his shaft.

"Lass, if you dinnae stop, I'll not be satisfied until you ride me again."

Mary whispered in his ear. "And what if I told you I've been longing to ride all these past hours?"

Grabbing her by the waist, he lifted her off his lap and, to her surprise, turned her to face away from him.

Instead of straddling her husband as she had intended, she was sitting upon his lap. "Gilbert, I want—"

"If I'm to uphold my promise and not impregnate you, I have to ensure that I can withdraw."

Looking over her shoulder, Mary asked, "but the other night."

Gilbert hitched up her skirts and reached between her legs. His fingers immediately sought out her core, which was already slick and ready for him.

Gilbert growled and then said, "The other night, you had already milked me of my seed, and it is easier to control upon the second round. Would you prefer we stop?" His fingers ceased their circular motion, and Mary pressed her hand over his, urging him to continue.

Stop. Was he mad? Her core ached. She was merely uncertain of how to go about things in this position. Gilbert spread his legs a little wider, and she felt his bulge nudge her bottom.

"Lass, place your hands on the ceiling."

She did as she was told, which resulted in her nearly shimming off his lap, but his arm about her prevented that from happening.

"Blast these falls." Gilbert apparently was well skilled, for his fingers between her legs never stopped as he continued to struggle with his breeches.

On a squeak, as Gilbert managed to find an ultrasensitive spot, Mary asked, "Do you need assistance, husband?"

"I'm going to shift slightly forward. Keep your hands on the ceiling."

Cool air hit her bottom as Gilbert adjusted her skirts. Mary let out a moan as she finally felt the tip of him prod her center. Easing back, Gilbert entered her, but his fingers continued to bring her the most pleasure. It was like riding him in reverse. She still had control of the pace, and she was eager to find her release. Her arms began to ache. She let her hands fall upon Gilbert's knees. With the additional leverage, she was better able to set the speed in which she rose and fell. Not for a moment had Gilbert removed his talented fingers. She was on the brink of experiencing the delightful explosion of tingling sensations when Gilbert pushed up, sending her over the edge.

With a deep growl, Gilbert removed his hand from her core and wrapped both hands about her hips and guided her to rotate them slightly as she moved back and forth. Would it be greedy of her to want to experience the bliss a second time? She didn't have to wait long as the weightless feeling overcame her. Floating back to reality, Gilbert plunged deep inside before releasing a moan as he pulled back—leaving her empty.

She wanted him to experience the pleasure he had just given her twice. Falling to her knees, she took him into her mouth, and he rewarded her with a deep rumbling growl that had her muscles at her core clenching once more.

With his hands threaded in her hair, he guided her to take more of him. He was no small man. Relaxing her muscles as her aunt had advised, she managed to take all of him. Over and over again. The tensing of his thighs indicated he was close to his release. Mary stroked his balls, and a salty burst of fluid slid down her throat. Swallowing, she slowly sat back upon her heels.

Pleased to see Gilbert's wide grin, Mary said, "I believe I've discovered a new favorite position."

Gilbert chuckled as he pulled up his breeches and adjusted his falls. "Lass, I haven't even begun to show you all the ways we can make love."

"You haven't?" Mary rose to sit on the seat, facing him. "How many more are there?"

"Too many to show you now, but I promise as soon as we are done with this blasted mission, we will spend many, many days abed." Gilbert reached for her and brought her to sit across his lap once more. Settling against the corner, he wrapped his arms about her and closed his eyes.

Mary rested her head against his wide shoulder. Was it selfish of her not to want to have children? Her own parents had had four children. Not one of them received an ounce of affection or love from either parent. Her mama had spent all her time appeasing Papa, while that man sought out his pleasure with other women. No. Mary would prefer to love her husband wholly and share a life of adventure.

GILBERT SLEPT the remainder of the journey. Once they reached Calais, André confessed his preference to remain on French soil. Since he no longer bore the responsibility of the item his papa had given him, he felt no need to make the crossing. The young man promised to remain a day or two at the port to delay the ruffians should he come across them. It was more likely they had already set sail, but Gilbert believed it would be a wise precaution just the same.

After swift goodbyes, Gilbert and his former soldiers boarded the *Quarter Moon* while Lord Hadfield escorted Mary up the gangplank. She had several questions for Lord Hadfield, but they would have to wait until they gained some privacy.

After they had set sail, Mary hunted Lord Hadfield down in his cabin.

Looking out the porthole, Hadfield said, "You will have to have Waterford teach you how to enter without detection."

If she had wanted to startle him, she knew how to be stealthy, but this was not the time to debate her skills. "Perhaps." Mary had come to retrieve answers. "Once we arrive in Dover, will we accompany you to meet with the other families?"

He swiveled to face her. "No. I've already placed you in grave danger."

"But that is to be my life now that I'm married to Gilbert. We are honor bound to protect you."

"The item you gave me. It holds great significance, and Lord Burke will stop at nothing to obtain it."

"Please cease speaking in riddles and explain."

"Very well. The bearer of the coin holds the ultimate veto power among the families. It has been hidden for decades. But now that it is in my possession, I will need to confer with the others to decide what needs to be done with it."

Lady Frances had made it clear that it was fated for the coin to remain in Lord Hadfield's possession. For out of the three, Lord Hadfield was the only one who would act out of pure selflessness, and that is why the coin had found its way into his hands.

"I don't understand the need to consult with others. It is you who possesses the coin. Why not keep it and oversee it all?"

"Human nature is fickle. Power. Money. Too much can challenge or, better said, tempt a person to do what they otherwise might not."

"I believe that nothing occurs by pure happenstance. It is not by chance that it is you who holds the coin. You are worthy of the honor of being the bearer of the coin."

"My thanks, Mary. That is a kind endorsement. But I can confirm I am no angel."

"I didn't say you were. However, your secret will be safe with Gilbert and me. You have our support. I would urge you to consider keeping it in your possession."

"What if it was best for one of the other families to retain the coin?"

"How would you determine that?"

Lord Hadfield appeared torn.

Mary repeated Lady Frances's sage advice. "When the time comes, you will know what to do."

Gilbert burst into the room and froze. "What the devil is going on in here?"

Lord Hadfield placed a hand on her husband's shoulder. "My thanks for keeping me safe all these months. When we reach Dover, your assignment ceases, and you are to take care of Lady Mary."

Gilbert asked, "You don't want us to accompany you to London?"

Oh, her husband was good at playacting.

Earlier, Lady Frances had shared with Mary Lord Hadfield's intention to alter Gilbert's orders. In turn, Mary had informed Gilbert of the true treasure and of Lord Hadfield's ability to lay claim and wield ultimate authority as the bearer of the coin. The brilliant solider that Gilbert was, he followed instruction beautifully—pretending not to know of Lord Hadfield's plans.

"No. You need to put those soldiers to work and enjoy some much-needed time alone with your beautiful wife. I will send word if there is a need for you to return to town."

Before Gilbert could answer, Lord Hadfield had turned and left.

"Lass, is everything settled between the two of you?"

"If you are referring to the matter of the coin that has Lord Hadfield's mind and heart in a conundrum, yes. I shared with him my opinion, and now it is up to him to decide."

"Well, if he were wise, he would take your advice and not think twice about it."

Her heart soared at hearing her husband's words. "You know exactly how to tell me you love me without using the tired old phrase of *I love you*. Promise you will continue to do so."

"I promise." He sealed the promise with a kiss that left her wanting more. She grabbed his hand and pulled him along the galley back to their cabin.

EPILOGUE

*S*eated at his desk in the freshly refurbished study, Gilbert opened the parchment that he was sure would be a summons to London. Mary had begun preparations for their trip into town three days ago. After being married to the woman for three months, he no longer inquired as to why she went about things that appeared to be out of order.

Avoiding the temptation to seek out his wife again, he quickly turned his attention back to the note in front of him.

> *Waterford -*
> *You and your wife are to attend Lady Grace Oldridge's*
> *betrothal party, one week hence.*
> *Be prepared to stay in town for the remainder of the Season.*
> *Sorry to cut your honeymoon short.*
> *Archbroke*

He read the note several times, debating if it was a forgery. In all the years Gilbert had worked for the Home

Office, he'd never before heard the home secretary utter an apology.

Being happily married must be the reason behind his superior's altered behavior. Gilbert knew he too had changed for the better since marrying.

Mary breezed in and plopped in the chair, facing him. "Why are you frowning?"

"We are to remain in town until the end of the Season."

"Yes, and that is why it is taking me an extraordinary amount of time to arrange everything."

Uncertain as to why their length of stay posed a problem, he trained his eyes on Mary's beautiful honey-brown ones, but he couldn't resist gazing down at her delightful body. They had spent most of the morning in bed, yet his body still hungered for her.

"Gilbert! Please focus."

"Lass, you look lovely. I admit I'm having a rather hard time remaining here behind this desk, resisting the temptation to take you to bed."

"Those activities will have to wait until you can retain more letters."

They had exhausted his supply of French letters much sooner than he had anticipated. He smiled. Perhaps it was fortunate that they were headed for town, for he wasn't certain how long he could refrain from having Mary again.

Eager to be on their way, he asked, "When do we leave?"

"The earliest will be at dawn."

"Dawn!"

"The staff will leave this afternoon. We need to allow them time to prepare and ready the town house." His wife's mouth curved into a wicked smile. "We will have to make adjustments for this evening. You are resourceful. I'm certain we will manage."

Mary stood and left him to resolve the problem of how to ensure their activities would not result in her increasing. Withdrawing before he spilled his seed would be the most feasible solution, but it was not always easily done in the heat of the moment.

He reached into his desk drawer to refer to the calendar he had meticulously maintained to keep track of her cycle. They had consulted with the local midwife as to how to best prevent a pregnancy. He had promised he would do everything in his power to honor her wish for no offspring. It came as no surprise to him that neither of them had a deep desire for children. Neither set of parents had been stellar examples.

He, along with his father-in-law, had corresponded at length and had finally agreed that papers were to be drawn up to provide for Mary if he was to meet his maker first. It was surprising what the Crown would grant to a duke. However, it was Hadfield who he ultimately had to thank. Hadfield had drafted the papers for the special concessions and assisted in persuading the Crown to provide its seal of approval.

Glancing at the calendar once more, he bowed his head. The midwife's chart clearly indicated today would not be the best day on which to partially engage in marital affairs. Abstinence was the only way to ensure he kept his promise.

MARY PACED in front of the fire in Gilbert's bedchamber. They had discussed the idea of her sharing the chamber since she had spent every night in her husband's arms. It was an odd notion. Her parents had maintained separate chambers, one at each end of the hall. Mary pondered as to why that was. Her mama clearly loved her papa—why Mary would never understand. Her papa was not one to show affection, unlike Gilbert who had no issue kissing her whenever he desired and regardless of who was about. His Grace was never open about such matters. Mary was fully aware that her mama had to bribe the servants to obtain information. She was grateful that Gilbert openly shared each evening the details of his day, the issues he had to deal with regarding the estate, his successes of the day, and even his fears.

Her marriage to Gilbert was everything and more that she had hoped for.

But tonight would be a test of sorts for them both. Were they indeed in accord?

Gilbert entered and stopped as soon as he saw her. Maybe she should have waited in her own chambers tonight.

He started to approach. "Lass, what has you worried?"

"I received a note from Theo today."

"What did Archbroke's wife have to say that has you frowning?"

"She requested my assistance while we are in town. I believe she and Lucy are scheming to somehow disentangle Lady Grace from her betrothed."

He entwined his fingers with hers and tugged her over to a chair. "That should come as no surprise. Lady Grace's heart belongs to Harrington, always has."

Settling herself upon Gilbert's lap, she said, "You of all people know how it feels when others interfere into matters of who one should or should not marry. If Lady Grace wants to break off the engagement, she is more than capable of doing so on her own."

"I would agree with you. But are we not proof that at times divine intervention is not enough and that human interference might be necessary?"

Grinning Mary asked, "Are you trying once more to tell me you love me?"

"No, lass." Gilbert took her face in his large hands and kissed her slowly, with so much feeling she wondered how she had ever doubted him. "I *am* telling you that I love you."

I HOPE YOU ENJOYED VISIONS OF LADY MARY. Ready to find out how the Agents of the Home Office defeat their arch enemy - Lord Burke'? Find out in Book 4 of the Agents Home Office series - Confessions of Lady Grace.

ABOUT THE AUTHOR

RACHEL ANN SMITH writes steamy historical romances with a twist. Her debut series, Agents of the Home Office, features female protagonists that defy convention.

When Rachel isn't writing she loves to read and spend time with the family. You will often find her with her Kindle, by the pool during the summer, or on the side-lines of the soccer field in the spring and fall or curled up on the couch during the winter months.

She currently lives in Colorado with her extremely understanding husband and their two very supportive children.

Signup for Rachel Ann Smith's newsletter for up to date information on new releases and monthly giveaways: www.rachelannsmith.com

Agents of the Home Office series
Desires of Lady Elise (Novella) - July 2019
Secrets of Lady Lucy - September 2019
Mysteries of Lady Theo - November 2019
Visions of Lady Mary - March 2020
Confessions of Lady Grace - August 2020

Printed in Great Britain
by Amazon